anny in love

anny in love

A NOVEL

Barbara Wright

ONSLOW SQUARE BOOKS
NEW YORK

ALSO BY BARBARA WRIGHT

Crow
Plain Language
Easy Money

Copyright © 2024 Barbara Wright

All rights reserved. No part of this publication may be reproduced, distributed, or transmitted in any form or by any means, including photocopying, recording, or other electronic or mechanical methods, without the prior written permission of the publisher, except in the case of brief quotations embodied in the reviews and certain other noncommercial uses permitted by copyright law. For permission requests, contact the publisher at the address below.

ONSLOW SQUARE BOOKS
200 Chambers Street 29E
New York, NY 10007

For more information about the author and her books
visit: barbarawrightbooks.com

Library of Congress Control Number: 2024907512

Printed in the United States of America.

ISBN print: 979-8-9904036-0-4

First Printing, 2024

Photography credits are found on page 293.
Book design by K. M. Weber, I Libri Book Design

To Lydia

ADMIRERS AND CURIOSITY SEEKERS waited in front of the red brick mansion beneath black umbrellas. They came alone, and they came in groups. They came in spite of the icy drizzle that softened the street's frozen hoof marks into mud. In great numbers they gave up their Boxing Day to pay their respects to William Makepeace Thackeray, author of *Vanity Fair*, who had died unexpectedly on Christmas Eve.

To be sure, celebrity played a part in their willingness to brave the cold. And the grand Queen Anne-style house behind the wrought iron fence failed to disappoint. But more importantly, Thackeray seemed like their friend. He created characters so real, so recognizable, that they couldn't help but wonder if he had taken their friends and family as models. *Yes, I know a conniving vixen just like Becky Sharp. Amelia is so sweet she's a danger to herself—just like my sister!*

Thackeray charmed, he startled, he amused; he plied his readers with witty satire, wicked vignettes, and abrupt swings from parody to pathos. His colloquial style established an intimacy with them, like a friend whispering in their ear. He made his readers feel less alone.

Now men of all classes and professions huddled shoulder to shoulder under umbrellas, wearing black armbands and all manner of hats—wool caps, silk top hats, and derbies. The costermonger held an umbrella over the head of the barrister. United in grief, they wished to show publicly their affection for Thackeray, dead at fifty-two.

Women, legion among his readers, largely stayed home due to the custom of the day, the holiday, and bad weather, but they sent along Christmas decorations from their hearths as tributes to the great author. Family wreaths hung from the spikes of the wrought iron fence. The pile of laurel, fir, mistletoe, and holly by the gate was large enough for a bonfire. Among the greenery were sprigs of dried lavender, roasted chestnuts, homemade ornaments from the family tree, as well as oddly personal items: a shaving brush, a quill pen.

Outstanding among the tributes were the slender yellow pamphlets, now limp and sodden in the rain. Because Thackeray's novels were published in parts, each was housed in these yellow wrappers. They were as closely associated with him as the green and duck egg blue folders were with Charles Dickens.

"My jaundiced livery," Thackeray had called them.

Advertisements inside—cod liver oil, patented self-adjusting shirts, cutlery, chamomile pills, and invisible ventilating perukes—were aimed at a different class than Thackeray's characters. Nevertheless, his readers had snapped up the installments, yearning to make the story last until the next release.

A murmur passed through the crowd, and people strained to get a glimpse of perhaps the most famous literary figure in England, the poet laureate Alfred Tennyson. With his long stringy hair and beard, with pouches pending beneath his eyes, he was instantly recognizable from engravings in magazines and newspapers. A close friend of the novelist's since their Cambridge days, he thrilled the crowd by arriving, not in a closed carriage, but on foot. Rain pearled on the shoulders of his black cape and in the folds of his velvet slouch hat. He was a vision of what a poet should be—abstracted, disheveled, slightly mad. As he trudged through the mud to the front gate, men collapsed their umbrellas one by one to allow him passage.

Tennyson had not invented grief, but he had given it a national voice in his poem "In Memoriam." He also understood that the true mourners in Thackeray's unexpected death were his daughters, Anny and Minny, still in their twenties, whom he had known since childhood. The wish to leave them well provided for had driven Thackeray his entire life. It was a cruel fate that he should die without a will, leaving his unmarried daughters to make their way in a Victorian world uncongenial to female talent and ambition.

one

DECEMBER, 1863

ANNY KNEW THE SECRET HER father suppressed as shamefully as if it were a criminal record: he was, at heart, a sentimental soul. The day before, she had received, under her study door, a hand-lettered invitation from her father, who adopted one of his early pseudonyms: "Mr. M. A. Titmarsh requests the pleasure of your company at the tree trimming, two o'clock sharp. 23 December, 1863." The invitation was accompanied by a charming pen and ink drawing of two little girls by a Christmas tree. Neither she nor her sister Minny was married, so no children brightened the household, but that didn't dampen his delight.

Together they had decorated the tree with marzipan sweets, paper fans, tin soldiers, whistles, and spinning tops. Paper cornucopias filled with walnuts and hard sweets were tucked away in the branches. The tapers on the tree would not be lit until Christmas Eve, transforming a rather pathetic looking sapling into a luminous spectacle.

That morning Anny dressed with special care, for the family would receive visitors in the afternoon and carolers in the evening. She chose the red velvet dress trimmed in black piping, with a ruffle at the floor that could be detached and cleaned separately after dragging up dirt from the London streets.

On the way down to breakfast, she met her father's man-servant on the landing. "He is dead, Miss. He is dead," he said, shaking.

"Charles, calm down. What are you saying?"

"Your papa. He's dead."

"You are mistaken."

"I'm sorry, Miss."

"It is impossible," Anny said.

He motioned for her to follow him into her father's room.

There she saw her father face up upon the bed in a long white nightdress, his large feet hanging over the end of the mattress. His hands were flung over his head and grasped at the brass rails as if he were trying to shake the bed to rouse someone. His face showed no hint of suffering, but the position of his body told another story.

Sitting by his side, she said, "Papa, it's me. Anny. Wake up. Please wake up." She stared at his face, ringed by an unruly mass of silver curls and thought she detected a quiver in his eyelids. He was only dreaming. Surely he was only dreaming. She gently shook him and waited for him to open his eyes and say something funny. He could always make her laugh.

When he did not respond, she tried to unwrap his fingers from the rungs but they were locked in place and felt cold and greasy to the touch. She let out a cry.

That week, he had complained of disordered digestion, but that was not unusual. He had Rabelaisian appetites and reeled from one party to another, waddling in turtle soup and swimming in claret. His six-foot-three frame sagged with years of indulgence. She had become accustomed to his bouts of indigestion and his troubles with his "bowowels," as he joked. No matter how bad he felt, he always made time to write. It was a superstition of his. If he didn't write every day, even if it was only a sentence, the power would be snatched from him. The novel he was working on was giving him trouble, but he doggedly kept at it. The previous week, he had come out of his study, pointed to a few scribbled lines and said, "There, that's been my day's work. I have sat before it 'til I nearly cried and nothing would come."

She had heard his steps overhead the day before as she was writing in her study. When he got stuck, he liked to pace, counting his steps from one end of the room to the other. Why had she not noticed a difference in his steps—a change in the rhythm or a heaviness of his gait? Something to alert her to his deterioration.

Her head throbbed as she tried to hold herself together and figure out what to do next.

She climbed the stairs to her younger sister's room. Through the door, she saw that Minny was still asleep. She paused with her hand on the cold brass knob, as if delay would alter the shocking news. Because the sisters had grown up without a mother, Anny had always felt protective of Minny, long after she needed or wanted protecting. As she stared at her sister sleeping peacefully, her hair tumbling onto the pillow from beneath her muslin nightcap, she saw a vulnerable child, and desperately wanted to shelter her from life's pain.

She perched on the side of the bed and gently shook her. "Min, wake up, darling. It's Papa. He's dead." She was too rattled to think of a way to impart the news more gently.

Minny opened her eyes, still half asleep.

Anny wanted to climb into bed and hold her, as she had when they were girls and Minny was scared or unhappy. But the metal hoops and struts of her crinoline made that impossible. Instead, she affirmed the truth of their startling change of fortune and held Minny's hand as they both cried.

"We have many decisions to make," Anny said.

"Such as?" Minny said, drying her eyes with the handkerchief Anny gave her.

"Whether or not we should let Mama know," Anny said.

"I can't believe you're even thinking about her at a time like this," Minny said.

"What do you think Papa would want?" In most matters, Anny knew her father's heart, but on this, she could not guess.

"Does she even know who he is?" Minny said. She had been a newborn when their mother lost her sanity.

Anny sighed. "I suppose I'll send a telegram to her caretaker and let her decide. She'll have a better idea of how the news will affect Mama."

Their father had never tried to hide the fact that he had a mad wife. He was not one to indulge in self-pity. When misfortune came his way, rather than mope or snarl, he looked on the bright side. "If things had been otherwise, I would not have been so close to my darling little gurgles. My *bleshings,*" he said, in that playful way he had with a mock lisp. He used to say, "Godblesh, and goodnight my shildren." Or, in a fake French accent, "Bong Swaw" and stoop for his adult daughters to kiss him before going to bed. Light-hearted banter one day and the next day silence. And life changed forever.

DOWNSTAIRS, THE ROOMS WERE fragrant with spicy scents. It took a wagonload of greenery from the countryside to fill the house to her father's satisfaction. Spruce and pine were tucked into the hooked arms of the gas chandelier, with mistletoe dangling beneath. Holly and bright berries graced the front windows. Garlands with red bows festooned the oak staircase. Bay laurel ringed the candles on the table. Even the gold mirror in the hall merited its own evergreen swag. Now the decorations seemed all wrong, like a wool overcoat on a summer day.

In the dining room, Anny was met by the cook who assailed her with questions: How many were coming for Christmas dinner? Should she stuff the Christmas goose? How did the missus want the wassail bowl prepared? With apple slices bobbing on the surface, the way it was last year? Anny knew she should say, "Stop. Please. Stop. Papa is dead." But she could not, for to say it would be to make it so.

"I can't think about Christmas now," Anny said.

Details, so many details. Charles was on his way to summon the doctor and the funeral director. Friends had to be notified. She needed to dispatch a servant to the mourning warehouse and have them send over a seamstress immediately. Everything would be closed on Christmas Day and Boxing Day. Traditionally, they gave the servants Boxing Day off, but how could she get along without them? Her thoughts crashed into one another.

She sat at the head of the dining room table so she would not have to look at her father's empty place. The *London Gazette* was neatly folded up by his silver teapot, waiting to be filled.

He never disappointed her. Never. And now, this. She felt betrayed. How dare he do something so unthinkable, without even allowing her to say goodbye.

Why, on the death of the man she loved more than life, who was her hero, her role model, and her protector, why at this moment did she feel so angry?

She could remember only one other time when she felt so thoroughly betrayed by him, and that particular memory was so upsetting that, even as an adult, she did not like to revisit it. She was three and traveling with the family in a stagecoach. Inside it was pitch black and stuffy. Her father sat across from her, their knees touching. Minny slept in the nurse's arms. Her mother must have been there, though Anny had no memory of her. A Frenchman with bad breath sat next to Anny. He pressed his nose against the window, moaning over and over that he had a fever.

Anny started to bawl. The Frenchman scolded her, which only made her cry louder. Her father lit a lantern to amuse her.

"If you go on crying, you will wake Baby, and I shall put out the candle," her father said. She could not stanch the sobs. The noise woke Minny, and she started crying, too.

With a loud whoosh her father blew out the lantern and plunged the interior into darkness. Anny was shocked. It seemed so unlike him. "Light it! Light it!" she begged.

"No. I warned you I would put the light out if you kept crying," her father said.

As an adult, Anny could only imagine what it must have been like for him to be trapped in the claustrophobic dark with two screaming children, an erratic wife, and a feverish Frenchman. He was bringing the girls to Paris to live with their grandmother after a disastrous trip to Ireland, when their mother's mental state had worsened. Gone was the illusion that his wife would get better. Gone were his dreams of patching the family together again. He was returning with a writing career in tatters, a mentally unstable wife, and two daughters under the age of three.

But as a child what Anny had felt was a fear that embedded itself so deeply that, more than two decades later, the memory still made her shudder.

Now, as she sat in her father's Chippendale armchair looking out at the room from his vantage point, the import of his death came crashing down upon her, and she put her forehead on her arm and wept. This time there was no one to ask her to stop.

THE REST OF THE DAY PASSED IN a blur. Two women fitters from Black Peter Robinson's Mourning Warehouse arrived after lunch bearing bolts of fabric. Minny and Anny needed a whole new wardrobe in black, including purses, hair clips, and fans.

"I would suggest you consider 'The Aesthetic' for both correctness of fashion and economy of price," the fitter said, showing her a black crepe design inspired by the Pre-Raphaelite painters. "Our buyers consult with top Parisian designers."

Anny stared at the catalog without reacting. Minny had

the better fashion sense, but she was in the next room being measured. At times like this, Anny felt the disadvantage of growing up without a mother.

"Of course, if you prefer Parramatta silk, I would recommend 'The Inconsolable.' Very *comme il faut*," she said in a Cockney French accent.

"Please. Anything. I can't think about it now." She just wanted to be left alone.

"Grief is no time to be dowdy," the woman said, taking the tape measure from her neck.

After the fitters left, Anny and Minny met with the funeral director, Mr. Radcliffe, a short, mole-like man with a pointed nose and no discernible waistline. He outlined his lavish plans for the funeral.

"Before you go any further, Mr. Radcliffe," Anny said, taking a deep breath, "I'm afraid our ideas differ radically. My father was a modest man. I want a simple ceremony for him."

Though he had outsize appetites in food and drink, her father was remarkably humble. Even after his novel *Vanity Fair* had made him famous, he could never get used to strangers recognizing him on the street. She and Minny could not convince him to buy new clothes. Recently, they had secretly given away a waistcoat that was so shabby they were embarrassed to see him in it. When he searched for the vest to retrieve a chamois to clean his spectacles, they had no choice but to tell him. He laughed good-naturedly and said that he was surprised that they had found the waistcoat wanting.

"Modest, perhaps, but famous, nonetheless, and deserving of the very best for his final ceremony," said Mr. Radcliffe, looking to Minny for affirmation.

"I've already made up my mind. We will dispense with the feather men and the mutes with wands," Anny said.

"Need I remind you that this creates a very impressive display? For a man of your father's stature . . ."

"That may be true, but it's not what Papa would want," Anny said. "And another thing. It will not be necessary for you to provide mourners' fittings."

"It is my professional responsibility to give you the best advice I can, Miss Thackeray. I'm afraid people will think you are not showing your father proper respect."

"Mr. Radcliffe, anyone who knows anything about me will know that first and foremost I have my father's interests at heart."

"But Anny, that seems so stingy," Minny said.

Anny paused a moment. "Well, perhaps we should provide hats, bands, and gloves. But I insist that everyone get the same grade. Silk or crepe, I don't care, but I don't want one quality for the family and another for friends."

"Certainly," Mr. Radcliffe said, scribbling a note in his book.

"We will, of course, need a hearse, but I insist that the coachman not carry a truncheon. And no black ostrich plumes for the horses," Anny said firmly.

"If cost is a consideration . . ."

"Cost is absolutely no consideration whatsoever."

"My dear Miss Thackeray, your father was a man of considerable importance. There is his reputation to consider. People expect a certain pageantry for the famous. It would not do to stint. People will think you are disrespectful." Mr. Radcliffe's lips twitched.

"Excuse me, Mr. Radcliffe, but my concern is not with what other people expect, but what my father would want."

"You have suffered a terrible shock. Have you no gentleman who can advise you? An uncle, a grandfather, or a trusted family friend? I fear, in your current distress, you may make a decision you will come to regret."

"I am perfectly capable of carrying out the arrangements," she said, knowing full well that she was completely inadequate to the task. But there was no one else to do it.

If her father were alive, they would have had a good laugh

together after Mr. Radcliffe left. They would have made up a story and acted out little vignettes, a game they both enjoyed. Her father had a merry narrative mind and a taste for the absurd. He had always been amused by the tales she told about the strangers she encountered: the man at the bakeshop, the little waif on the street. He believed that people's flaws made them more interesting and, ultimately, more sympathetic. Because of him, she had developed the habit of close observation, which served her well in her own writing.

Now there was no one to rehash the meeting with Mr. Radcliffe, to imitate the quivering of his lips, and the funny little hiss that escaped through the gap in his front teeth. Without her father to make her laugh, the man seemed intolerable.

In the past, she had not had trouble dealing with men. She had cordial relations with George Smith, her publisher at the *Cornhill*, who had serialized her first novel the year before. She was used to socializing with her father's friends, London's great men of letters.

"Shall we order straw for the street outside? If you change your mind, we can always accommodate you," Mr. Radcliffe said.

"There's no need to muffle traffic. That won't help calm our nerves. More importantly, Papa wouldn't want it. One final matter. A carriage for Minny and me . . ."

His sudden intake of breath resembled a hiss as much as a gasp. "You are aware, Miss Thackeray, that it is not customary . . ."

"Please. Go no further," Anny said.

He looked at Minny, whom he suspected might be an ally, but she did not offer a differing opinion.

It was not common for women to attend funerals. They were considered too emotional. But if her father had taught her nothing else, it was to have opinions. One of the advantages of being raised without a mother or brothers was that her father invested his considerable intelligence and ambition in his girls. "My sister and I will attend, and I will hear nothing to the contrary."

They agreed on a casket—extra long—with a simple brass engraved plate. After he left, Minny said, "Are you absolutely sure about the funeral arrangements? I'm afraid we will appear miserly."

"You know Papa. He hated airs of any kind. The door guarded by mutes in hats with long weepers? That's just the kind of thing he would find ridiculous."

"But other people don't necessarily know that. They might think we don't care. That's what Mr. Radcliffe suggested. You were bossy with that poor man."

"That poor man, as you say, was trying to force me to do his bidding."

"Well, you made all the decisions without consulting me."

"Why didn't you speak up? I'm not a mind reader." She was short with Minny. Grief exhibited itself as bad humor.

"You never asked me. You acted as if my thoughts didn't count."

"I could use your opinion on the memorial card. I thought maybe we could take a canto from Alfred Tennyson's 'In Memoriam.' Papa admired that poem so."

"That's a terrible idea," Minny said with a pout.

"Why do you say that? Have you read it?"

Although Mr. Tennyson had been coming to their house since they were little girls, Minny had never taken an interest in his poetry.

"You don't take me seriously," Minny retorted. "You're just like Papa."

"Oh Minny, darling, let's not quarrel now. It's more than I can bear."

"You know what I mean. Papa never praised every blessed word I ever wrote, every stupid poem, every scrap of doggerel. To hear him talk, you'd think you were the next Charlotte Brontë. He never asked me to be his scribe."

"I was fourteen when I started taking dictation for *Esmond*.

You were only eleven and had no interest in writing. And don't forget, you copied out part of *Philip* to post to American publishers."

"Only because you were out of town." Minny bit her lower lip to keep it from trembling. "Why should you have the last word on the arrangements? What makes you the arbiter of his memory and what he wants and doesn't want? Maybe, just maybe, he told ME what his favorite poem was."

"All right, what poem do you propose? We'll use anything you suggest." Anny was tired. So tired. She just wanted this day to be over.

Minny paused. Then she put her face in her hands and sobbed. "Oh Anny, I'm so sorry. I didn't mean it. I don't know. I just want him back so we can ask him."

THAT NIGHT MINNY WENT TO BED early, but Anny chose to sit alone in the parlor. The apples nestled in the mantel greenery were sprinkled with gold leaf that glittered in the fire's light. The day had utterly exhausted Anny, but she was not yet ready for bed. She dared not light the candles on the tree for fear that carolers would stop by for a warming cup of wassail. She could not bear a visit. Not tonight, even though Fanny had prepared the wassail bowl.

In the dark, light from the fire shimmied up the boughs of the Christmas tree. Every year, without fail, her father looked at the spindly fir and said, "I think this is the prettiest ever."

The public would never believe how this hard-edged, irreverent wit felt about Christmas. But they had not seen him at St. Paul's, his face wet and his shoulders shaking as the charity children filled the sanctuary with their sweet voices.

Less than a week before, he had taken Anny to the cathedral on the underground railway and bribed the beadle to let them sit in the Dean's box, all carved oak and soft cushions. If only she had known that this was to be her last outing with him, she would not have indulged in her own petty thoughts and selfish concerns.

In the dust-filled shadows, the children paraded through the arched aisles wearing white robes over their patched rags. Candles lit up their angelic faces. Afterwards, her father said, "I've seen coronations, the grand opening of Crystal Palace, and the Pope's procession of cardinals, but I've never seen a grander sight than this."

He was happiest when he was with children. Even though he kept company with famous painters, writers, and thinkers, it was around children that he could be totally himself. Charles Dickens once remarked to her on the particular delight her father took in young boys, and what an excellent way he had with them. This was after he had visited Eton, where Mr. Dickens's son was in school. "Your Papa told me that he never saw a boy without wanting instantly to give him a sovereign." She knew he was being kind in telling her this, but it made her sad. Her father had no sons. He spent his life surrounded by women— his daughters, his mother, his grandmother—everywhere he turned, women and more women, though not the one woman he needed most: his wife. She wondered if he regretted not having a son to invest his ambitions in, though he often said how well his daughters suited him. "What would I do without my Little Women?" he was fond of saying.

Her father and Charles Dickens were not the rivals the press made them out to be. In fact, Dickens's novels were as much a part of their household as his own. Growing up they had named their cats after their favorite Dickens characters. Minny christened a fat gray tabby Nicholas Nickleby. There was also Martin Chuzzlewit, a black kitten named Pip, and the half-starved tom, Barnaby Rudge.

Every Christmas eve, the family read *A Christmas Carol*. Her father's voice, which could be rather stiff when he lectured in public, took on warm, expressive tones when he read aloud to his daughters. Each of them assumed different parts, though he reserved the part of Scrooge for himself.

Through the window, she heard the hearty strains of "Deck the Halls" coming from a house down the street. The carolers had passed over their dark house and moved on. Still, she chose not to light the candles on the tree. The sight of the tree ablaze would make her too sad. But she could not escape the scent of cinnamon, nutmeg, and roasted apples that evoked memories of Christmases past.

As usual, she had put off wrapping presents until the last moment. The slippers she had embroidered for her father were not under the tree and now it was too late. It pained her to remember her dear Papa, who adored her and complained about so little, scolding her for always being late. Less than six months before, he had said, "I have asked you in vain year after year to come down at nine o'clock. It has chipped off a little piece of my affection for you. When I am gone you will remember this and do it —but then it will be too late." She had been devastated. After a good cry, she went to his study and said, "Do forgive me, Papa." He looked up from his writing, smiled, and held out his hand, that dear hand with rosy knuckles and long fingernails—how he loathed cutting them. Of course he forgave her, but she had not reformed, and still had the wretched habit of leaving things until the last moment.

She felt a catch in her heart as she realized: her father was not a procrastinator. His gift to her was wrapped and under the tree. By the light of the fire, she found the package and shook it. The thump inside was definitely not a necklace, as the size of the box suggested. She held it to her chest. Dare she open it? It was his last offering to her, and therefore more precious. Her first instinct was to save it unopened, but curiosity won out, and she loosened the raffia ribbon, removed the paper, and opened the box. Inside was a cedar penholder with a metallic receptacle for the slip nibs. She rolled the smooth wood between her fingers.

As a writer, her father had a deep bond with his pens. Like a necromancer's wand, the pen allowed the spell to happen. His favorite, a gold one, he kept for six years. He always said that he could never think so well as when he held a pen in his hand.

He could not have known that he would be dead before he could give this gift to her. It was so like him. He had a talent for the right phrase, *le mot juste*, and the perfect gift.

What she felt was an inviolate connection to him, a fatherly reassurance that she could make her living by her pen, now that the responsibility of supporting her sister, her mother, and a household of servants was on her shoulders. His parting gift to her was the confidence that, with her own special pen, she might, just might, be able to do it.

THE DAY OF THE FUNERAL ARRIVED, wintry and bright. Anny sat beside Minny inside the chapel and listened to the eulogy, her head slightly bowed. The logwood dye of the black veil gave off a slight humus smell of forest duff. Jagged fragments of light colored the stone floor, cast by the sun through the stained-glass window.

When she was six years old, her father had given her a kaleidoscope for Christmas. How she loved that magic tube. With every twist, the colored fragments rearranged themselves to form beautiful patterns in endless variety.

Minny had wanted her own kaleidoscope—she always wanted what Anny had. They quarreled, snatching the tube back and forth, until it slipped from their hands and shattered on the floor, spilling out pieces of glass. Without the light behind it, the glass lost its magic. "What's wrong with my girls? It's silly to quarrel. I'll get you both your own kaleidoscopes," their father had said. And he did. It was not until many years later that she learned of the severe difficulty this had caused him. At the time, he was a young father, cobbling together a living from writing freelance articles for *Punch* and *Fraser's Magazine*. Deep in debt from their mother's illness and private care, he had not yet written the novel that would pull him out of financial distress. He had used his last five pounds to buy the kaleidoscopes.

In the chapel, Anny looked down at Minny's lap. She clutched a handkerchief in her black-gloved fist. She had been so young then, too young to be blamed for her covetous behavior, while Anny had no such excuse.

Now Anny looked at the random chips of color on the stone floor and thought: What was death, but a severing of future memories? From now on, all of her memories of her father would be in the past. And already some were slipping away.

The light dimmed in the chapel and the colored shapes on the floor disappeared as the sky clouded over. After the final prayer, Anny realized she hadn't the slightest idea what had been said.

Outside, the somber procession made its way along the path, accompanied by the crunch of gravel underfoot and the occasional rattle of a dry leaf still attached to the bare branches. Over two thousand mourners had gathered. A sour smell rose from the canal on the other side of the moss-covered wall.

The procession followed the pallbearers to the humble part of the cemetery where Anny's sister Jane was buried. Born a year after Anny, she died at the age of eight months, and their father had never gotten over it. His spectacles became moist when he was asked about little Janie. Had she lived, she would be twenty-five, and it was fitting that he should be buried beside her, as he had requested, rather than in Westminster Abbey.

As Anny approached the gravesite, she saw, amidst the solemn black figures, a bevy of women in bright shiny dresses, bunched together in the front row by the grave. She was perplexed. Women weren't supposed to attend funerals. The crowd parted so she could get closer. Suddenly, she found herself surrounded by ladies in low-cut frocks of blue, green, and red. Plumes decorated their hair. Their cheeks were bright with the red antimony so frowned on by the better classes. Some had faces streaked with the running lampblack used to darken their lids.

She was blocked from reaching the graveside by these women, jockeying for position as they must have done in the narrow back alleys where they plied their trade.

Literary London had turned out in full force for the funeral. Dressed in black silk top hats and buttoned frock coats, Tennyson, Dickens, Browning, Carlyle, and Trollope were all here to witness this humiliating scene. Anny was mortified. How dare these women cheapen her father's death with this tawdry display?

A hand touched her elbow and she turned to see a blue-frocked woman who led her through the knot of prostitutes. "Move aside, love. There you go. Make room for the daughters," she said. Soon Anny and Minny secured a place in the front row. Anny turned to thank the woman, and looked into her streaked face. There she saw, not a maudlin display, but genuine affection and grief.

It was at this moment that Anny broke down. The tears she had worked so hard to hold back rushed down her cheeks, for what she realized was that, as close as she had been to her father, as much as she had labored to make his life pleasant and attend to his every need, there was a side of him she did not know. His marriage had been ruptured by insanity, yet he could not remarry. Neither a bachelor nor a widower, he was forced to seek female comfort amidst the bright kaleidoscope of colors now surrounded by a sea of black. In her insularity, she had never considered the salient part of her father's life that marked every day he had lived: his loneliness.

two

JANUARY, 1864

ANNY SET THE SHAVING BRUSH in the wooden box and closed the lid. For the past week, she had avoided making decisions about what to keep and what to sell. Her father had died with no last will and testament, forcing the estate to auction off the house and its contents and sell his copyrights. The sisters had to find placements for the servants and move into more modest lodgings.

Minny had already identified the items she wanted to keep. As Anny roamed about the house—altogether too grand for her taste—she considered the Louis XVI clock, the circular marble table supported by columns of carved mythological figures, the cabinets filled with Dresden china, and the small collection of masters by Watteau and Aelbert Cuyp. Her father, who had such simple values, also had a love of fine things, and a habit of spending beyond his income. He had taken great pleasure in combing London's curiosity shops and silversmiths, and had decorated the house with antiques from his beloved eighteenth century. Anny wanted none of these newly acquired old things. But when she happened upon his shaving brush, with its dear dents in the sterling handle, she crumpled onto a chair and cried. She could so clearly picture him in front of the mirror, shaving with a few quick strokes and wiping the razor on the sleeve of his robe.

Two years before, he had designed and built this Queen Anne-style house on Palace Green, with arched windows that overlooked the elms of Kensington Palace. The bright red brick he had chosen looked vulgar on the rare sunny days in London. But most days fog blurred the gray and brown stones of the neighboring houses. Then the red brick seemed like a stroke of genius.

He loved this house, "all made out of an inkstand," he had proudly proclaimed. A family friend who never joked about anything suggested that he call the house Vanity Fair, after the book that lifted him from poverty and made such a house possible.

Their father was perfectly happy that neither of his daughters had married. He depended on them for companionship, comfort, and domestic stability. Anny served as his scribe, proofreader, secretary, and hostess. Minny managed the household budget and the servants. She could be counted on to bargain with the butcher and check the bell pulls before visitors arrived. She knew not to give her friends the Liverpool port when the Balfour wine would serve just as well.

Minny's shrewdness in running the household freed up Anny to concentrate on her writing. It was at Palace Green that she had finished her first novel, *The Story of Elizabeth*, which she published in serial form under a pseudonym so as not to trade on the famous Thackeray name. How lucky she was that her father was still alive to witness the novel's enthusiastic reception. He went into a blind fury over the one negative review in *Athenaeum*. He had been so proud of her, claiming to anyone who would listen that she had all of his better parts and none of his worst.

Minny loved the grand house on Palace Green, commensurate with their father's stature as one of the country's great writers. But Anny viewed it as a financial sinkhole. It had cost far more to build than their father had budgeted. While he was alive, she had fretted constantly over how hard he had to work just to support it. "If anybody knew how I hate the sight of a 'New book by Mr. Thackeray' I think they would be kind enough not to buy a single copy," she had complained to a friend. "I'm sure 'writing-books-and-going-out-to-dinner-to-shake-them-off' is the real name of his illness."

When her words found their way back to her father, he had been furious. "It is absurd to expect a man to give up work at fifty-two," he said, and admonished her for taking her concerns outside the house.

She was distraught now when she thought back on his displeasure. Why was it she only remembered their disagreements? There had been so few, but they cut her to the quick.

At the time, she had no idea he was so close to death. Granted, he never denied himself food or drink, and he rarely exercised like his friend Charles Dickens, who took a brisk ten-mile walk every day, leaving his companions gasping to keep up.

Anny constantly worried about her father's discomfort, but never, even for one moment, about his mortality. Why hadn't she taken his condition more seriously? She thought back on his bouts of shivering, the pain in his gut, the little blue pills he took, the manly disorders he kept to himself. She was stricken to think how blind she had been. She was closer to him than anyone in the world, yet she hadn't put together the clues. "Oh Papa, dear Papa, can you ever forgive me?" she said aloud to the empty room. She looked in the mirror. Her tears made the black crepe collar of her mourning dress bleed, staining the creases in her neck purple. She was only twenty-six but felt ancient. Her father had given her the certainty of love, and without that, her world felt thin and perishable.

AS THE ELDER SISTER, ANNY TOOK charge of her father's estate. The bewildering demands of lawyers, American and English publishers, auctioneers, and movers overwhelmed her. She lost important papers and was late to appointments. She was taken advantage of by the estimators. When the publisher George Smith offered a handsome sum for the copyrights to all of William Thackeray's works, she felt an enormous burden lift.

She thought Minny would be delighted when she told her, for the offer put the sisters on sound financial footing. Instead, she burst out in anger: "You've already accepted his offer, haven't you?"

"I trust Mr. Smith completely. He's been a true friend to me and to Papa," Anny replied. Mr. Smith had published Anny's first novel and owned the *Cornhill Magazine*, which their father had edited for two years. "It's an incredibly generous offer. We can keep all of Papa's letters and drawings and loose bits."

"So I'm right," Minny said, hand on hip and mouth set. "You have. Made arrangements without consulting me."

"It's an astonishing sum, don't you agree? I felt certain you would be in favor of it."

"You presume to know what I think, but I can assure you, you do not."

Anny was stunned. Throughout their childhood, Minny had let Anny speak for her. That had been the pattern for twenty-three years. Anny was the older, boisterous sister, Minny the quiet, well-behaved one who rarely asserted herself. Somewhere along the way, when Anny was not paying attention, Minny had grown up. It happened quite suddenly, as things did with Minny.

Her sister had not learned to talk until she was three, and the family worried she might be backward. Instead, she had waited silently—listening, observing, and absorbing—and then astonished everyone by speaking in whole sentences, skipping the stage of baby phrases.

She took her own sweet time growing up. A mere two years ago, when she was twenty-one, she was still wearing her hair in plaits and liked to play with kittens and children. Then one day, inspired by a marble statue she had seen at the 1862 London Exhibition, she began to wear her auburn hair in loose wavy loops on top of her head, and people marveled at what an uncommonly beautiful young lady she had turned into, overnight. Anny was reminded of the old garden adage about clematis, a flowering vine that seems stunted the first year, puts out insignificant new shoots the second year, then explodes in the third year, covering the trellis with showy blossoms. *Sleeps. Creeps. Leaps.* That was Minny.

In the family, Minny had the reputation as the pretty, non-intellectual one. Because Anny was closer to their father in temperament and interests, he unwittingly encouraged this view. True, Minny avoided discussions of ideas, but she was undeniably clever. She picked up French more quickly than Anny when they lived with their Thackeray grandmother in Paris. Her letters displayed a felicity of expression and an acerbic wit worthy of her literary heritage.

The three Thackerays had formed a tight bond. Love had unquestionably been at the foundation. But Anny now saw that her relationship with Minny had been colored by their father in ways both good and bad. Now that he was gone, she found that she didn't really know who her sister was.

"Do you want me to try to renegotiate Mr. Smith's offer? I suppose we could sell the copyright for each novel to individual buyers," Anny said.

"No, but I want to be consulted in the future. He's my father, too."

ANNY LEFT THE SORTING OF HER father's study until the last minute, knowing that this would be the hardest room to face. The valuers were scheduled to come the following day, and the sisters would leave the day after that for a visit with their father's old friend Julia Cameron on the Isle of Wight.

The grandfather clock downstairs struck midnight. The servants had laid the fires and gone to bed. Her sister had turned in long ago. She could delay no longer.

When she entered his snug little kingdom, she felt herself relax. Unlike the other rooms in the house, his study was shabby and comfortable, filled with foolish knickknacks and keepsakes. He had left his tattered house slippers beside a bandy-legged cane-bottomed chair. A ragged sweater hung on the back of his desk chair.

She needed to pack up the contents of the desk, but she didn't want to disturb anything, almost expecting him to come back and start working. She ran her fingers lightly over the penholders, the writing slope, and the solid silver inkstand in the shape of Mr. Punch. Each item was a talisman. A mother-of-pearl box held the sand he used to absorb excess ink from his *Vanity Fair* etchings. She could never let that go. Never.

His shelves were crammed with books set sideways, upright, slanted, and tucked behind other volumes. Bookland—that inexhaustible country, he was fond of saying.

He was not attracted to special editions or leather-bound volumes with gold embossing. His books were worn and annotated. He kept a worm-eaten copy of Boswell by his bed to lull him to sleep when he awoke in the night.

She needed to sell off most of his library, but how could she part with his dear books? These were the ones he cared about. They shaped him, taught him, inspired him, and consoled him. Did he carry fragments of these books with him to the other side? Perhaps it was not so far-fetched, for it was the soul, and not the body, that was altered by the best writing, and that was the part that lasted forever. She was comforted by this view of heaven, where bits and pieces of his beloved books lived in him, the same way parts of his novels lived in others.

What to save and what to keep? The decision about his papers, journals, and correspondence was easy. She felt a special responsibility to be a good steward of his archives, even though she had given him her solemn promise never to write his biography or authorize another to do so.

One bundle tied in blue silk ribbon caught her eye. She unfolded a couple of letters and saw that they were addressed to his mother. With the friendly coals glowing through the fender and the stack of letters beside her on the chair, she abandoned all plans to finish organizing and sorting that night and started to read.

The sisters had moved in permanently with their father when Anny was nine. The correspondence dated from that time. In letter after letter, their father anguished over finding the right governess for his daughters. "This is not the woman to rule such a delicate soul as my dearest Anny's. What a noble creature she is, thank God," he wrote. He described another governess as honest and eager to do her duty, but not fit to guide Anny's mind. Yet another: "The child is the woman's superior in every respect and subject to a vulgar discipline which makes her unhappy. My little women are delightful. And the governess—a nuisance." He found yet another governess wanting: "Anny can run rings around her intellectually and the poor girl cannot keep up. I am convinced that my Anny is destined to become a Man of Genius. I must find someone more suitable to guide her."

Anny smiled at his reference to her as a "Man of Genius." Then she felt a catch in her throat. Her wish to please him did not end with his death. His ghost would trail her throughout her life, reminding her that she had to live up to his expectations.

One of the few governesses who made an impression on Anny was a clergyman's daughter, a real beauty with long flowing hair and dark eyes. Anny smiled when she read her father's description: "Mama, do not worry. She does not have what one would call a handsome face."

He could have sent his daughters to boarding school, but he enjoyed their company too much, and was finally able to find a permanent governess who was a family friend.

The lamplight was low and the candle burned to the nub. Anny knew she should go to bed, but she wanted to look at one more letter. Then one more. Reading them, she felt soft and herself again.

The next letter she opened was dated August 1840. When she finished reading it, her hand fell by her side and the letter slid to the floor. If only she had gone to bed when the clock chimed midnight. Then she would have remained ignorant of the incident that her father had kept secret all these years.

It occurred on a steamship crossing to Ireland when Anny was three, and Minny was two months old. Anny knew, from bits and pieces she picked up from relatives, that her mother never recovered from her sadness over Baby Jane's death, and was overcome with gloom after Minny's birth. Her father took the family to Ireland in hopes that their grandmother could nurse her daughter out of the doldrums. What her father had never told Anny was that, on the crossing, her mother had passed over from melancholy into outright madness.

By the flickering oil lamp, Anny picked up the letter off the floor and reread her father's account: "The poor thing flung herself into the water (from the water closet) and was twenty minutes floating in the sea, before the ship's captain saw her and turned around. O my God what a dream it is! I hardly believe it now I write. It is better you should know it from me, than from any of the gossips who might suddenly pour it out upon you in Paris."

Anny pondered the picture the letter painted of a young penniless father with a wife raving in one steamship cabin and an infant and toddler screaming in the next, tended by the seasick nurse Brodie. At night he slept tied to his wife by a ribbon so he could tell every time she moved. Despite the horrors of the trip, her father expressed the naïve belief that through force of will, he could make his family whole again.

Anny closed her eyes and leaned her head against the chair. The silence was complete. Ever present was the question, Did madness reside in her own veins, waiting for some wound to release it? This thought must have occurred to Minny, though they had never discussed it.

Now Anny was faced with a decision: should she tell her sister what she had discovered in the letter? Though Minny insisted on being treated as an equal, Anny felt protective of her. Their father had chosen to keep the incident a secret. Now she would do the same.

Minny, who had inherited her mother's great beauty, was also most touched by her neglect. She claimed to have no memories of their Irish mother, and made it a habit to leave the room or cover her ears when their father told stories about her. Anny had vague visions of being dragged around the room in a cart and yelling "Taytoes" at the top of her lungs. She remembered her mother's playing cat's cradle with her and singing with the organ grinder in the street. What Anny didn't know was which of these memories were her own and which ones her father, by telling and retelling the stories in such vivid detail, had planted so that she mistook them for her own.

Her mother now lived with a caretaker on the outskirts of London. Minny refused to see her, but Anny visited out of a sense of duty—mainly to her father, who worked so hard to do right by her. She tried to invest this pale husk of a person with a daughter's love, but, truth be told, she had no feelings for the woman who had always lived away, had never remembered her birthday, cooled her feverish brow, nursed a cut, helped dress a doll or trim a Christmas tree. The characters in her father's novels seemed more real to her.

Of all her memories, real or planted, what she was left with after reading her father's letter was this one image that she knew to be indisputably true: her mother, bobbing in the Irish sea, held aloft by her voluminous skirts, her red tresses swirling about her head like seaweed.

"MY DEAR DARLING GIRLS, I'M SO happy you could come and be with me." Julia Cameron rushed at Anny and Minny with extended arms as they got off the steamer at Yarmouth.

"I wasn't expecting you to meet us," Anny said.

"I can't have my sad girls take a cab in this damp cold. You must be pampered. I insist. I'll get my man to collect your baggage."

She herded them toward the waiting carriage and tucked them under lap robes with foot muffs to warm their feet. When she spotted the postman lugging a large leather sack toward the ferry, she said, "Pardon me, I must make sure these letters make today's delivery," and bolted in his direction. She was a voluminous correspondent, writing over three hundred letters a month. Anny loved to get her missives, which, very much like Mrs. Cameron herself, were full of effusive observations and opinions, all delivered in a gushing style without punctuation. When she ran out of ink, she used pencil, and when she ran out of paper, she turned the letter upside down and wrote between the lines.

Anny watched with amusement as she raced toward the postman, trailing drapery as she went. She was a squat woman in her fifties with plain brown hair and a mole by her nose. She refused to wear crinolines, those topsy-turvy monstrosities of fashion, and dressed unconventionally in loosely draped mantillas and bright Indian shawls. When she reached the postman, she gesticulated wildly, then reached into her bag and offered him a tea cake, along with a stack of a dozen or so letters, and, no doubt, some unsolicited reflections on the weather.

"I see she's quite unchanged," Minny said dryly.

"Yes, thank goodness," Anny said. There was nowhere she would rather be than with her father's old friend Mrs. Cameron, whom they affectionately called Cammie. She had been counting on her contagious—Minny might say overbearing—zest for life to elevate her spirits.

Her letters delivered, Mrs. Cameron returned to the carriage.

"Do you have word from your husband? Has he arrived safely?" Anny asked.

Mrs. Cameron doted on her husband, Charles, who was twenty years her senior. They had raised their family in India, and then purchased a coffee plantation in Ceylon. After Mr. Cameron retired, they moved to Freshwater on the Isle of Wight. A coffee blight had recently forced Mr. Cameron to return to Ceylon with their sons.

"It will be months before I hear. I'll be so glad when they finish that Suez Canal and I don't have think about Charles riding up the Nile to Cairo, then crossing the desert on camelback to board another steamer in Suez."

"Are you worried?"

"The true worry is this wretched coffee fungus. I don't know how long it will delay them or what it will mean for our financial circumstances."

The carriage traveled through the interior of the island on narrow lanes flanked by bare trees and brambled hedges. All at once, the lane opened out onto a great bald expanse of low grass. Beyond it, the sea filled the horizon. Detached jumbles of rock rose near a small stretch of beach framed on both sides by towering chalk cliffs tinted exquisitely by the winter sun.

"Smell that," Cammie inhaled deeply. "This salt air is a tonic, even for the heaviest heart."

She had a theory that the sea could cure anything, from consumption to indigestion. Certainly it was an antidote to grief.

The carriage pulled up in front of Dimbola, an ivy-covered

gabled house with large bay windows overlooking the sea. Inside, the rooms had the feel of a maharaja's palace, with inlaid mother-of-pearl furniture, ivory statues, and rush matting on the floor. Intricately carved sandalwood screens released a sweet woody fragrance. The large house caught the winter winds full force, making it impossible to heat. Indian shawls in every room provided guests protection against the drafts.

Cammie had offered Minny and Anny a wing of the house, but they chose to stay in the same room. Since their father's death, they had shared the same bed.

"I must show you my new toy," Cammie said over tea. "My daughter was afraid I would be lonely after Charles and the boys left for Ceylon, so she gave me something to keep me occupied. Grab a couple of shawls and come with me."

They followed her out back to a glass chicken house sheltered from the winds. "Behold my photography studio. I have liberated the hens and taken over."

Minny gave a little gasp. Her tenderness toward animals was well known.

"Don't worry, dear. The hens have been repatriated and will not end up on your dinner plate, I can assure you. I need their eggs."

To make a photographic print, she explained, the paper was first submerged in egg whites, and then in a silver nitrate solution, before being affixed to a glass plate negative.

The glass house looked like a miniature Crystal Palace, altogether too grand for the likes of fowl. But as a studio, it was perfect. The winter sun through the panes warmed the room. In the center stood a wooden camera, the size of a tea caddy, set atop a tripod. Robes and other costumes were draped over screens and thrown about the studio haphazardly, along with hats, turbans, swan wings, and enough props to mount any number of theatrical productions.

"I have so many ideas, I don't know where to begin," Cammie

said, when Anny asked about the props. "But first I need to gain some technical expertise so I can transfer what's in my head onto the plates."

She demonstrated how to tilt the large glass plate to coat the surface evenly with wet collodion. "Can you believe it? This is the same yellow syrup used as an adhesive to close small wounds and hold surgical dressings."

She lifted the black cloth at the back of the camera. "Would you allow me to take your photograph, Minny?" she said.

"If you don't mind, I'm going to excuse myself," Minny said. "I'm exhausted after all the travel."

"Of course. I understand, dear."

Anny was amazed at how firm her sister was, without being impolite. Anny, too, was worn out after arranging the details for the auction in London, then traveling by train and ferry to the island. But she didn't feel right leaving her hostess so soon after arriving.

"I received this camera on Christmas, the same day I received news of your father's death. Joy and sadness, all on the same day. Isn't that the way life works? My deep regret is that I will never be able to take his portrait. The world will miss that great man, but I will miss him more."

Anny wiped away a tear and sat on a tufted velvet chaise.

"Dear, if you stay just like that, I'll take your portrait."

"Oh please, Cammie," she pleaded. "My eyes are puffy, my skin is drawn, and this mourning dress makes me look deathly pale. I'm afraid I am a woman who needs the highest fashion to compensate for what Mother Nature has denied me."

Mrs. Cameron patted her arm conspiratorially. "We ugly ducklings are the ones history will remember," she said. "Mark my words."

Anny smiled wanly. The same Thackeray features in Minny, so well proportioned and comely, presented themselves in clumsy alignment in Anny. Their father could talk all he wanted to about the importance of inner beauty. She was no fool. Good looks did matter and to pretend otherwise was balderdash. Minny had them; Anny did not.

"Can I see one of your photographs?" she asked.

"I'm still perfecting my technique. I paid half a crown an hour to a farmer to be my first subject. My dear, I won't even tell you how many half crowns I went through while I tried to master the focus and this wet collodion coating. Patience is not my forte. After experimenting the whole afternoon, I finally got the image I wanted and then ruined the whole thing by rubbing my hand over the filmy side of the glass. Oh, I was so put out with myself."

"I wouldn't have the nerve for photography," Anny said. To have the image there on the plate and know that at any instant the whole thing could be ruined by a speck of dust or a slip of the hand. You're a braver soul than I." She admired her friend's passion. She was not sure she would have the courage to take up a new art form so late in life. "Maybe you should start out photographing children. It's much cheaper, and you could learn with them," Anny suggested.

"I'm not sure I could get the young ones to sit for ten minutes without moving. One flutter of an eyelash will blur the picture."

"Ten minutes? I'm not sure I could sit still for that long."

A FEW DAYS PASSED BEFORE Alfred Tennyson came for a visit. He lived in a grand house called Farringford, a short distance through the woods from Cammie's house. He arrived by the back path that Cammie had had built specifically so he could avoid his Cockney admirers, who, in the summertime, congregated in front of Farringford's gate, hoping for a glimpse of the famous poet.

He proposed to Anny that they take a walk.

"Let me just let Mrs. Cameron know where I'm going."

"Good gracious, no!" Mr. Tennyson said, looking trapped. "The woman is relentless. I'm afraid she will try to recruit me for one of her portraits."

Anny laughed at his consternation. "She tried to enlist me as well. But I had mourning as an excuse."

"I have no doubt she will be a great success, but I don't want to be one of her victims."

"Do you have the fortitude to resist her?"

"A better soul there is nowhere on earth, but there are limits to what I will do." Anny happened to know that Cammie was the only person, other than his wife, who called him by his Christian name.

"I'll leave a note." She went to get her bonnet and cloak.

They walked up the steep hill to High Down. The dormant grasses were tinged silver by the frost. She loved the spring, when hyacinths and self-sown daffodils brightened the Down, but the bleak midwinter produced its own stark beauty, and she didn't have to share it with the hordes of holiday-makers who swamped the island the rest of the year.

At the edge of the Down, the land dropped off a hundred vertical feet to the sea. Below, the chalk cliffs glinted in the sun. Gulls flashed their white breasts and planed down sideways toward the sea.

From on high, she could hear the crackle of waves rearranging the flint shingles along the shore. The sound reminded her of the gravel underfoot on the paths to her father's graveside. She thought of him every day. It was the little bits she missed the most, things so familiar it had not occurred to her they would not go on forever. "What has become of all my penholders?" "Has anybody got a needle and thread?" Odd, what the mind chose to remember.

With Mr. Tennyson, she felt a deep comfort. As they walked across High Down, she did not feel the need to talk. The wind flapped his black cloak out like some giant bird. When his squash hat blew off, he went running after it and she held her breath, afraid that he might follow it over the edge, but he caught the hat before it joined the gulls.

They paused to rest on a flat chalk seat that had been carved by the wind.

"Are you too cold?" he asked.

"No, I'm fine," she said, and pulled her bonnet tighter on her head.

"Tell me, truly, how are you getting along?"

She thought for a moment. She could not lie to an old friend. "I wish I were a poet like you, and could string together words as a bulwark against grief."

"Alas, I have no wizardry of words in me. Only sadness. I, too, miss him."

They sat in silence. She felt wind blow tears from the corners of her eyes.

Finally, he spoke: "I had great respect for your father's work, but an equal respect for him as a man. I always admired how close he was to you and Minny. Your father's love was unequivocal. I can say that about few men, and even fewer great men. William was a man in full."

Whitecaps gleamed on the blue water like plumes of snow, and the caw of gulls rose from far below on the beach.

Of all her father's friends, she felt that Mr. Tennyson understood matters of the heart most deeply. She trusted his words, not because he was a poet, but because he was one of her father's oldest friends. She couldn't remember a time when she didn't know him.

"Some strive for fame and immortality," he continued. "We all fall into that trap. I know I'm guilty. And your father certainly achieved fame, and may yet achieve immortality. Only time can answer those questions. But to achieve decency, now there's a true accomplishment."

"I don't know who I am without him," she said, looking out to the sea, sparkling under the cold sun.

"You are an intelligent woman. I have confidence you will figure it out."

"You are a true friend to us," she said, simply.

She could tell he was moved, but covered it with his gruff voice, which still carried the tinge of his Lincolnshire boyhood. "We're almost to the village. Shall we have tea?" he said.

They walked until they came to a fissure in the cliffs, where a steep path led to the beach. The overturned fishing boats, with their black hulls and high keels, looked like a school of sharks.

The inn was open, but deserted at this time of year. They warmed themselves by the fire in the front room beneath the stuffed carp and cuttlefish hanging on the wall.

"I love the winters here," Mr. Tennyson said. "I can't come here in the summer. Those blasted Cockney pests make it impossible. Are you hungry?"

"Mrs. Cameron is the best, but truly, her meals are shockingly bad. It's bacon and eggs for breakfast, bacon and eggs for lunch, and then, for a change of pace, bacon and eggs for dinner," she said. The hens, which had been moved from the glass house to make room for Cammie's studio, were by all evidence, copious producers.

Over tea, he regaled her with tales of his early days at Cambridge, when William Thackeray regularly entertained his friends with puns, satirical poems, humorous toasts, and bawdy limericks. He was widely admired for his wit and his ability to make people laugh. Mr. Tennyson remained his friend when he lost his fortune, partly through gambling, and partly because of a bank failure in India.

She took solace in hearing stories of the man her father was, before she was born.

The day was losing light by the time she returned to Dimbola. Cammie rushed at her before she could take off her cloak.

"Oh, I am in a transport of delight. Where is everyone? They've abandoned me. You must come at once. You must see this immediately. I've had my first success. This little girl's a marvel. You were absolutely right. I should have started with children."

Anny waited in the dining room. Before long, Cammie returned holding a dripping print by the corner. "I will be strong as a charwoman before this is over, hauling those buckets of water from the well. It took seven trips to get enough water to develop this photograph. But look. Just look at this child."

She set the wet print down, oblivious to the white damask tablecloth. A pungent chemical smell hovered about her.

"Shall I put something under this? I fear photography may be perilous to table linens," Anny said, but Mrs. Cameron was on to the next thought.

"That sweet, sunny-haired child. I had to make several attempts. But she sat for long stretches without wiggling."

"However did you manage that?"

Cammie had a way of cajoling and bullying to get her way. The victim could be Mr. Tennyson, or it could be a child—she made no distinction, which was part of her charm.

"The photograph is a complete success, owing to the docility and sweetness of my best and fairest little sitter. Oh, I must give her a present. What shall I give her?" She looked wildly around the room, and then raced away.

Anny gazed at the wet sepia print of the little girl, who had moved to the island to live with a local family. In the photograph, she was gazing off into the distance. Her unruly hair and plain coat gave her the waif-like appearance of a street child. Light glanced off the top of her head and fell in splotches on her cheeks, chin, and the side of the nose, as if dabbed there by painter's brush.

Anny could not stop staring at the image. She recognized, in the child's wistful look, the isolation of the motherless.

Cammie returned to the dining room carrying a paisley shawl in shades of red and orange. "What do you think?"

She seemed to have an endless supply of Indian shawls. Perhaps it was not the perfect gift for a child of seven, but Anny had noticed that often, Cammie's unconventional slant on life proved to have merit.

"I'm sure the child will appreciate it."

"No, I mean how do you like the photograph?"

Anny admired Cammie's single-minded focus. Her new camera consumed her, filled her with fire. Her five children raised, her husband in retirement, she had nothing to hold her back. She started late and exuded impatience. Now that she had completed her first successful photograph, she felt the need to go on to the next, as if one lifetime were not enough to discover all that needed to be discovered. In her rush to create, she had little interest in being to Anny what Anny craved most of all: a mother. That part of Cammie's life was behind her.

"Oh, the photograph," Anny said. "It's exceptional." The image of the little girl had about it a wonderful depth and mystery.

"I can do this. I know I can," Cammie said.

"I have no doubt," Anny said, happy for her friend.

"I know I come across as a flibbertigibbet, but I was born to do this. I have such plans. I know I can make beautiful things."

Her flashing eyes lent a beauty to her face and Anny recognized the complete absorption that accompanied the thrill of creating. In the days since her father's death, the creative urge had abandoned her. Could ideas all of a sudden shrivel and die? What would it take to get the words flowing? She feared the condition might be permanent.

"I must finish printing and framing this photograph for the child's father. You won't be offended if I miss dinner? I'll have Cook fix you and Minny some eggs and bacon."

FOR THE REMAINDER OF THEIR STAY, Cammie spent the majority of each day in her studio and darkroom. She emerged briefly for interludes of reminiscing and—her favorite—gossip.

"Have you heard? Il Signor is engaged to be married to Ellen Terry, a sixteen-year-old actress."

"Il Signor?" Anny said in amazement. That was Cammie's nickname for the artist George Frederick Watts, known as Britain's Michelangelo. "Isn't he a little . . . How old is he, anyway?"

"He's thirty years older than his child bride," Cammie said.

Mr. Watts was a friend of her father's, but he looked older, especially when he walked. He took small shuffling steps and stooped his head forward, either from infirmity or too many hours staring at a canvas.

"Nelly's a dear. She's from a family of actors and grew up on the stage playing Puck, Cupid, and little boys before adolescence," Cammie said. "Our painter has taken it into his head that he will save her from the moral depravity of the stage and give her an education."

"Poor child," Anny said. "Perhaps she does not want to be saved."

"Il Signor is my artistic advisor and biggest devotee," Cammie said. "I worship that man. His encouragement has given me wings to fly. But this marriage is a natural disaster in the making, and I don't know how to tell him."

"I'm sure I don't."

"Just a few months ago, he asked me what I thought about the idea of his adopting her," Cammie continued. "I said she was too old. 'What if I married her?' he said and I told him she was too young. Next thing I know, they're engaged. You see what kind of influence I have over the man."

three

SUMMER, 1864

$\mathcal{B}$ACK IN LONDON, THE SISTERS oversaw the selling of the grand mansion on Palace Green and moved into modest lodgings on Onslow Square, the same street where they lived when their father was a struggling journalist. G. F. Watts married the child actress Ellen Terry, and they spent their honeymoon at Freshwater. Anny couldn't wait to get back to the relaxed, egalitarian atmosphere of the island and its famous inhabitants.

She was not alone. Many men of distinction sought out the island and were content to put aside their celebrity for a time and be treated as equals with the rest of the inhabitants. When they came to pay Mr. Tennyson a visit, Cammie cajoled them into sitting for their portraits. Her perpetual state of disarray and want of affectation allowed the men to let down their guard, and she was able to capture on the glass negative the peculiarities of their personalities while retaining the ineffable mystery that is at the heart of genius. In the seven months since Anny's last visit, Cammie had produced penetrating portraits of G. F. Watts, the dramatist Henry Taylor, and the Pre-Raphaelite artist William Holman Hunt. So far, Mr. Tennyson had refused her pleadings, but Cammie had shown the other portraits at the annual exhibition of the Photographic Society of London.

Cammie's absorption in her new art did not diminish her hospitality. At the end of the summer, she invited Anny and Minny to stay in a cottage she owned down the lane, called The Porch. From the front windows, the sisters had an unimpeded view of the sea in the distance. They went to sleep at night to the sound of waves and awoke to the salt breeze blowing in from the bay.

The day after they arrived, the sisters set off to meet their cousins at the shore. Anny noticed a tall, slender man a few years older than she walking down the sandy lane. He was mumbling and gesticulating, deep in an imaginary conversation.

Anny recognized Charles Dodgson, the well-known photographer Cammie had introduced her to at the Photographic Society exhibit in June. Eschewing the full bushy beard in vogue for men, Mr. Dodgson was clean-shaven and had delicate lips and fine features. Dressed formally in a coat, top hat, and gloves, he carried a black bag, like a doctor on a house call.

Anny called out to him, and he waited for them to catch up.

"D-d-don't mind me. I'm just talking to myself," he said with a flush.

"Well, at least you're assured of an intelligent answer," Anny said with a smile. "Are you headed to the bay?"

He nodded. No one had told him that people dressed more casually on the island. Cammie made it a point never to wear a crinoline, and Anny had left her metal and whalebone hoops at home.

"Do you mind if we accompany you?" She fell in step beside him. He had ramrod straight posture and walked with one shoulder lower than the other. "This is my sister, Minny Thackeray."

"P-p-p . . ." His upper lip trembled and with an extreme effort, he pushed out the word "Pleasure," though it was clearly anything but.

"We're staying at Mrs. Cameron's cottage," Anny said, trying to smooth over the awkwardness of his stutter. "She calls it

The Porch, but there is no porch. Only a covered stoop. Classic Cammie."

"I like that idea," he said, brightening.

"It's quite illogical. To call something by an attribute that is missing," Anny said.

"Precisely. What could be more delightful."

Anny knew that Mr. Dodgson taught mathematics at Christ Church, Oxford, and loved logic, mathematical puzzles, and riddles.

When they reached the beach, they parted ways.

"Queer fellow," Minny observed. "Is he one of Cammie's curios?"

"He's quite well-known as a photographer. Even though he's young enough to be her son, he's probably her biggest competition."

Anny found their cousins near the inn, a low building nestled under tall cliffs topped with prickly yellow gorse. Holiday-makers now replaced the smugglers and fishermen who frequented the inn in times past.

Minny collected her bathing costume and went with the cousins to rent one of the bathing cabins on wheels lined up at the water's edge. A mule backed the wooden cubicle into the surf until the water reached just below the floor. The enclosure offered women a place to change clothes and lower themselves into the sea to swim in private, unseen by male eyes.

The ridiculous bathing costumes consisted of long sleeves, pantaloons, and a knee-length skirt with buckshot sewn into the hem to keep it from puffing up in the water like a moorhen. The fish may have gotten an eyeful of ankle, but otherwise, Anny couldn't understand how anyone could possibly be scandalized by the sight of women covered from neck to toe in sodden flannel.

She chose to skip the swim and read her novel under a black parasol. It was a beautiful day, with a slight breeze. Pools of purple from the cloud shadows rested lightly on the blue sea, interrupted by the occasional ruffle of white.

Anny watched two little girls, like delicious slips of seaweed, cavorting barefoot at the water's edge. Their skirts had been pinned up, but their petticoats were wet at the hem. How lucky they were, Anny thought, to enjoy the pleasure of cool water against bare skin. In a couple of years, their mothers would forbid such delights.

After several hours, Anny decided to return to The Porch to get in a few hours of writing before she was expected at Cammie's for tea. As she left, she noticed Mr. Dodgson sitting on a rock, surrounded by a dozen or so little girls. Among the men dressed in straw hats and rolled up trousers, Mr. Dodgson, in his formal coat and top hat, looked more like a carnival barker than an Oxford don.

He was helping a child pin up her skirt to wade in the water. After he finished, he pulled out a handkerchief. The little girls watched in rapt attention as he transformed the handkerchief into a mouse and made it jump in his palm. With a wave of the hand, he made the handkerchief disappear, and his child audience squealed in delight.

Anny decided not to interrupt him. She was surprised to find, later that afternoon, that Cammie had invited him for tea. He arrived shortly after she did, carrying a portfolio of photographs under his arm.

"I trust you and your sister had a pleasant day by the shore," he said.

"Quite. I saw you as I was leaving and thought of saying hello, but you were busy helping a little girl pin up her skirt."

"Yes, I always carry extra safety pins in my b-b-bag for that purpose."

"What else do you carry in that bag?" Cammie said.

"Books, wire puzzles, and magic tricks to keep the children entertained."

"I see you've brought photographs instead of magic tricks to indulge the adult children," Cammie said.

"Photography *is* magic, don't you agree, Mr. Dodgson?" Anny said.

He ran a gloved finger along the surface of the dining table, leaving a visible trail. When he blew on his finger, particles dispersed like a dandelion seed head.

"Oh, don't be so fussy. A little dust won't hurt the prints at this stage," Cammie said, as she haphazardly spread out some of her own work.

He placed his photographs on the table, adjusting each one with exacting precision so that the edge was parallel to the table and an equal distance from the one beside it.

Mr. Dodgson got out a magnifying glass and bent over Cammie's portrait of Nelly, Mr. Watts's young bride. She was wearing an off-the-shoulder peasant blouse. Leaning her head against the wall, the child beauty gazed down in an attitude of deep despondency. Her long loose hair was pulled back, exposing a vast expanse of skin and neck. The light caressed the side of her face. Cammie titled the portrait "Sadness."

Mr. Dodgson stared at the image for a long time. "Beautiful," he said. "I have wanted to meet Miss Ellen Terry ever since she played the role of Mamillius in *The Winter's Tale* when she was nine. Would you provide an introduction?"

The opportunity presented itself much sooner than anyone expected. When Cammie saw Nelly walking down the lane, she took Mr. Dodgson outside to meet her.

Upon returning, she looked more closely at Mr. Dodgson's photographs. "He's a wizard with the camera. A pity he doesn't like my work more."

"He said your portrait of Nelly was beautiful," Anny said.

"He was talking about the subject matter, my dear."

Anny looked out the window and saw the photographer and the child bride sitting side by side in the garden. He was reading aloud from a green Moroccan journal. Every so often, he leaned over and showed her a drawing.

"Mr. Dodgson appears to have taken quite a fancy to Nelly Watts," Anny said.

"As much as he can to someone over the age of ten," Cammie replied.

"What makes you think he doesn't like you?" Anny asked. "Aside from the fact that you are half a century beyond the optimum age?"

"He is a proper gentleman with an established reputation. I am an upstart. He finds it distasteful that I had the audacity to copyright my photographs and enter them in the exhibit at the Photographic Society. Well, if I don't protect my work with copyright, who will?"

Cammie picked up a print of the famous dramatist Henry Taylor, which had appeared in the exhibit.

"He pronounced my portraits horrid, as if word wouldn't get back to me. He deplores their lack of focus."

"Perhaps he doesn't understand your vision. Or worse, thinks your skirts prevent you from having one."

Cammie's shimmering impressionistic images were very different from Mr. Dodgson's precise, unblemished approach, but they both worked in the finicky wet collodion process and had much to learn from each other.

"I must work on Alfred to get him an invitation to dinner tonight. Mr. Dodgson tends to put people off with his old-maidish airs."

"Why make an effort to include him if Mr. Tennyson doesn't like him and he doesn't like you?" Anny said.

"Oh, he likes me. He just doesn't know it yet. I will win him over, you'll see. I am the overbearing mother he wished he didn't have."

"But can't escape," Anny said, smiling.

"The man is a genius. You should see him with children. He is a completely different person. He teases and charms them with stories and riddles. They adore him. That's why his photographs of children are so natural."

Cammie had a knack for collecting geniuses. Once she got it in her head that you had talent, there was no way to escape her clutches.

"He could learn a thing or two from me about self-promotion. History will not remember a singularly dry mathematics don who puts his students to sleep droning on about Euclid's *Elements*."

While Cammie slipped out the back gate to wheedle a dinner invitation from Mr. Tennyson, Anny took a closer look at Mr. Dodgson's photographs. Most were exquisite portraits of little girls. One was barefoot in a nightdress, reclining on a couch. Another wore a formal frock. Another slept peacefully in bed. All radiated beauty, innocence, and purity.

She could see how the buttoned-up Mr. Dogdson would clash artistically with Cammie, who was intuitive and messy. When Giuseppe Garibaldi had come to visit Mr. Tennyson earlier that year, Cammie had rushed out from her darkroom and fallen to her knees in front of the Italian revolutionary hero. Extending hands stained from silver nitrate, she entreated him to sit before her camera. He withdrew in horror, mistaking her for a common beggar. She looked down at her blackened hands and said, "This is not dirt, but art!"

Cammie had a way of mythologizing herself, so Anny was not sure the incident was true in all its particulars, but who cared—it made a good story, and that was what mattered to the denizens of Freshwater.

Before long, both Mr. Dodgson and Cammie returned. His face brightened when Cammie told him she had secured a dinner invitation for him from the famous poet.

"What is in that green leather journal?" Anny said.

"It's a story I wrote for children. I was thinking about calling it *Alice's Adventures Under Ground*."

"Oh, it's about child miners?" Cammie said.

"Not at all. The title isn't final. I was also considering *Alice's Hour in Elfland*."

"Children love elves. I'm sure it will be quite popular," Cammie said.

"Well, actually, there are n-n-no . . ."

They waited until he pushed out the word *no*, by force of will, and then proceeded smoothly from there. "No elves in the book."

"Well, whatever is in the book, Nelly was enchanted," Anny said, hoping to put him at ease and forestall another round of stammering.

"It's about a little girl who falls down a rabbit hole and finds herself in a strange world where everyday rules of logic don't apply. She encounters a mad hatter, a Cheshire cat, a mock turtle, and plays a game of croquet with flamingos as mallets and hedgehogs as balls." He became animated as he described the book, and the stutter disappeared.

"What a wonderland!" exclaimed Cammie. "I shall be the first to buy a copy."

"Speaking of books, I need to return to the bay," Anny said. "I managed to leave my novel behind this morning, and I'm sure by now it's yellow and swollen beyond recognition."

She left Cammie and Mr. Dodgson exchanging technical tips.

ON THE LANE, ANNY RAN INTO NELLY heading to High Down. Her loose blond hair flowed behind her bonnet, and her fresh rosy skin made her look even younger than her sixteen years. Anny caught up with her and linked arms affectionately. "How have you been getting on?" Anny said, feeling a responsibility to make her feel welcomed on the island.

"Mr. Tennyson has been so nice to me. He taught me to say luncheon instead of lunch. And Dodo is especially kind."

"Dodo?"

"That's what Mr. Dodgson asked me to call him. He put that bird in his book to make fun of himself and his stammer. You know . . . Do-Do-Dodgson."

Anny smiled. She would find it hard to refrain from calling this staid logician Dodo.

"I saw him reading to you in the garden. Did you like the story?"

"It's quite brilliant, really. One moment this little girl named Alice is nine feet tall, and the next, she shrinks to three inches. She always seems to be the wrong size for whatever she wants to do. That's how I feel here, among all these talented people."

"I'll tell you a secret. When I was your age, I wanted more than anything to be a boy—a clergyman, so I could write a sermon that would make people's hair stand on end."

"You are wicked," Nelly said, giggling.

"Wouldn't that be fun? To make people's hair stand on end? Or do something, anything, really, to make people remember me. When my father first brought us to the island, I thought: Everyone here is either a poet or a genius or a painter or peculiar in some way. Is there no one who is commonplace here?"

"I wish I knew how to be peculiar."

Poor Nelly, Anny thought. She seemed quite overwhelmed. It could not have been easy to be this raw, unpolished beauty thrown among this cast of talented eccentrics.

"I have an idea. Let's go to the Needles, just the two of us," Anny said. The novel she left at the shore would have to wait.

"You would go with me?" Nelly said.

"Of course. Why wouldn't I? It's my favorite spot on the island."

The three white chalk outcroppings called the Needles rose out of the sea on the westernmost tip of the island. The rock structures had been named by someone with a questionable grasp of metaphor, for they bore no resemblance whatsoever to needles, but looked more like icebergs. A red and white striped lighthouse had been built at the farthest point.

Anny followed Nelly up the hill until they reached High Down. The grazing sheep were oblivious to the gorgeous view of the island spread out before them. The straits were busy with yachts, brigs, and a steamer ferrying provisions, carriages, and people back and forth from the mainland. The sun caught a gull's wings, adding flashes of white to the sails that dotted the blue water.

Nelly took off her straw hat and turned her face to the wind. Her golden hair billowed behind her.

"Let's stay up here forever," she said, twirling far from the ledge, where the earth ended abruptly and dropped many feet to the sea. She seemed so terribly young. Given her druthers, she'd no doubt rather be playing knights and jumping gates with Mr. Tennyson's boys.

"What would your husband do without his muse?" Anny said.

"He could easily find someone else to sit for him."

"You don't enjoy it?"

"It is dreadfully dull. One day I sat for hours and hours in armor and never realized how heavy it was until I fainted. I never should have married."

"Why did you?"

"One day after posing for him all day, he gave me a long, long kiss, and I knew I had to marry him immediately, because I was going to have a baby."

Good gracious me, Anny thought. Does the child not know where babies come from? Anny was a bit fuzzy on the details herself—this was one area of her education that her father had neglected—but she did know enough to know that you did not get babies from kissing.

"And are you? Going to have a baby?" asked Anny.

"I'm waiting."

"Perhaps a baby is more likely after your wedding night," Anny said. They had been married for six months.

"That night!" she said in horror. "How I cried and cried and my husband asked me to please stop, because it made my nose swell. I guess I'm no good as a muse with a fat red nose. But up here, on the top of the world, it doesn't matter how I look."

She danced up the hill, carefree and happy.

Anny remembered when she was sixteen, full of passion but little wisdom. At that age, she had already written several romantic novels and a play. Her father advised her—wisely, she now saw—to tuck the manuscripts away and not pick up her quill until she gained more perspective. "The first novel you write is not necessarily the first one you publish," he had told her. She cringed when she thought of her overwrought depictions of handsome suitors and beautiful maidens so different from herself.

Unlike Nelly, she would never be anyone's muse. Her father had called her "a fat lump of pure gold" or "My Great Fat Deedle-Deedle." He said it affectionately, and she never let on how much it hurt her. He was fond of telling people that his dear fat Anny was the greatest girl he had seen anywhere and that he was brutally happy she wasn't handsome enough to make an early marriage likely. He never said anything like that about Minny.

Anny paused a moment, as if she might be struck down, entertaining an unkind thought about her father, whom she adored and missed dreadfully.

She sat on the ground, dotted with chunks of chalk shorn from the cliffs and scattered about by the wind.

A fresh wave of grief hit her, more fierce for being unexpected. And she was reminded anew that she would have to live her life without her father. He had given her the gift of fascinating friends, but she was not that far removed from Nelly, struggling to figure out who she was among this coterie of strong personalities.

IT WAS STILL LIGHT WHEN SHE returned from the Needles, and she had just enough time before dressing for dinner to look for the book she had left at Freshwater Bay that morning.

The empty bathing machines, lined up side by side beyond the high tide mark, had the sad air of a deserted carnival. She walked along the pebbled beach, searching in vain for her book among the seaweed, driftwood, and feathers. Either it had been swept out by the tides, or had found its way into the hamper of another holiday-maker.

She walked along the deserted beach until she reached a place where an outcropping of rocks prevented further progress. The late afternoon light lent a rosy radiance to the chalk cliffs. Waves crashed against the rocks near shore, and sent a spray of water in her direction. She backed farther into the cove.

Something about the smell of the salt air and the sea mist jostled loose a memory.

She is a little girl, barely three. It is night and she is surrounded by water. Someone is holding her at arm's length so that all she can see is the sea and the moonlight unfurling a pathway of liquid silver. Terrified, she reaches out for a breast, an arm, a shoulder, anything solid, but all she feels is air. She cannot swim. She can barely walk.

She slips from the hands that are holding her and descends into total darkness. Underwater, she thrashes about. She can't breathe. She can't see. It only lasts an instant. Then, in a great spout of water, she is pulled out and enveloped in someone's arms. They belong to her mother, who is weeping, covering her with kisses and saying over and over, "My Baby, My Darling. Please forgive me. You must. You must." It is just the two of them, the silver moon, the water, and the night sky.

Was this real or invented? Memory or nightmare? Now, in the secluded cove surrounded by high chalk walls, she found herself shaking uncontrollably. Her whole life, she had tried to protect Minny from the pain of being cast off by their mother, but suddenly the danger dwelt much closer to home.

MINNY WAITED IMPATIENTLY BY the front door while Anny dressed hurriedly after returning from the cove. Her sister hated being late. For Anny, it was a habit. Even after her father complained about her tardiness shortly before he died, she had not reformed.

When the sisters arrived at Farringford, the guests were already seated. Anny found her place card beside Mr. Dodgson. As he stood and helped her with her chair, she suppressed a naughty urge to call him Dodo.

Waiting for the soup to be served, he picked up his knife and rubbed the blade with his damask napkin. Anny feared he might feel compelled to give the butter dish a buffing. Mrs. Tennyson would be mortified. Luckily the poet's wife was engaged in conversation and did not notice.

Across the table, her sister sat between two students who were visiting with their Classics professor. Minny had an eye for fashion and a knack for selecting frocks that were becoming on her, even in mourning. With a flutter of the eyelids and a downward glance, she held the young men in her thrall. She exuded fragility and the need for protection and brought out men's gallantry.

At the far end of the table, Nelly was seated beside her husband, who had a long beard with a patch of pure white hair beneath his lower lip, as if he had dribbled milk on himself. Now, as he nodded off to sleep, the tip of his beard dipped precariously near the soup.

"Oh dear," Anny said, under her breath, knowing his child bride would not know how to attend to the situation.

"A veritable dormouse," Mr. Dodgson observed.

"Pardon?" said Anny.

"The Dormouse in my children's story keeps dozing off

during a tea party," he said. "My character is not the only one to pass social occasions in a perpetual state of torpor."

Anny was surprised that he had noticed Mr. Watts. She went to their end of the table, leaned down between the snoozing artist and his wife and said in a loud voice, "Nelly!"

Mr. Watts startled awake, looked at her with groggy eyes, and grumbled something unintelligible.

"I wanted to tell your wife what a capital time I had, going to the Needles this afternoon," Anny said.

"Yes, Yes, um, er, well . . ." He rearranged his napkin in his lap.

Tragedy averted, Nelly squeezed her hand conspiratorially.

Back at her seat, Anny said, "Tell me more about the Dormouse. Was that the story you were reading Nelly this afternoon?" she said.

"It's just a children's book," he said modestly.

"My father's children's book *The Rose and the Ring* is still one of my very favorites—silly and spirited with a healthy dose of absurdity."

"Mine is filled with puns, riddles, and all kinds of nonsense."

"I adore riddles. Ask me one."

"It's n-n-not that interesting, really." She found his awkwardness endearing in a strange way.

"Perhaps not, but let me have a go at it."

After a little back and forth, he relented. "As you wish. How is a raven like a writing desk?"

"Hmmmm." She thought for a moment and came up short.

She got the attention of the assembled guests and posed the question to them. Word games, pantomime, charades, and amateur theatricals were a staple at Freshwater. Soon everyone joined in on the fun.

"They are both used for bills and tales," Mr. Watts said.

Not bad for a catnapper, Anny thought.

His answer set off a competitive rush. The group enjoyed sharpening their wits and playing off each other.

Cammie chimed in: "The notes for which they are noted are not musical notes. Dear me. Does that make sense? That one got away from me."

Mr. Tennyson made his offering: "Mmmm. A raven and a writing desk. I suppose one is good for writing books and the other is better for biting rooks." There was a murmur of approval.

"In rhyme, no less," said one of the students, admiringly.

Anny thought of an answer that had not come to her earlier. "Edgar Allan Poe wrote on both," she said triumphantly, proud of her answer. She looked toward Mr. Dodgson for his approval, but she was seated by his bad ear, and he gave no sign that he had heard it.

"Nevermore!" blurted out the student beside Minny, and started reciting the poem, until a collective groan caused him to stop.

Minny remained silent but the student at her other side entered the fray. "They both have black hearts."

"What does that mean?" said the professor of Latin and Greek.

"I don't know. It was a wild guess," the student sputtered and looked mortified.

"It's all in fun," Anny said. She didn't like to see someone belittled. It was contrary to the spirit of Freshwater.

"That old crab should stick to teaching the Classics— Laughing and Grief," Mr. Dodgson said in a whisper. She looked at her straitlaced dinner companion for signs that the pun was intentional. The beginnings of a smile formed at the edge of his mouth, and she saw that he was not as dull as he seemed.

When the responses died down, Mr. Dodgson looked to the end of the table and said, "Nelly, what do you think?"

The child looked startled. There was a moment of silence, as everyone looked in her direction.

"Not all riddles need have answers," she said.

"Brilliant!" Mr. Dodgson broke out. "Exactly."

Nelly beamed in triumph and her husband looked as if he had gas. "If there's no answer, why put it in the book?"

"My child readers will understand," Mr. Dodgson said.

"What, pray tell, is the moral of this . . . this children's book?" said the Classics professor, spitting out "children's book" as if he couldn't wait to expel a bitter substance from his mouth.

"There is none. I don't know about you, but I'm never so out of sorts as when I'm being preached at," Mr. Dodgson said.

The moralists and preachers among them fell silent.

After dinner, the guests retired to the drawing room for dessert. Anny was hoping someone would suggest a game of charades to give Nelly a chance to show her acting flair. But Mr. Tennyson, who appeared to be in bad humor after the attention paid to Mr. Dodgson's riddle, perked up considerably when someone entreated him to read one of his poems.

Mr. Tennyson took his place in the carved throne-like chair beneath the great oriel window. Guests spread out on the window seats and on scattered chairs and sofas. In the flickering candlelight, with the sound of the sea in the background, he began to recite a poem to the rapt audience.

> Come into the garden, Maud,
>   For the black bat, Night, has flown,
> Come into the garden, Maud,
>   I am here at the gate alone;
> And the woodbine spices are wafted abroad,
>   And the musk of the roses blown.

His booming voice rose and fell, casting a rhythmic spell over the room. On the second verse, one of the Classics students joined in. He had memorized the poem, along with almost every schoolboy in England. Not to be outdone, the other students added their voices. When the professor cast a dark look their way, they tapered off, leaving Mr. Tennyson to finished the poem alone, and the evening ended with an abundance of good feeling.

THE SISTERS RETURNED TO The Porch and dressed for bed. Moonlight brushed the waves, distant but visible from their window. Minny pulled back the coverlet, scattering a couple of Cammie's cats who had taken up residence at the cottage during their stay.

"Shall I brush your hair?" Anny asked.

"I would like that."

She took off her nightcap and let her auburn tresses tumble down her back. A fluffy gray cat jumped back on the bed and crawled into her lap.

"You seemed to be getting on capitally with the young men on either side of you," Anny said as she ran the brush though her sister's hair in long steady strokes.

"The only person they were interested in impressing was King Alfred. The cult of Tennyson. I was merely a trifle to pass the time. What about Mr. Dodgson? He might actually be attractive if he didn't look as if he swallowed a poker."

"I find him fascinating, but not for the reason you suggest. He is two different people and the most imaginative one is not accessible to adults. I have a feeling his book will be quite good."

Anny picked hair from the bristles and placed it in the porcelain hair receiver by the bed. Cammie saved it for the villagers to weave into wall hangings, brooches, and wreaths.

"That clenched young man could never write a story to please children," Minny said. The cat in her lap purred and lifted its head into her hand as she petted it.

"Apparently he has. Nelly was spellbound when he read a section to her. Did you see those little girls who gathered around him at the beach? He helped a couple of them pin up their skirts to wade in the water. He keeps safety pins in his bag."

"I find that disturbing. Ouch. You're too harsh," she said as Anny encountered a tangle.

"Me?"

Minny laughed.

"Well, I wish him and his children's book the best," Anny said.

"The b-b-best." Minny countered.

She thumped her sister on the back with the brush.

Minny turned serious. "At dinner, when everyone was talking about the raven and the writing desk, I couldn't help but think of Papa. Remember the way he used to cut his own quills as part of his writing ritual? I don't know if they were raven quills."

"Why didn't you say something?" Anny said.

"I'm not like you. I don't have the intellect to spar in that literary company. But the image of Papa at his writing desk was so strong, it was almost like a vision."

The sensation Anny had experienced in the cove that afternoon had felt so real, she couldn't say whether it was a vision or a memory. She had not found an opening to tell Minny about the letter revealing that their mother had tried to take her own life. Now was not the proper time to tell her that she may have tried to take Anny's life as well.

The moon moved in and out of the clouds, varying the ambient light in the room. Minny's hair crackled and separated with each stroke of the brush. "Do you remember anything about Mama?" Anny said.

"Why ask such a thing?" Minny said, suddenly cross. "I was an infant when she was taken away."

"Any fragment or image—anything?"

"That's enough. You're hurting my scalp." She shooed the cat off her lap, and pulled back her hair, tying on the nightcap.

Anny continued: "It's just that, with Papa, there's room after room—a mansion, really—crammed full of memories. But with Mama, there's barely a cupboard's worth and it seems so sad."

How disturbing, then, to discover, on the mostly empty shelves, a vial that might or might not contain poison.

Did her mother try to save her or drown her? She would never know. And the one person who could tell her was dead.

four

1865 AND 1866

"ANNY, HOW COULD YOU?" Minny cried. The dining room table was piled high with bills. The monthly accounts ledger, which they had dubbed *Le Grand Livre*, was opened between them.

"I don't know what happened. Oh, I'm hopeless."

Every January, Anny made a New Year's resolution to make a budget, and then failed to stick to it.

"You forgot to enter the books from Marks & Hinton," Minny said, waving a bill at her sister.

"I meant to." Anny promised to be more vigilant.

"And what is this donation to the Children's Foundation?"

"They do such good work. And they need extra money at Christmas."

"Well, we are way overdrawn, and cannot pay the rent. There's no reason in the world we should find ourselves in this position!" Minny blinked back tears of frustration.

After their father's death, the copyrights to his works had sold for more than anyone imagined, leaving the sisters well provided for. By all rights, they should have been able to get along handsomely on their generous monthly allowance. But money flew out of Anny's hands and she couldn't account for it. At the end of the month, she was always coming up short, even though she earned a steady supplement from her essays, shorts stories, and sketches.

"Look at this wine bill," Minny said, pointing to a line in the ledger. "We're going to have to start doing things differently." She managed the household accounts and was conscientious about expenses. "No more wine at parties."

"You know how deadly dull the dinner parties are at the Cranmores. All the guests staring forlornly at their water glass," Anny said, pushing away the dreaded *Grand Livre*.

"Then we must find other ways to economize. Something has got to change. I can't go through this every month."

The sisters were rescued from their financial straits by their Ritchie cousins, who agreed to rent the house on Onslow Square for a few months while the sisters moved to less expensive lodgings. The boisterous Ritchie clan was the closest the sisters had to family. There were eight children, four boys and four girls. The older girls were close to Anny and Minny in age. The sisters had many happy memories of summers at the Ritchie house: Pinkie playing Mozart on the grand piano in the parlor, Blanchie in the deep bow window seat chanting Latin at the top of her lungs, Nellie galloping over the hill on a pony. The cousins mounted elaborate theatrical productions in the attic, played games of croquet on the lawn, and enjoyed picnics at the seashore.

Richmond, the second to the youngest, was the cleverest of the Ritchie cousins. He had earned a full scholarship to Eton at age eight. When dressed in the required top hat and tails at school, he looked like a pint-size prime minister, but on holiday, in his knickers and houndstooth jacket, he looked like any young boy. Now eleven, he had come to London to stay with his mother and sisters in Anny's house.

"You are welcomed to help yourself to any of the books in my library," Anny said.

"I will be very careful with them," he promised solemnly, observing the shelves.

He had lost his father early, and, as his godmother, Anny felt a special responsibility to him. Growing up without a mother, Anny had had many teachers.

"There's one book I think you'll find particularly interesting." She took a volume from the shelf and opened it at random. "This was my father's school book when he was not much older than you," she said. Richmond peered at the pages. The margins were filled with caricatures drawn in pencil.

"He was a wicked boy, defacing schoolbooks," he said.

"Sometimes it's permissible to be a little wicked," she replied, knowing that this precocious boy was cursed with the bugbear of perfectionism. "Even at that young age, Papa could convey character with a dot here and a few quick strokes there."

Richmond watched her raptly. With dark curly hair and velvet eyes, he had a curiosity unmatched by the other cousins.

"Before he became a writer, Papa wanted to be an artist. Most people don't know this, but he applied for a job as the illustrator for the *Pickwick Papers*, and Charles Dickens did not hire him. It was the first time they met. Papa referred to the incident as Mr. Pickwick's lucky escape. That failure was what propelled him to concentrate on writing instead of illustration, and we're all the better for it."

"If he'd have known that Uncle William would become his main rival, perhaps Mr. Dickens would have hired him," the boy said.

No wonder his family called him Whizz. Anny noted the way he soaked in the details. It was intoxicating, feeding young minds, and she saw the attraction of teaching as a profession.

"Papa was a fairly good draughtsman, and did the illustrations for *Vanity Fair* and *Pendennis* himself. He could have made a middling living as a draughtsman, but he went on to become a truly great writer, and that might never have happened if he had not experienced that blight to his early prospects. Failure can sometimes lead to good fortune."

She wished to introduce the benefits of failure because bright boys like Richmond, so accustomed to getting things right, often shied away from challenge for fear of floundering.

"Drawing continued to be a passion throughout his life. It relaxed him," she said. "After a long day of writing, and always on Sunday, he'd fetch his drawing board. I have fond memories of when I was around your age, standing on chairs to hold draperies to cast shadows. Or washing the chalk off the boxwood blocks. I'll never forget that beastly day when I washed away a finished drawing while the messenger waited in the hall."

"So you make mistakes too," Richmond observed.

"Too many to count."

CAMMIE CAME CALLING THAT WINTER after a meeting of the London Photographic Society. She sailed into the house, chattering at full speed.

"That crusty congregation of nattering old fusspots. They can criticize me all they want, but it is my work, not theirs, that will delight and startle the world. I am waxing mad in my own conceit you will say."

Actually, Anny didn't have time to say anything, for Cammie was off on a tear, about how the members didn't take her seriously or understand what she was trying to achieve.

Without stopping to catch a breath, she pressed a leather binder upon Anny and continued her tirade. Anny opened it and read the inscription in Cammie's bold handwriting: "Fatal to photographs are cups of tea and coffee, candles and lamps, and children's fingers."

It was an astonishing gift—a collection of her most recent photographs. As usual, Cammie casually gave it to her without pausing for a reaction.

"I am so touched. You must have barely left the darkroom since I last saw you." Cammie produced new work the way she produced words, as if time were inadequate to accommodate her torrent of ambition, ideas, and passion. "Oh, look. There's Mr. Tennyson. You finally wore him down, I see." The portrait showed him in a scruffy cowl with wild hair, clutching a book. He looked like a vagabond before a bench of magistrates.

"Yes, he's dubbed this the Dirty Monk, but secretly I think he fancies it," Cammie said. Mr. Tennyson was not vain about his appearance. He had more important things to attend to.

"And there's a Madonna and Child. Beautiful."

"Later, my child, later," she said, brushing aside any praise. Like criticism, it was irrelevant to her. "First tell me, how are you and Minny getting on?" She looked around the small parlor. "This place suits you."

Anny was able to get Cammie to stop talking long enough to surrender her coat.

"Is Charles Dodgson part of the Photographic Society?" Anny asked.

"No, but he's the worst. He thinks I have fame on my mind, as if fame were pronounced 'the last infirmity of noble minds.'"

"I thought you'd made it your mission to make an ally of him."

"I would, if I could get him to stop stealing my subjects. He's been trying to wangle another photo session with the Tennysons. Well, Alfred is mine!" she said, throwing the end of her shawl over her shoulder and taking a seat by the fire. "He did manage to weasel his way into Nelly Watts's good graces and convinced her to sit for a portrait at the beginning of the year. In her wedding dress, no less! That brown silk affair that Holman Hunt designed for her. Can you believe it? What poor judgment on Dodgson's part. Less than a month after the child's rupture with Il Signor. I've seen the photograph. If you ask me, the background looks like sticking plaster."

Anny had heard rumors that the couple had separated after less than a year of marriage. It was Mr. Watts's doing. By all accounts, Nelly was thunderstruck. Anny should really go visit the poor girl. She must feel like a pariah. What an unkind blow to a lively girl whose only crime was to be young, naïve, and beautiful.

"The muse is used, then abused," Anny said, and then, apologetically, "The Dirty Monk would wrap me on the knuckles for that rhyme!"

"My lips are sealed," Cammie said.

"Do you know what happened?"

"Heaven knows, he would never tell me. I think it was something about Nelly's insane excitability keeping him from his work. I have it on good authority that he offered her 300 pounds a year if she stayed chaste, and 200 if she returned to the stage. When you come out to the island—You are coming, aren't you? Soon I hope!—you must respect the embargo on uttering Nelly's name. Il Signor has strictly forbidden it."

THAT DECEMBER, ANNY RAN INTO Charles Dodgson at a gallery opening in London. He stood gazing at a Pre-Raphaelite painting, holding his gray gloves behind his back. She recognized him by his off-kilter posture, with one shoulder slightly lower than the other. He was the only man in the room without a beard.

She rushed up to him and started gushing about his children's book, which had just been published a few weeks before. She had fallen in love with the feisty heroine Alice, who navigated a world of outlandish characters with curiosity and verve—the conversational rabbit, the mad hatter, the raging queen. She wanted to become better acquainted with the man who wrote under the pen name of Lewis Carroll, a wildly imaginative rebel so different from the stuffy photographer she had met at Freshwater.

"Oh Mr. Dodgson. I adored your book. I've never read anything like it! What an imagination you have!"

He looked as if she had deposited a dead rat at his feet. "I doubt there will be many more like you," he said.

"But there will. Children and adults. I am certain of it. The story is magical," she said, undeterred.

"I am fed up with the whole business. I recalled the first printing and sold the first two thousand copies as wastepaper. The print quality was totally unacceptable. Substandard. I insisted that the book be done right, even though I had to b-b-bear the entire loss. It cost me six shillings a copy, or 600 pounds, to reprint the book. If I make 500 pounds by sale, this will be a loss of a hundred pounds, and the loss of the first 2,000 will probably be a hundred pounds, leaving me 200 pounds out of pocket, which I may never recover."

Anny's head was spinning with figures. Only he could make a discussion of *Alice's Adventures in Wonderland* boring. Cammie may consider him a genius, but she placed him in the highest ranks of priggery and fuss.

THROUGH THE WINTER, ANNY kept a regular writing schedule, thanks to Minny, who did many of the things a wife would do. A good thing, too. Their father had once summed up Anny's domestic accomplishments with a drawing of a goose.

Women of their class were expected to paint, play the piano, and write pretty letters—but only in the drawing room and never for money. Anny was raised differently. She saw no shame in being an ink-stained wretch. She was paid for the essays, articles, and short stories she published in the *Cornhill*. The extra income allowed her and Minny the luxuries that made life more enjoyable—a couple of servants, new hats and dresses, an unlimited number of books, and the ability to travel without financial worries.

Writing novels, however, was more personal. She had no illusion that her work would change the world, the way her father's had. She did not write fiction for recognition. She wrote because it gave her life meaning. On her worst day, the effort was more fulfilling than needlework or any number of drawing room pursuits expected of ladies of her class.

Lacking her father's gift for narrative and character, she approached story as she did life—through visual impressions. These revealed themselves to her in flashes, like Cammie's photographs: blurry, evocative moments that she snatched from time and froze into permanency.

Certain places haunted her from childhood. Like magic lantern pictures, they emerged by a chance association out of the darkness when the lamp was lit. She struggled to make the images as vivid on the page as they were in her imagination.

One such image was from the fishing village on the Normandy coast where she and Minny spent summers with their grandmother. A windblown house perched on the edge of a cliff with steep steps to the sea. The abandoned château had many windows, weathercocks, muslin curtains, and wooden balconies. It belonged to a widow whose husband left it to her in his will. Why did no one live there? How did the widow's husband die? What was the story behind their marriage? She began to write a novel to answer the questions.

IN THE SPRING, GEORGE SMITH invited the sisters to a dinner party. As publisher of the *Cornhill Magazine*, he could be counted on to assemble a fascinating group of writers, artists, and intellectuals. Minny was not feeling well, so Anny went without her, chaperoned by a family friend.

She arrived late, as usual. Mr. Smith ushered her over to Leslie Stephen. She and Minny had been introduced to him at luncheon at his mother's house. He had a long red beard and piercing blue eyes and was unusually tall, like her father, but more athletic.

Minny had been greatly impressed by his international reputation as president of the Alpine Club. It interested Anny more that he read widely and was intimately familiar with the works of Tennyson, Browning, Dickens, and Trollope.

"I understand that you two have already made your acquaintance," Mr. Smith said, and left to mingle with the other guests.

"It was a great pleasure to meet you and your sister. Is she here tonight?" he asked.

"I'm afraid she was not feeling well and elected to stay home."

"Please give her my regards."

Anny was drawn into a circle that included the poet Robert Browning and the novelist Elizabeth Gaskell. She wanted to return to Mr. Stephen, who looked a little lost, but she could not gracefully escape. Dinner was announced, and she was delighted to find her place card next to Mr. Stephen's. She saw dear Mr. Smith's hand in that.

Light from the silver candelabras cast a glow over the lavishly set table. Individual tureens of soup were placed in front of each guest.

"I hope you did not find me to be currying favor when I named *Vanity Fair* as my favorite novel at Mother's house. I meant it sincerely," he said, watching to see where she put the lid to the soup tureen.

"I fancy myself a good enough judge of character to know that." She was aware that he had resigned from Cambridge after he lost his faith and felt he could no longer continue to be a man of the cloth, which was a requirement for a mathematics don. A man who refused to feign belief to retain a prestigious university position was not the kind of man who would fib about his favorite novel.

"I confess to being a bit out of my element here," he said. "I'm afraid I spend all of my time alone on top of a mountain or closeted away with my books."

"I hope there is no entailment on that property, for that is where I spend most of my time as well. In the closet with my books."

"I saw you talking to Mr. Browning. I couldn't help but notice how comfortable you seemed with him."

She was pleased to note that he had been watching her.

"He was my father's friend. I've known him all my life," she said. She felt totally at ease with the poets, writers, and intellectuals of her father's circle. She was less successful with men her own age.

"I've read all of Mr. Browning's poetry and know most of it by heart. The intellectual capital in this room is overwhelming." He stretched his neck, as if his collar bound him too tightly.

"There's no reason to be intimidated," Anny said. "No one else in this room has conquered the Schreckhorn."

"You know about that?"

"I read your article. I'm not that interested in mountaineering, but I was riveted by your descriptions. I wrote several down in a little notebook I keep of memorable phrases. Ice clouds like cobwebs, shooting out mysterious fibers—what was it you compared it to? The way a spider projects its net of gossamer. Brilliant! You certainly have an eye for detail."

"I can't tell you how happy it makes me to have my own words quoted back to me." His thin lips quivered with delight.

"Even if I mangled them royally?"

"Coming from a person of your literary lineage, it is an incredible compliment," he said.

Like so many, he had been swept up in the Thackeray mystique. Part of her, though, wished he had referenced her own novel or *Cornhill* articles.

"I'm trying to make a name for myself," he said. "More than anything, I want to be worthy to sit here at this table." His struggle reminded her of her father, before the success of *Vanity Fair*.

"In case you haven't noticed, you *are* sitting at this table. Why do you think Mr. Smith asked you to contribute to the

Cornhill? My father published you in the magazine, did he not? Your talent is obvious."

"Do you really think so?" He looked at her intently, eager for praise. His unruly hair and scraggly beard gave him the air of a mad prophet.

It surprised her that such a shy, bookish man had become one of the leading figures in the golden age of alpinism. "How did you become interested in mountain climbing?"

"A combination of good fortune and opportunity." He explained that he was at the height of his physical fitness at a time when the sport was gaining in popularity, appealing as it did to the era's fascination with nature, exploration, and leisure. The new French train line to Geneva made it easier for him to reach the Alps. There, he apprenticed himself to local guides, who taught him how to climb on ice and snow, scale vertical rock walls, and manage fields of loose scree. For the past seven summers, he had made nine ascents. He was the first to conquer the Schreckhorn and the Rothorn.

"I owe my success to my guides," he said. "A third-rate guide will always be superior to a first-rate amateur."

She found he lacked pretension and was charmed.

"I fear that last summer was my last serious climb," he continued.

"Why would you give it up?"

"Oh, I'll never abandon climbing. The Alps have been my school and my cathedral. But I need to focus on my career now, and I no longer have the time to maintain my fitness at the level necessary for a serious ascent. But it has proved to be excellent training for writing."

"Really? How so?"

"In both activities, there's a sense of anguish, exhilaration, and sudden inspiration. You start out having no idea where you're going or if you'll get there, and along the way there are serendipitous turns, unanticipated challenges, and numerous risks. And then when you reach the summit, you are flooded by astonishment, both at the incomparable beauty, and at having pushed yourself beyond what you thought possible."

She was swept up in the romance of his description. "At least there is no danger of losing one's life in the business of manufacturing phrases," she said.

"I was perhaps too cavalier. For death, there is no training."

When she got home that night, she couldn't wait to tell Minny about the dinner party. She found her sister asleep in her room. Anny rarely woke her but she felt exuberant. She sat down on the bed and shook her gently. Minny stared at her with hooded eyes as Anny described the guests and the menu.

"I saw Leslie Stephen again. He didn't impress me the first time I met him, but tonight I found him to be quite the scholar mountaineer."

"Anny, please," she said, peering up at her with a pale, wistful face. "I need to rest." Minny had a weak constitution, and the frequency of her illnesses worried Anny.

"Can I get you something? Some water?"

Minny shook her head. "I just need to sleep. I'll feel better in the morning."

Anny went to bed and dreamed of mountain peaks.

SEVERAL WEEKS LATER, AN INVITATION arrived for the sisters to join Mr. Stephen and his brother for a boating outing on the Thames. Anny was in high spirits.

"I'm not sure I feel up to it," Minny said.

"Of course you do! The fresh air will do you good. You can't remain on the settee day after day." Minny had been in ill health throughout the spring and avoided socializing.

"You go," Minny said.

"No, that would not be proper. The invitation is to both of us."

"If you insist."

They met Mr. Stephen by the docks and waited for his older brother, Fitzjames. The sisters knew him as the man who had helped untangle their father's estate.

Leslie helped Anny into the bow of one of the boats, and then took Minny's hand while she stepped into the other boat.

"You have strong hands, Mr. Stephen," Minny said.

"Please, can we use our Christian names? There are too many Stephens and too many Thackerays on this river," he said.

His older brother arrived late with his daughter Margaret skipping beside him. The little girl jumped in beside Anny, while Fitzy offered a flurry of apologies. He climbed into the boat with Anny and took the oars while Leslie installed himself in Minny's boat.

"That's a pretty dress you have on," Anny said to Margaret, cursing her luck in ending up in the boat with Leslie's brother.

"Thank you." The little girl pulled her skirt wide to show off the three layers of ruffles.

Before long, they were out of view of St. Paul's dome and gliding through beech groves, alongside banks fringed with white cow parsley and meadowsweet. Sunday afternoon was a popular time for leisure activities, and the Thames was crowded with pleasure barges, skiffs, punts, and rowing boats.

The child was deeply engrossed in reading *Alice's Adventures in Wonderland*, ignoring the scenery around her.

"Do you like the book?" Anny asked.

"I wish there were ten thousand more just like it," she said.

Her father said, "She's read it six times."

"Seven," the child corrected him.

"I know the author Lewis Carroll. That's not his real name. It's only a pen name."

Margaret looked at her oddly, and Anny realized that for her,

Alice's story sprang full blown from the page to her imagination, without the help of an author.

"You know, someone wrote down the words that make up that story."

Mr. Dodgson had told Anny how the book came into being when she met him at the gallery. As she predicted, it had become an instant bestseller.

"The author was rowing the three Liddell sisters on the Thames, just like we are now, except they were going from Oxford to Godstow. Their father is dean of Christ Church College, where the author, Lewis Carroll, teaches mathematics. On this particular day in July, it was hot, and the ride was long, and the little girls were really, really bored."

Fitzy's daughter nodded gravely, no stranger to boring boat rides.

"The middle sister, Alice, was about your age. How old are you?" Anny asked.

"Nine."

"She was ten. Anyway, Alice begged him to tell them a story. So he began spinning a tale to make the time pass quickly. He put Alice down the rabbit hole with no idea what would happen to her after that. He just started making things up, working in names of people in the boat. Alice's sister Edith became an eaglet. Her sister Lorina was turned into a Lory. The other man in the boat, Mr. Duckworth, was a duck."

"What animal would I be?" said the child, holding her place in the book with her finger.

"Let's see. Margaret." She thought a moment. "Does anyone call you Maggie? You could be a magpie."

"I hate the name Maggie. I don't want to be a chattery old magpie."

"You could be an egret. Marg-egret."

"There's already an eaglet," the child pouted.

Anny looked wistfully toward the boat in front and saw her

sister and Leslie deep in conversation. They were certainly discussing something more compelling than avian character possibilities.

They rowed to Maidenhead. After strawberries and cream at a fashionable restaurant and a game of croquet on the lawn, they returned home.

FOR THE FIRST TIME SINCE HER father's death two and a half years before, Anny felt in the mood to celebrate, so she feted her twenty-ninth birthday in grand style with a picnic. Tables were spread under the trees beside a charming half-timbered inn in Surrey. Guests arrived by carriage from the railroad station. The luncheon table was sumptuous, with platters of lobster smothered in homemade mayonnaise and cold poached chicken with a tarragon cream sauce. Bees buzzed around the layered trifle, and butterflies alighted on the lips of the champagne bottles. The sun through the trees cast a magical confetti of light over the table, the lawn, and the assembled guests.

That summer, the first chapter of Anny's second novel, *The Village on the Cliff*, was serialized in the *Cornhill*. She had not written the ending yet, but as she looked out over the assembled guests, all here to celebrate her birthday and her novel, she felt a sense of contentment.

Leslie and Fitzy Stephen were there, and as Anny accepted congratulations from her friends, she kept track of Leslie's whereabouts out of the corner of her eye, waiting for the right moment to approach him. She was curious to find out what he thought about the first chapter of her novel. But every time she caught a glimpse of him, he was fetching something for her sister—a luncheon plate, a cup of tea, some water.

When she finally saw him alone and started toward him, she was detained by Mrs. Sartoris, her father's old friend and an internationally acclaimed opera singer. "What a grand beginning to the novel. Your father would be so proud," she said.

Anny glowed. While writing the novel, she often felt his presence admonishing her to be lively, be authentic, be real. Under his tutelage, she had learned to avoid the novelist's sins of grandiloquence and tall talking.

"The writing advice you gave me was so wise. You were absolutely right," Anny said warmly, giving the older lady's arm a squeeze. "I read the manuscript out loud, as you suggested, and a number of things struck me that I might otherwise have passed over."

"When you've written something awkward or false, your voice will let you know it. Your voice is the real you," Mrs. Sartoris said.

If anyone knew about voice, it was Mrs. Sartoris.

Anny spotted Leslie towering over her sister and approached them.

"I'm so glad you invited me," Leslie said. "This is a capital picnic."

"I have Minny to thank for that."

"I'd also like to congratulate you on your novel," he said, but offered no details. She was fairly sure he had not read it.

"Yes, my sister is a genius!" Minny jumped in. "Her characters are so open, so empathetic. Just like Anny herself. No wonder people can't get enough of her writing." Anny felt warmth toward her sister, her first and biggest admirer.

"I understand she has quite a following among women," Leslie said.

"Not just women," Minny said. "Anthony Trollope declared her characters sweet and charming and quite true to human nature."

"Is he a family friend?" Leslie said, as if this were the only conceivable reason for such praise.

"Let me introduce you to some of the other guests," Anny

said to Leslie, hiding her hurt feelings. "Do you know Mrs. Cameron's niece and namesake, Julia?" She nodded toward a woman Minny's age, draped in a stunning white dress with a sprig of larkspur behind her ear.

Cammie worshipped beauty, and had taken more photographs of her niece than any other subject.

"She could be the Sistine Madonna with those flawless features."

"Would you like to meet her?" Anny said. She felt he should mingle with more people than Minny.

"I've never cared for perfection. I prefer to stay with the people I know," he said.

Great beauty could be intimidating, Anny realized. That was not its only drawback. She thought of Nelly Watts, whose dazzling looks captured an artist thirty years her senior. When her magic as a muse wore off, he tossed her aside. Nelly's career and marriage prospects were over. It was a high price to pay for beauty.

The picnic guests assembled on the lawn for a game of blind man's bluff, and Leslie joined the circle next to Anny.

Unwilling to give up her place beside Leslie, Anny declined to be "it," so Minny volunteered. Someone tied a blindfold around her eyes and twirled her around three times.

Minny staggered about on the lawn, the skirt over her steel hoop crinoline swaying like a Japanese lantern. Half a dozen men and women got in the circle with her. One woman tiptoed close and let out a peep. Minny turned and stumbled toward the noise with her hands in front of her.

Leslie joined the game. With his long legs and athletic ability, he was a playful participant. He crouched near Minny, leaped toward her, let out a whoop, and then retreated, just as she swung toward him. The crowd reacted with laughter.

Minny seemed to gain nourishment from the cheering crowd and played her part with gusto.

One by one, people dropped out of the game until Minny was left alone in the ring with Leslie. The guests had noticed what Anny had been slow to acknowledge: Leslie was smitten by her sister.

Now friends encircling the pair shouted out hints to Minny—left, right, behind you. Leslie pranced around Minny and popped up at unexpected places. He reached his long arms around to tap one side of her arm then jumped to the other side.

A pink hydrangea blossom fell from her hat. Leslie picked it up, held the blossom like a powder puff, and lightly dusted her cheek. Minny tottered toward him and was on the verge of falling. He caught her, and she reached out and clamped her hands on his arms. The guests clapped and cheered.

With the blindfold still on, she was face to face with Leslie. Now she had to guess whom she had captured.

She patted his arms and worked her way up to his beard.

"It's a man, obviously," she said. "But every man here has a beard."

The top of her head reached his collarbone. She moved her hands up to his face and ran her fingers over his cheeks. The only touching allowed was in this wholesome game, and she was making the most of it.

"It's someone tall," she said. Murmuring broke out. The promise of romance added to the crowd's enjoyment.

"Make a guess," someone called out.

She patted his chest. Anny knew perfectly well that Minny knew who he was.

"It's Fitzy," Minny guessed, doing her best to prolong the game.

"Close," came a hint from the spectators.

Really, she was being unbearably dense, which Anny found profoundly vexatious.

"Surely you can figure it out," someone shouted from the circle, as if reading Anny's mind.

Now Minny had her hands cupped over Leslie's ears, in the perfect position for a kiss, which, of course, would never be allowed. She ran her fingers through his hair. This was closer than either sister had ever been to a man their age. Anny cursed herself for having proposed this wretched game.

Finally, when Minny could no longer, in good taste, continue the charade, she called out, "Leslie Stephen," and the picnickers whooped and shouted. Leslie untied her blindfold.

Anny watched with a forced smile. What is the sound of a breaking heart? Not a dramatic shattering, or loud crash. Just a barely audible crack. She was twenty-nine. Ahead she saw nothing but loneliness.

THE SELF-STYLED MATCHMAKER Mrs. Huth had taken a fancy to Minny. She and her husband, a wealthy German banker, had bought their father's house at 2 Palace Green, furnishings and all. They invited the sisters to go with them to Chamonix, Switzerland, in August. Leslie Stephen was staying nearby in Zermatt. Mrs. Huth arranged to meet him there.

No railroads or carriage roads connected the two villages, so they had to make the three-day journey on twisting mountain roads. Their party made quite a spectacle, with the ladies on mules, followed by Mr. Huth and the guides, who wore vests and chimney pot hats. The maids and porters stayed back with the pack mules laden down with leather trunks and crinoline hoops packed flat like Chinese lampshades.

The caravan passed green meadows, snowy peaks, thick forests, and drifts of rhododendron with leaves as glossy as holly.

Leslie met them near Täsch, where the road curved around a little bluff. He accompanied them back to a pine chalet with green shutters and balconies that overlooked the Matterhorn.

The following day Leslie, Minny, and the Huths set off with

a mule and a local guide. Mrs. Huth, in her lavish gown, made no nod to traveling comfort, and sailed along the path like a ship in full rig. The metal edges of her crinoline clipped the alpine flowers along the sides of the path. Minny wore a walking dress and shoes suitable for the terrain.

Anny stayed behind to write. Another installment of her novel was due by the end of the month. Like her father, she worked best under deadline. But that day she could not settle down to write and spent a frustrating afternoon in the drafty room that reeked of tar pitch and mothballs.

By sunset, the party had not returned. Through the window, Anny watched the high snowfields catch the rosy light until each peak shone like a signal fire across the delicate twilight.

Night had fallen completely when Minny came to Anny's room, breathless. She fell backwards on the bed with her arms outstretched. "It was so wonderful," she said, looking at the ceiling. "We watched the sunset together. I was cold and he gave me his jacket." She sat up on the bed. " I do believe he cares for me. Oh, it is too much to hope for."

"How could he not?" Anny said with as even a tone as she could manage.

"Do you really think it's possible?" Minny hugged her sister and left.

The moon made the snow-covered Matterhorn gleam like some horrid ghost that might poke its crooked nose in through the window. Anny closed the curtains and went to bed without dinner.

On the last day, Leslie organized an expedition to the Riffelhorn. The inn packed a hamper of cold cuts, cheese, and bread, with champagne wrapped in wet newspaper to keep it cool. They spread out blankets on a high Alpine meadow dotted with gentians, harebells, dianthus, and lacy ferns.

Leslie stretched out his long legs and lit a pipe, leaning on his elbow and gazing at the snow-covered peaks. Seated beside him, Minny looked particularly lovely, her cheeks flushed from the mountain air. Mrs. Huth seemed very satisfied, as if she alone were responsible for the success of the young couple.

After they had eaten, Mrs. Huth rose and said, "I believe I will have the guides take us back to the inn. I need to pack for tomorrow's journey." She looked her husband's way and he rose. Anny needed no prompting. "I'm sure we can trust you to bring Minny back safely," Anny said to Leslie.

He stood up abruptly. "Actually, I need to pack as well. I'm leaving tomorrow to meet a friend in Transylvania."

No one spoke. The tinkle of a cowbell sounded from a distant meadow.

"Transylvania?" Anny said finally, as if she had never heard of the place. "For how long?"

"Three months." The answer landed in stunned silence. Minny could not even manage a smile.

The group broke up in disarray. Leslie stayed behind and the others returned to the inn. Minny went straight to her room.

"How dare he! What was he thinking? I wish we had never come," Anny said to Mrs. Huth, forgetting she had ever had feelings for Leslie. He had humiliated her sister and she wouldn't stand for it.

"No need to get overly worked up," Mrs. Huth cautioned.

"Surely it wasn't just me. Were you not expecting him to make Minny an offer?"

"I must admit that all signs pointed in that direction," Mrs. Huth said.

"Was he only flirting with my Min? She's heartbroken."

"Now don't be annoyed. We must act as if nothing has happened. For, in fact, that is exactly what has transpired—nothing."

"I can't abide his playing with her emotions. It's intolerable."

"Let it pass, dear," said Mrs. Huth, with the resignation of an experienced matchmaker. "There's nothing we can do about it."

Anny went up to Min's room. Through the door she could

hear her sobbing. She knocked and went in. "I dared let myself believe he loved me. What a fool I was!" she said.

"He's nothing but a craggy old mountain goat, and you can't let it bother you."

"What did I do wrong? I truly loved him."

Anny sat on the bed and hugged her. "I don't know if we'll ever know what happened. We'll just have to carry on."

AUTUMN PASSED QUICKLY. With the deadlines of serialization looming, Anny worked long hours on the novel she was close to completing. A full schedule of social engagements kept the sisters busy. One of the things their father had left them was a large and diverse circle of friends.

The first of December arrived in a swirl of ochre fog. The acrid air seeped through the window cracks and coated the furniture with a thin layer of greasy soot that doubled the work of the household staff.

On one such dreary day, Leslie Stephen came to call. Anny saw his card on the silver tray. Minny was out for the afternoon. The maid left to inform him of that, but returned and said that it was Miss Anne Thackeray that he wished to see.

She went downstairs and found him standing in the hall with his hat and his kid gloves in his hands.

"What can I help you with?" she said, coldly.

"May I have a word with you?"

"As you wish."

They went into the parlor. He stood with his back to the fire and she sat in the straight-backed chair that forced her into good posture.

"How is Minny?"

"Fine," she said.

"No, tell me truly. How is she?"

"How dare you come back and stir the pot all over again.

Have you no heart? If you have no honorable intentions, then do her a favor and leave her alone."

"I'm surprised by your anger," he said. He wiped his brow, leaving a sooty smudge on the white handkerchief.

"And what did you expect? Running off without warning in Zermatt. Did you not consider what that would do to my Min?"

"I . . . I . . . I wasn't sure she cared for me."

"Even someone as dense as you could see that she had feelings for you. On the trail to Zermatt, she stopped every stranger on the path and asked if they had seen a Mr. Leslie Stephen of the Alpine Club. And then . . . and then . . . to lead her on for no reason and then drop her." Anny vacillated between telling him to never contact Minny again, and begging him to reconsider.

She continued: "Can you honestly tell me you did not know her heart?"

"Well, I may have had an inkling."

"I knew it!"

"But I became . . . became . . ."

"Afraid?" she offered.

"Confused. I needed time to clear my head and figure out how I felt. I was not sure I'd like losing my independence or that I was ready to be brought to heel."

"Had you no thought for Min's feelings or what it would do to her to leave so abruptly and disappear for months? You are nothing but a selfish bore."

"I dared not take the chance of falling in love," he said, as if love were a matter of will. "I had planned the walking trip with my friend beforehand, but I was miserable the entire time. All I could do was think about Minny. I didn't realize the extent to which she had worked her way into my heart."

He looked at Anny with pleading eyes. She returned the gaze with no emotion.

"Oh, I've made a royal mess of it," he said, yanking his beard like a bell pull. "I convinced myself that I was not worthy. Who would want a fusty old bachelor with poor job prospects? Certainly not a creature as lovely as Minny. I want to provide for her properly, but earning my living by the pen, I'm not convinced I can. And I could never bear to depend on her income. That's intolerable to me. I'm also quite aware that she is used to socializing at a certain level of society. I'm from a line of evangelical clergy and not used to that milieu."

"If you don't love her, for heaven's sake don't marry her. But if you do, none of that matters. You will find a way to work things out."

"I never thought of it that way," he admitted, continuing to tug on his whiskers.

After he left, Anny collapsed on the chair in a state of agitation. She had never before given a piece of her mind to a man in such an unbridled fashion. She was overcome with passion in Minny's defense, but once he was gone, she wondered if, by interfering, she had done more harm than good.

She began shaking all over as if stricken by the ague and went to bed early. She didn't mention the visit to Minny for fear of upsetting her.

The next evening, she was in her study, trying to finish the final installment of her novel. Minny came in and twirled around in front of the fireplace. "Oh you won't believe it. Leslie has asked me to marry him."

"Heigh ho. That's capital," Anny said, trying to strike just the right note of surprise and enthusiasm.

"Oh, I'm the happiest person in the world." She looked at Anny. "Are those tears in your eyes?"

Anny hugged her. "I'm going to miss you," she said. "But I'll get used to it."

"Nothing is going to change between us. I'm determined," Min said fervently. "We must continue living together at Onslow Square, the three of us. I couldn't be parted from you any more than I could part with my left hand."

"You will feel differently when you're married. You may find you have no need for your left hand. And there's Leslie to consider."

"He wants whatever will make me happy. My mind is made up."

FOR THE NEXT TWO DAYS, ANNY adopted a cheerful countenance to hide her anguish. Much as she fancied herself Minny's protector, it was Minny who provided the stability that allowed Anny to work. Without her, she would be lost. Who would rein in her spending, who would temper her impulsiveness or organize her life? Luckily, she had the excuse of a deadline and no one thought anything amiss when she shut herself away in her study.

The plot of *The Village on the Cliff* took a twist at the end that surprised her, but seemed just right. The English governess is widowed and finally in a position to pursue the man she's secretly loved. Instead, she magnanimously encourages him to go after his own true love.

She planned to dedicate the novel to Minny, before she traded in her famous last name to become Mrs. Leslie Stephen.

She needed a final paragraph. That was all. But she could not come up with the right words.

She dreaded the following day, when she had to put her manuscript in the post. She dreaded the week after, when she would have to endure the pitying whispers about the younger sister becoming engaged first. She dreaded the fast-approaching holiday season. Her father's untimely death had forever ruined Christmas for her and always brought a fresh round of grief. Near, intermediate, and distant—all she saw was gloom.

Her world upended, she wrote one ending paragraph, then another, until she had many different versions, all saying more or less the same thing. She was in a jangled state when Alfred Tennyson came to call.

She threw herself on his mercy and begged him to help her with the ending. He pulled up a chair to her desk and spread out the numerous versions.

Slowly he began to read through them. She fancied she saw him grimace. "Everything seems ridiculous. I can't make sense of anything," she said by way of apology.

He straightened his back and pulled up his sleeves. The tip of his beard brushed the desk.

"May I?" he said.

"Of course."

He dipped the pen in the inkwell and started circling and numbering sentences and drawing arrows. The surface of the desk was completely covered by pages of her failed attempts. She could hear her father now, complaining about the waste of paper. Mr. Tennyson picked up one sheet, then another, and wrote the final paragraph in his own hand.

"See what you think of this," he said, and handed the page to her.

She read what he had cobbled together from her discarded efforts. It was a miracle. Such minor adjustments brought everything into focus. "Yes, that's exactly what I was trying to say," she said.

"That's what you *did* say. The words are yours. I just changed the order."

"I'm astonished."

"Trust your heart. It's wiser than you think."

She had never found it to be a reliable companion.

"Life is mysterious," he continued. "Just when things seem the most hopeless, the seeds of change are growing. You can't see it at the time, but looking back, you will."

He couldn't know that Anny hid in her heart an affection for Leslie. Yet somehow, he said exactly the right thing. That was his genius.

She read the final paragraph again:

And Nature, working by some great law unknown, and only vaguely apprehended by us insects . . . brings about the noblest harmonies out of chaos. And, so, too, out of the dire dismays and confusions of the secret world come results both mighty and tangible.

five

1867

NEVER WOULD ANNY HAVE imagined that living as a threesome would prove to be so difficult. After a June wedding, Leslie moved into Onslow Square. She and Min had had their spats when it was just the two of them, but they had lived in relative harmony and had enjoyed a special relationship. Suddenly she was superseded by this . . . this . . . interloper, this usurper. His masculine presence dominated everything. The syrupy smell of his pipe tobacco trailed him into every room, and his border collie Troy was always underfoot. Anny was forced to accommodate his changing moods, his bottomless need for affirmation. Minny mothered him and attended to his every wish, but he demanded Anny's attention as well, and she stubbornly refused to give it.

Minny had strong opinions about the decoration of houses, but she wisely left Leslie free rein to arrange his attic study the way it suited him. He was inordinately fond of his writing space, with its slanted roof, a pipe rack on the writing table, and alpenstocks leaning against the wall. A stuffed goat head hung over the fireplace, with curved horns and quizzical eyes that stared at him as he worked. "Leslie's patron saint," Minny quipped.

He read in a low rocking chair with his gangly legs stretched in front, leaning back so far he was almost horizontal. When he finished a book, he'd snap it shut, lurch forward on the rocker, bound to his desk, and, in a frenzy of composition, fill pages of foolscap with his tight, nervous script. He could complete a six-thousand-word article in a single sitting.

Anny's habits were less methodical. Images came to her in swift impressions as she pottered about the house. When she had a flash of inspiration, she reached for the nearest scrap to record it before the image vanished. Numerous merchant bills of sale had aided in this burst of creativity, as had the margins of a handmade Valentine. Here was evidence that Mrs. Thomas Carlyle had come calling and, judging from the turned-down upper left-hand corner, had delivered the card in person instead of sending a servant. Scribbled on the back was a description of a French village where Anny had spent summers with her grand-mother. Black-rimmed mourning cards, birth and marriage an-nouncements, and RSVPs fell prey to her instant need for paper. The maids had been instructed never to throw away a piece of paper, no matter how small.

Her publisher, George Smith, never complained about the queer patchwork that arrived in the post for typesetting. The manuscripts were written on foolscap, the backs of old apoth-ecary scripts, shopping lists, and envelopes, and held together with straight pins, a needle and thread or, in one case, the perfo-rated edges of stamp paper. Mr. Smith took this to be evidence of her quirky genius.

Leslie was not so kind. "That's not writing. That's collage!" he exclaimed.

The disorder drove him mad. He could not conceive of a mind so scattered. One evening before dinner he confronted her. "Is it too much to ask you to contain your scraps? I'm starting to feel hemmed in by this paper blizzard."

"It's how I work best. You keep to your study and I'll keep to mine," she said.

"Fine. But you have a habit of overflowing. For the life of

me I don't know how you manage! Bits and pieces everywhere. A stranger observing you would think you don't know what you're doing. I know otherwise, but for Heaven's sake, can you not contain this . . . this . . . insanely chaotic habit of composing on confetti. The other day I stumbled upon evidence of Robert Louis Stevenson, henceforth forever memorialized, not as our dinner guest, but for offering up the back of his place card for a description of daffodils on the Isle of Wight."

"Please, you two. Enough," Minny pleaded, stepping in as peacemaker. "Leslie, darling, Anny has always worked like this. It's unreasonable to expect her to change." Then, turning to Anny, she said gently, "Dearest sister, could you not at least try to gather your notes and put them in one place? It will be easier for you, and easier for Leslie. What about the ginger jar that Papa loved so—the one with the wide mouth, and dragons intertwined around the girth?"

Anny vowed to reform. Slowly she learned how to engage Leslie without surrendering her opinion or taking offense. Their arguments flared up quickly, but were always resolved before dinner. He was the brother she never had—infuriating but invigorating. There was an undertone of generosity and goodwill to their arguments, as there was to his advice. The Jane Austen lecture, for example. "Her merits are such as you might study to advantage—particularly the careful way in which the stories are worked out," he advised her.

"I adore her novels, but I am not Jane Austen, nor do I wish to be."

"I'm only suggesting that you bring some discipline to the study of her work."

While he was quite liberal in dispensing advice, he was thin-skinned about receiving it. She was careful to keep her own counsel about any improvements he might make in his own writing. But she respected his opinion. Otherwise she would not have asked him to read her work-in-progress, *Five Old Friends*, a re-imagining of Cinderella, Sleeping Beauty, and other classic fairy tales.

"I should think you would do well to choose a topic more commensurate with your talents," he said, before he read the manuscript.

"I want to reinterpret the tales for adults. Fairies, myths, and legends are much in vogue at the moment," she said, refusing to be patronized. "Besides, there's nothing wrong with children's literature. Lewis Carroll has outsold everyone we know. People are mad for his book." She had heard that Queen Victoria was so taken with *Alice's Adventures in Wonderland* that she insisted Mr. Dodgson give her his next book. He sent her *An Elementary Treatise on Determinants*.

Leslie read Anny's manuscript immediately. When he finished he said, "These are good. You have your father's gift. You remind me of him at every turn. But you're wasting your talents on these trifles. You should do something more ambitious. Something with a story and vigorous characters acting on a large canvas. I'm quite sure you could do it, if you put your mind to it."

An idea had been germinating of a story set in the Old Kensington of her youth. She started jotting down ideas and stuffing them in the ginger jar as Minny suggested.

Anny's spirited discussions with Leslie sometimes caused friction with her sister.

"He would never think of asking me my opinion on a Ruskin essay," Minny complained one afternoon when they were alone.

"You might offer your own opinion and then ask for his," Anny suggested.

"Well, I find him tiresome."

"Leslie?"

"No, Mr. Ruskin."

"His *Seven Lamps of Architecture* was such a part of our childhood," Anny said. "I can picture it so vividly, on the round table in the middle of the parlor on Young Street. Remember the room with bowed windows, glass-fronted bookshelves and that carpet with an oak leaf design?"

"You have a remarkable memory for detail. How do you do it? For me, the past is a blur, but for you, it's as vivid as if it were happening this very moment."

"I remember that book in particular because you and I were convinced it was made of slabs of molten chocolate. I didn't read it until much later. At the time I was more interested in the copies of *Punch* or the brides and veiled ladies and ghosts and brigands in the red silk Annuals."

"I was terribly frightened of Mr. Ruskin," Minny confessed.

"Well, tell Leslie that. He loves to hear stories about the famous people we knew growing up."

"That won't spark a discussion."

"Well then, pick an author you like—Dickens, or one of the Brontës. There's plenty to discuss there." As young girls, she and Minny had been enchanted with the idea of two sisters who were both novelists. "Leslie told me the other day that he found *Wuthering Heights* to be rather coarse—all that unseemly passion. Emily's sister Charlotte is even worse, in his opinion—more alive to the physical side of romance than is proper for young ladies."

"He told you that?" Minny said with a little gasp.

"To tell you the truth, I find him to be rather prudish about women. He seems to think that the merest hint of passion will make us collapse on the fainting couch and call for smelling salts."

"Anny, I forbid you discuss such things with Leslie. It's not proper."

"I was only telling him about the mix-up with Miss Brontë and Papa."

When Charlotte Brontë was writing under the pen name of Currer Bell, their father had guessed that she was a woman and sent her an admiring letter through her publisher, George Smith. *Vanity Fair* was her favorite novel, and she was so touched that she dedicated the second edition of *Jane Eyre* to him. This set off a tempest of rumor, since most people in literary circles knew that their father had a mad wife, and assumed that the author had based the deranged wife in the attic on Anny's mother.

"You should have let *me* tell him that story," Minny cried, as if Anny had snatched her childhood from underneath her.

"What were you—nine or ten—when she came to the house? Do you even remember her?"

"I knew that she was famous, and Papa was famous, and I had some childish fantasy that they might marry each other. But to tell you the truth, I can't recall much about that evening."

"I can see the scene so plainly: Papa pacing up and down the hall, my heart beating wildly as we listened for the rattle of carriage wheels, for I loved *Jane Eyre* above all other novels, even Papa's, though I certainly didn't tell him that. I said something about being excited to meet the famous authoress and Papa was quick to correct me: 'She's no more an authoress than a writeress. She's an author—and a marvelous one at that.'"

"What was I doing at the time?" Minny said.

"I don't know." The younger sister crossed her arms and pouted, as if Anny's lapse of memory had erased her from the story.

"It was a hot summer evening," Anny continued. "I remember that detail because I was astonished when Miss Brontë arrived, quite remarkably, in mittens. I couldn't understand why she'd be wearing mittens on such a hot day. She must have been about thirty at the time, a pale wisp of a thing in a moss green dress and so far removed from my idea of a genius. She could barely reach Papa's elbow and he had to stoop to escort her to the table. The guests all waited for the brilliant conversation to commence. Apparently, Miss Brontë's genius did not include a sense of humor, for the evening was oppressively dull. After she left, Papa was so upset he donned his hat and slipped out to his club. Leslie was fascinated by the anecdote."

"It's my story as much as yours, and I want to be the one to tell Leslie."

"But you don't remember it," Anny reminded her.

Min stomped her foot. "That's not fair."

"In the future, I'll be more careful. But I felt I owed it to Leslie after he confessed that he found the mad wife in *Jane Eyre* to be unnecessarily bestial. Clearly, he didn't know about Papa and Miss Brontë. Imagine if he had said something similar to a colleague who knew the story. He'd be deeply embarrassed."

"It's so easy for you to talk to him. You read all the time and he respects your opinion. He treats me as though I don't have anything worthy to contribute."

"So read a few books. This house is filled to the brim."

"That won't change anything. Leslie reminds me of Papa. Always seeking out your opinion and never mine."

"Oh, Min," she said, finally understanding. But before she could think of how to reassure her sister, she was overcome by sorrow. Four years after their father's death, she was still not used to the strange rhythms of grief. She could go for weeks without thinking about him, and then the least scrap would set off waves of sadness.

She hugged Minny tearfully and said, "I miss him dreadfully. Do you ever wonder what life would have been like, had he lived?"

AT THE BEGINNING OF THE SUMMER, Minny learned that she was expecting a child. "Oh Min, Papa would be so thrilled," Anny said, squeezing her tight.

"How am I going to support a child with this penny-a-lining I'm doing?" Leslie fretted. He became prickly around matters of money.

"You'll figure a way," Anny said, irritated that his nerves overshadowed his joy.

By August, Minny had cut out most of her social activities

and spent most of the day resting on the sofa. Anny watched her carefully, not ready to become alarmed just yet. Minny had never had a strong constitution.

One day, Minny ordered luncheon in her room. Anny kept her company while she ate. It was a high fog day, with the east wind blowing in exhalations from the Essex and Kent marshes. The damp air trapped particles from the soot-spewing factories, giving the air a bronze glow, as if lit by distant fires.

Anny noticed that Minny was short of breath, though she had done nothing more strenuous than push away the luncheon tray.

"Are you quite all right?" Anny asked, concerned. "You look as though you're having trouble breathing."

"I can't seem to get enough air. My corset may be too tight."

"Take that thing off right now," Anny said. "It can't be doing you or your child any good."

"You can be so bossy," Minny complained.

"It's common sense. You'll feel fifty percent better, just by a simple change of undergarment."

"But then I won't look fetching."

Even in her sickly state, Minny was more beautiful than Anny could ever hope to be. Their father had never called her "My Little Lump of Fat."

"You're not going out in society during your confinement. Why would you care?"

"Leslie cares."

"Surely he doesn't want you trussed up in whalebone and steel while you carry his child."

"But he likes my figure. He's said so many times. He has no idea how hard I work to look good for him."

"My love, he doesn't want to see you in pain. Just wait until I lace up Troy like a sausage and pull the strings so tight the poor creature can't chase after squirrels or curl up at his feet. Leslie will realize in no time what you're putting yourself through."

"You just want me to look ugly for Leslie."

Anny gasped. "Min, surely that's not what you think!"

But it was. Anny left the room in tears.

CAMMIE'S INVITATION TO COME TO Freshwater came at the perfect time. Leslie and Minny needed time alone, and Anny wanted to escape the metallic haze of London for the clear blue sky of the island. She installed herself at The Porch.

Cammie continued her maniacal pace, staying up until two in the morning working on her photographs. When famous guests of Mr. Tennyson were unavailable, she combed the island for subjects. No visitor or villager was safe; she coaxed the known and the unknown into sitting before her lens.

One day, Anny accompanied Cammie to the reading room the two women had set up for villagers in Freshwater. Anny was donating several copies of her novels while Cammie carried some books from her library. Hobbling along the lane in the opposite direction was an unkempt white-haired man much in need of scrubbing. "Stop! There he is. Time!" Cammie said. She had conceived of a tableau with Father Time and had found her mark. She thrust her books on top of Anny's pile and approached the astonished old man. "I am Mrs. Cameron. Perhaps you have heard of me. You would oblige me very much if you would let me photograph you. Will you let me do so?" He helped carry the books to the reading room and then returned to the glass house. Mrs. C. cleaned him up, draped him in costume and sat him before the camera.

In the summer, tourists flocked to Freshwater, hoping for a glimpse of Alfred Tennyson, who was, by far, the most famous poet in England. Mass market consumption of poetry had reached frenzied levels. Now that people enjoyed more leisure time and improved transportation, his fanatical readers traveled to Freshwater, hoping to get a glimpse of the poet's house or a piece of the man himself. Tennyson abhorred the "Cockneys," as he called them, though his fans were not all Cockneys. Fashionable ladies also sought his autograph and once mobbed him and took his hat. The more aggressive celebrity seekers scaled the fence and scoured the lawn at Farringford, hoping to find a dropped pencil, a remnant of clothing, or a souvenir to remember the great man by. Some went so far as to strip branches from the tree he had planted with Garibaldi. Mrs. Tennyson had taken to wearing a whistle when she was on the grounds so she could alert him to encroaching visitors. He escaped by way of a specially built spiral staircase hidden on the far side of the bay window.

He rarely went into the village in the summer and confined himself to the private path to Cammie's house and the well-trod trail to High Down, where he could walk undisturbed.

He welcomed Anny's company on his walks and shared with her his sense of wonder. Astronomy was a strong interest of his. From a telescope on the rooftop at Farringford, he gazed at the heavens and explained to her how stars rearranged themselves across the sky, depending on the season. "See the Big Dipper?" he said, pointing over the Solent to the only star formation she could call by name. "In winter, it will be over there" he said, pointing to a different part of the sky.

In their daily walks, Mr. Tennyson taught her the names of wildflowers and showed her how to recognize trees by their bark. He was sensitive to the differences in the flight patterns of different birds, and pointed out how a compact wedge, against the sunset, suddenly narrowed sharply into a thin line.

Once, when he forgot his spectacles, he asked her to look and tell him if the field lark came down sideways upon its wing. How many times had she watched these birds land among the gorse, yet she had not the slightest idea of the answer to his question. She learned from him how to look, really look, at something, and not just glance, get a general impression, and fill in with what she already knew.

On their walks they sometimes shared long periods of silence. Other times they talked nonstop. But there was always a deep comfort to their companionship.

Upon occasion, he would stop close to the ledge of the cliff and try out a few lines of poetry, releasing the words into the void, only to have them swallowed up or blown back, depending on the direction of the wind. Then he would make adjustments and speak again, unselfconsciously trying out different words and rhythms.

One evening, as they were returning from High Down, a shepherd approached with a flock of a dozen sheep. Anny watched as her companion plunged into the bushes.

"Mr. Tennyson. Are you quite all right?" she said.

He parted the branches and looked out at the bleating flock. He emerged, looking uncharacteristically diffident. His hair stood out wildly on his head. He reached for his slouch hat, which had been snagged on the bush.

"I thought it was a group of tourists."

Anny couldn't help herself. She broke out laughing. "I see you forgot your spectacles."

"You have no idea. These blood-sucking Cockneys. They treat me like a pig to be ripped open for the public. Thank God the world knows nothing of Shakespeare's life. We know everything we need to know from his work."

"Aren't you being a tad bit oversensitive?" she said, still smiling. "These are, after all, umm . . . sheep."

"You're no better than a Cockney yourself," he said, with a flash of anger.

"And you're nothing but a country bumpkin!" she said, and parted from him at the path to Cammie's.

She found Mrs. C. hurrying through the garden with an exposed glass plate.

"I'm afraid I've had cross words with Mr. Tennyson," Anny said. "He is not at all in love with me just now."

"I must get this into the developing bath before the collodion dries," Cammie said. "I shall be back straightaway, and you can tell me all about it."

She descended into the coal house, which she had converted into a darkroom.

Anny waited on a bench by the sweetbriar hedge. Unlike her famous poet neighbor, Cammie was more accepting of visitors to the island. When a local policeman alerted her that tourists were picking roses from her sweetbriar hedge, she replied, "That is just what they are there for!"

Before long, Cammie emerged from the coal house and sat beside Anny. "Give me a few minutes more, and I'm all yours." She extracted a notebook from her pocket. "If I don't write down the precise amounts of gold chloride immediately, I'll forget. Ah, the decrepitude of age. Shall you never experience it." She entered some figures into the book. Her hands were a fright, with ugly burn scars from working with highly flammable chemicals. Even the maids with their raw lye burns had smoother hands.

"Now I'm all yours," she said, tucking her notebook away. "What has our Alfred gone and done?"

"I'm embarrassed to say."

"Don't be. This spring he accused me of picking his wild hyacinths," Cammie said. "Imagine! Thousands and thousands of the lovely blue teardrops covering the hillside. As if he'd miss a few. Emily was horrified when she found out about his accusations and wrote me a lovely letter of apology. I don't know what Alfred would do without that woman. If people only knew what she does to keep him in line!"

Anny gave a brief account of Mr. Tennyson's dive into the bushes.

"Yes, without his spectacles he's blind as a mole," Cammie said, chuckling.

"I shouldn't have called him a country bumpkin. I wonder the bears didn't come and devour us both."

"He may growl and snap, but he's harmless. It's not in his nature to hold a grudge."

"I adore that man—he is noble and simple like Papa, and he lets his friend's children thump him."

Cammie gathered her trailing drapery and stood to go.

"Julia Duckworth is here for a sitting. Do go and speak to her before you leave."

Julia was Cammie's goddaughter and favorite model. In a family of beauties, she stood out. Her striking aristocratic looks had intimidated Leslie at Anny's birthday picnic but had inspired many artists. G. F. Watts had painted her. The Pre-Raphaelite painter Holman Hunt and the sculptor Thomas Woolner were so smitten that they had offered proposals of marriage. What was it about beauty that rendered men weak-kneed and foolhardy? For artists, it was a professional liability. Anny knew more than a few who seemed incapable of painting a beautiful woman without falling into temporary insanity and mistaking the condition for love.

Charles Dodgson worshipped beauty as well, but only the unspoiled perfection of prepubescent girls. To Anny's knowledge, he had never asked one to marry him, though Cammie—always a source of rumor but not necessarily a reliable one—had heard speculation about why the family of Alice, his muse, abruptly cut off all contact with him a year after the trip that sparked *Alice's Adventures in Wonderland*. It had to do with the family's suspicion that a marriage proposal might be in the offing. At the time, the child was eleven—a year away from twelve, the legal age of consent.

Alice had a family to protect her. The discarded child bride Nelly Watts did not. By contrast, Julia came from an established family that descended from a chevalier in Marie Antoinette's court. She had a strong sense of who she was, and beauty was not the attribute that defined her. The marriage proposals of famous artists did not tempt her. She waited for the right man, and found him in the barrister Herbert Duckworth. They had recently married and were reportedly madly in love.

Men were not the only artists in love with loveliness. Cammie, too, was infatuated with Julia's face. She had photographed her niece in every mood and hue: in light and in shadow, from the side and straight on, full bodied and in tableaux. Mostly she concentrated on her face, with its defined cheekbones and ethereal eyes. Whether Julia was depicted as a prim maiden or a slightly dangerous beauty with mussed tresses, the blurry sepia images of her face, emerging from a smoky mist, suggested the mystery of womanhood in its many forms.

Julia's mother and Cammie were two of the seven famous Pattle sisters, who made a splash in society when they moved from India to London. Half French and half English, the sisters were excitable, cosmopolitan, fluent in several languages, and known for their eccentric dress. Anny's father met the sisters when he was a bachelor and had dubbed them, collectively, "Pattledom." All were ravishingly beautiful, except for Cammie. Her nickname was Talent, even though it would be more than two decades before the nature of her gift would reveal itself.

Cammie's father was a scamp and a gambler and drank himself to death in India, leaving behind a wife and seven daughters. The wife decided that he should be buried in England and had his body preserved in rum for the voyage. The barrel sat at the head of the intricately carved crinoline staircase of the family home in Calcutta. The bung had been pulled too tight and it exploded as Cammie's mother descended the staircase, dousing her with rum and sending her husband's corpse tumbling down the steps. She had him repickled in another cask. It took four strong men to carry the cask on board, and only one to off-load it in Southampton. A rum shortage en route had forced the sailors to tap every available source of liquor. After the voyage, Cammie's mother was never the same, and spent the last part of her life raving and babbling.

Anny had always felt a special connection to Cammie. Both had mothers who had gone mad. But she was never entirely sure that the story was true in all its particulars. All of Pattledom loved a good yarn, even at their own expense. The tale bore a suspicious resemblance to the oft-repeated story of Lord Nelson, killed at the battle of Trafalgar in 1805 and pickled in a cask of brandy that was emptied during the journey to England.

Julia might be able to tell her the truth about her grandfather. Anny found her in the glass house, relaxing on the chaise longue. She had served as her aunt's model frequently enough to know that she was expected to wait and see if Cammie was happy with the results, or needed to reshoot.

The two friends caught up on family news. Julia was still in the midst of newlywed bliss and had even more news to relay: she was expecting a child. Anny rejoiced with her friend, even as she silently lamented that on her side of the ledger, she had little happiness to share.

"There's something I've been meaning to ask you. About your grandfather," Anny said.

"The exploding casket," Julia said.

"Yes, how did you guess? Is the story apocryphal? I know Mrs. C. is not above embellishing."

"What have you heard?"

Anny gave her the details as she remembered them.

"There are several variations, but that is more or less in line with the family lore," Julia said.

"And your grandmother?"

"She died before I knew her, but she was said to have gone mad after she brought my grandfather's body back to England. Sometimes I think we're all mad. Every last one of us."

"I sincerely hope not," Anny said, for this tapped into an unspoken fear.

"And what about you?" Julia asked.

"What, mad?"

"No, no. I mean, how are getting on? You are living with your sister and her husband are you not?"

"I'm slowly learning to get along with Leslie, but in this threesome, I am the superfluous 'some.'" She and Julia had a strange relationship. They did not see each other often, yet when they did, Anny found herself confiding intensely personal thoughts in a way that she hadn't planned.

"I need to figure some things out for myself," Anny continued. "It's as if my real life is hiding out there somewhere, but I can't find it."

She waited for Julia to say something perceptive, as was her habit. But this time, her great happiness muted her natural wisdom.

Six

1868

HERE IT WAS AGAIN: *Le Grand Livre*. The big brown leather volume rested like an open coffin on the dining room table. Anny dreaded the book even more, now that Leslie sat on the other side of it. Minny had ceded control of her half of their father's trust to Leslie, and he now presided over the monthly financial conferences. The New Year was but a few days old, and already Anny was forced to borrow a hundred pounds.

"Money seems to evaporate in your hands. You are a single woman. You must learn to manage your affairs better," he said.

She didn't need reminding that, at age thirty-one, her marriage prospects were limited. Though too young to have crystallized into an Old Maid, she could practically smell the dust accumulating.

She was overdrawn for the most noble of reasons. The previous fall, after she left Freshwater, she had leased a charming ivy-covered cottage in Henley, thirty-five miles from London. She wanted to give Leslie and Minny some privacy. At first she delighted in having a place of her own. She got a lot of writing done. Autumn was glorious, the weather unusually warm and clear. As the season advanced, however, darkness fell earlier and earlier. When the trees lost their leaves and winter set in, the long solitary evenings sent her into despair. The cottage was damp and she had underestimated the problem of earwigs and mold. By the end of November, she could bear it no longer and returned to Onslow Square.

Leslie gave her a stern professorial look and wagged the stem of his pipe at her. "I will advance you the hundred pounds, but you must promise to be more diligent in getting a tenant for the Henley cottage."

"I will certainly try, but it's unlikely that I will find a devotee of earwigs in the dead of winter," she said.

"You must live within your means," Leslie said. "Neither a borrower nor a lender be."

He may have resigned as a member of the clergy, but he retained the reformatory zeal of a man of the cloth. "I thought you didn't believe in the Bible," she said.

"No, but I believe in Shakespeare," he said. "*Hamlet*."

"Oh." She flushed, embarrassed by her mistake.

She hated, hated, hated dealing with Leslie about money. She had leased the Henley cottage for his benefit, to give him and Minny time alone to settle in.

"I will repay you with proceeds from my new book," she said. Her collection of fairy tales, *Five Old Friends and a Young Prince*, was with George Smith, waiting to be published.

"I wouldn't press you about money, but with the family growing, I feel the need to marshal our finances," he said.

Leslie closed the financial ledger and left for his attic study while Anny went in search of Minny. She found her stretched out on the velvet settee in the parlor, looking out at the dreary winter day, suffused with greenish vapors.

"I can't bear to deal with Leslie over the accounts. He's so . . . so . . . annoying. *Il m'énerve*." Speaking French cast them back to the time of their childhood when they lived with their grandmother in Paris. Minny spoke to her animals in French, possibly for the same reason. "Can't you take back that job?" Anny begged. "*Le Grand Livre* was your idea in the first place."

"Darling, he's my husband."

"But it's Papa's money."

"Be fair, Anny. You can't deny that Leslie is working hard. He's doing what he loves, and the money will eventually follow."

Those were Anny's words exactly, spoken to Minny a few months after her marriage, when she was fretting about Leslie's lack of earning power. Anny had explained that Leslie would take a certain amount of time to establish himself, but his penny-a-lining, as he called it, for *Fraser's Magazine*, the *Pall Mall Gazette*, and the *Saturday Review* would pay off in the future. Already he was earning a reputation as a man of letters.

"I can't stand to deal with the man," Anny said. "I'd rather eat glass shards than borrow money from him."

"Are you overdrawn? Again? Anny! If I were in his place, I would be no kinder."

"At least you would not be so moralistic."

"He's trying to be a good steward of our money. That's his job as my husband. Darling, I wish you could be married once just for a week, to see how pleasant it is, and then I should like your husband to disappear, for I couldn't stand to share you with anyone. It seems as if Leslie and I have lived together all our lives. We're like a single person."

"Well then that person is a skinless arrogant prig!" Anny said and went outside to regain her composure. Only someone who knew her intimately could figure out how to so perfectly rub her the wrong way.

THE FINAL MONTHS OF CHILDBEARING turned Minny into a near invalid. That was another reason Anny had wanted to move back to London. Minny's health had never been robust and Anny wanted to make sure her sister did not overexert herself during her lying in.

One day, Anny brought Minny watercolors and brushes so she could paint. Seeing her stretch out on the sofa brought back memories.

"Do you remember when you were sick with scarlet fever at that hotel in Naples? All your pretty curls fell out and Papa took you to have your head shaved. I cried and cried, but you were perfectly happy and liked to take off your wig and pop your bald head into the guests' rooms. One day you dressed up like a little Turk with a turban and surprised me. I screamed, for I was easily alarmed."

"Yes, those were good times," Minny said.

"They were terrible times," Anny said. All three of them had been sick in bed for days. The hotel staff was terrified of becoming infected and offered limited service. Their father abandoned his plans to finish his novel. Minny was too young to remember, but they had been wracked with worry over her condition, for she was the most fragile member of the family.

"It's one thing to be ill for no purpose, but now I have a purpose," Minny said and put her hands on her belly. "I am quite cheerful in my misery."

ANNY KEPT UP A DIZZYING SCHEDULE of dinner parties, opera, theater, and social engagements. Why she had ever thought she could survive in a solitary cottage in Henley, she'd never know. One evening, she announced that she was going to the Huths for dinner. Ever since they had purchased their father's house and furnishings, she experienced a rush of memories every time she visited.

"Shall I ask Les to accompany you?" Min said. She was stretched out on the sofa with her needlework in her lap while Leslie read by the fire. His black and white border collie, Troy, was curled at his feet.

"Good heavens, no. I wouldn't think of it. The dear man despised being trotted out to these occasions when you were still able to go out in society, and you ignored his pitiful remonstrances."

"Is that true, darling?" Minny said, turning to her husband.

"If the wit of man has invented a duller form of entertainment than the dinner party, I have yet to discover it," he said, leaning down to scratch Troy behind the ears.

"Look at your husband," Anny said. "He's the picture of contentment. Just be happy that he'd rather spend a cozy night by the fire with you."

"But you can't go to the Huths unaccompanied," Minny said. "What will people say?"

"It's not what they'll say. It's what they won't say: there goes a musty old spinster. A chaperone would indeed be entirely superfluous."

"Mrs. Grundy will be turning over in her grave."

"In that case, she must get a lot of exercise. If I'm going to garner the approbation of the entrenched Grundyists, I really must think of something more daring than going unaccompanied to dinner at the home our father built."

She went to get her coat and Leslie met her in the hall by the front door.

"Thank you for taking my side. It is pleasant to have, if not an auxiliary, at least a fellow sufferer under Minny," he said. "I know you sympathize with me because you've had to endure the same tyranny. Your dear sister is bent on bringing me to order, and I'm afraid I balk at any reform." He was just now beginning to understand that despite Minny's demure demeanor, she managed to get her way.

"Take advantage of her confinement," Anny smiled. "After the child is born, she will drag you, balking and sulky, into society."

"When that day comes, I will depend on you to be my ally. You understand me."

"That is something you will have to take up with your wife," she said, not willing to take sides.

BY MID-FEBRUARY, MINNY BEGAN to weaken further. Her complexion turned chalky and her cheeks grew hollow as her belly grew bigger. She no longer had the strength to climb to Leslie's attic study and was content to stretch out on the chaise in the bedroom and work on her needlework. More often than not, she declined to come down to dinner and had food sent to her room.

The grim February weather did nothing to cheer up her confinement. The smog was always worse in the winter, when thousands of chimneys spewed coal dust into the air. Day after day, a canopy of yellowish green smog hovered above the city, so thick you could almost spoon it up like split pea soup. The air smelled of rotten eggs and filled the house with a contaminated vapor that made the furniture slippery to touch.

One afternoon after she finished writing for the day, Anny heard giggling from the bedroom. She peeked in and found Min up from her nap and leaning against the headboard with her fingers spread over her belly.

Min looked up with a smile and said, "This little chap is so active. I've already decided. I'm going to name him after Papa."

Anny felt a catch in her heart. The child who would carry her father's name would belong to Minny, not her.

"It may be a girl," she pointed out, sitting on the edge of the bed.

"No. It's a boy. I'm certain."

"How do you know?"

"I know. He's so real to me. I didn't think it was possible to love anyone more than Leslie." She looked at Anny and quickly added, "And you, of course. That goes without saying. But I can't shake the feeling, I can't help but worry . . . what if . . ." She rearranged the covers and took a deep breath. "What if I'm a bad mother?"

Anny reached for her sister's hand. "Oh, darling, you'll be unsurpassed as a mother. You have the most loving and tender nature, and I've seen how you enter naturally into the little amusements of children. When the time comes, when you have your own child in your arms, you'll know exactly what to do."

"How? I have no example."

"It will come naturally. You'll see."

"If there's one thing we learned from Mama, it's that motherhood is in no way instinctive."

Anny felt her blood still. "Don't think about it for a single instant," she said.

"Sometimes I catch Leslie staring at me, and I know he's thinking," Min said.

"What?"

"He's thinking: Will giving birth turn her into a raving lunatic like her mother?"

"Oh, Min. That's not true. Leslie's so excited about the baby. It's one of the things that endears the old boy to me. He can be such a cold bath of water, but about the baby, he gets all soft and sentimental. Don't tell him I said so. He'll deny it. The poor dear is convinced he's not the sentimental sort."

"But what if the baby is . . ."

Anny waited without speaking.

"Not right," Min whispered, finally. "Then how will Leslie react?"

"Oh Minny. Don't say such things. I won't hear of it," Anny said. "It's not good for you and not good for the child."

"Well, I don't care what my baby turns out to be. He's mine and I will love him, no matter what!"

If ever anyone needed evidence of Minny's fitness for motherhood, Anny thought, it rested now in her shining face.

ANNY'S EARLIEST MEMORIES WERE of her mother, not her father. She remembered her sitting at the piano, her auburn hair shining and her pale white hands flying over the keyboard. She remembered snuggling as her mother sang to her. In those days, her father was a blur. She had a vague recollection of being carried on her mother's back into a dark room where a man sat hunched over a desk. He lifted his head and scowled. Now that she made her living by the pen, Anny knew how writers hated to be interrupted. But as a child, his unwelcoming reception confused her. It was her mother who was all sunshine and song. After she gave birth to Minny, the light and music never returned.

Their father placed their mother in the most progressive care available, including a sanatorium on the Rhine that specialized in water treatments, and a clinic on the outskirts of Paris stressing gentleness and freedom of movement for the patients. Nothing worked. At their grandmother's house, she was referred to as "Poor Mama" so often that Anny thought that was her actual name. She called her grandmother Grannie and her mother "Poor Mama."

She remembered visiting her mother once when she was four or five and her mother was living with a doctor in the village of Chaillot. The grounds were filled with winding paths, a pond with an arched bridge, and flowers everywhere. She roamed about until she came upon her mother sitting on a terrace by a narrow house with big windows and blue shutters. Her mother bowed her head and leaned forward so that her gorgeous red tresses, highlighted with threads of gold, cascaded forward to expose the startlingly white nape of her neck. A woman in a starched white apron and white cap brushed her mother's hair from the neck forward.

Anny watched silently, her hands clasped behind her. Hair

hid her mother's face, but she seemed so serene, sitting by a bank of purple-flowering bushes with an overpowering smell.

The nurse motioned for Anny to ran her fingers through her mother's hair. She did, feeling the silken smoothness of it. Without warning, her mother sat bolt upright. Her hair whipped back from her face. She was young and beautiful but when she saw her daughter, her face turned ugly. Trembling, Anny backed away. Her mother began to yank at fistfuls of hair, as if trying to pull it out by the roots, and cried out from the pain of it. The nurse tried to restrain her. As they struggled, Anny ran away, retaining forever that cloying smell that in later years she identified as lilac, a common bush that never failed to turn her stomach each spring when the strong scent permeated the neighborhood. After that, the doctor recommended that the family not return.

Anny did not see her mother again until she was a young woman and her mother lived with a caretaker in a flat on the outskirts of London. At her father's gentle urging, she began to visit her regularly. Min, however, refused.

AT THE END OF FEBRUARY, ANNY went to Bedfordshire for the weekend to visit the Rothschilds at Mentmore, which, with its gothic style and square stone towers, reminded her of the House of Parliament, only smaller and more opulent, since it was filled with the Rothschilds' art collection. She had just unpacked her bags when she received an urgent telegram calling her home. Minny had given birth prematurely to a son, who had not survived. Her sister was gravely ill. The desperation in Leslie's words was clear: "We need you. Stop. I need you."

She caught the next train to London and arranged to have her luggage sent later. When she arrived home, she went straight to Minny's room without taking off her coat. Leslie met her in the upstairs hallway.

"We came close to losing her," he said. His red beard quivered and he took a moment to compose himself. "It's infernal that women should have to undergo all this pain. Any male I know could never withstand it."

"I must see her," Anny said, reaching for the doorknob.

He grabbed her upper arm and squeezed so tight she felt a bruise forming. "Not now. She's finally getting some sleep."

"I won't disturb her. But I must be there when she wakes up," she said, ignoring his pleas.

She entered quietly and sat in the semi darkness, watching Minny's chest rise and fall. The room had the stale odor shared by so many sick rooms. She had misjudged the gravity of her sister's condition, just as she had with her father, and she was not going to let her only remaining family member die under her watch.

After a while, Minny's eyes fluttered open. Anny pulled a chair next to the bed and held her hand.

"You're here," Min said, plaintively, and Anny understood what she meant: *You were not here when it counted.*

"Ssshh. There's no need to talk," Anny said, alarmed by the sallow color of her sister's face.

"He came out of my womb and onto my breast—my own flesh and blood, but so small, so cold." Her voice was barely a whisper.

"Don't. You'll tire yourself," she said, but Minny did not stop.

"I wanted to hold him, but the midwife took him from me, saying it was not good for me, but that's not true, Anny. It *would* have been good for me. I know it would have." Anny smoothed her damp hair away from her face. "I locked my arms around Billy and tried to keep him with me for a little longer, but I was too weak. Now I'll never know what it's like to hold my own baby. If only I had held him, then maybe it wouldn't hurt so much."

Anny squeezed her hand. She could think of no comforting words.

"Why was I born weak, Anny? Why?"

Anny put her hand against her sister's wet cheek.

"If something happens to me, will you take care of Les?" Min said. "He needs someone."

"Nothing is going to happen to you. You're going to get stronger."

"But if I don't, will you promise?"

"I will not," Anny said, and cast off Minny's hand abruptly. "You must get better. You must! He depends on you."

All at once it became clear to Anny how perfectly suited Min was for Leslie. She mothered him, calmed him, cosseted him, jostled him out of his moods. It came naturally to her. More importantly, she gave him daily reassurance—he could not hear it enough—that he was talented and worthy of respect. He blossomed under her caressing care. Without her, he would be lost.

Minny turned her head away from the wet spot on the pillow and fell asleep. Anny slipped out.

SLOWLY, THROUGH THE WEEKS, Minny strengthened. The extra bedroom was turned into a sick room, and Anny moved her writing table in. But she found it impossible to work, even when Minny was sleeping. She envied Leslie's ability to block out everything and produce articles on deadline. She simply could not muster that level of concentration. When Minny was awake, she read stories and poems aloud to her, and scanned her face daily to search for the return of color to her cheeks.

One day, Minny sat up in bed of her own accord and watched a robin sunning himself on the windowsill. The bird shook itself rapidly, as if shaking off water, and then tucked its head into its body, so the eyes were near the breast. Min watched carefully and requested pencils and a sketchbook. By the time Anny returned with the supplies, the robin had flown off, but she knew her sister was out of danger.

It was another month before Minny felt strong enough to

travel. Anny and Leslie decided that a change of air would do her good, and they went to the country to stay with the Ritchie cousins.

During the week's visit, Min thrived, enjoying a full life without ever leaving the house. Blanchie was home with her new baby in arms. A giggly Gussie was in love, and shared whispered confidences with Min in the corner, while Pinkie, just turned seventeen, practiced Bach partitas on the piano. The male cousins amused themselves with outdoor sports while the female cousins spent hours at the round table in the parlor working on an elaborate collage. Minny's artistic ability was greatly prized. The cousins cut out round faces from a group photo of the family and glued them onto the bodies of the fantastical creatures that Minny painted.

Leslie was out of sorts in this big noisy household. His childhood had been one of austerity and denial, so different from Anny and Minny's youth, filled with opera, dances, theatrical performances, and sumptuous food. Their father was wondrously droll and had created a lively home atmosphere with his love of jokes, playful repartee, and comical poems, not to mention outings to museums, the zoo, the park, and frequent dinner parties.

Anny felt sorry for Leslie. His father, a member of the Clapham sect, had once smoked a cigar and liked it so much that he never smoked again. When Leslie asked him how he could justify taking snuff, he could find no good reason, other than that he liked it, and emptied the box of snuff out the window. Leslie had told this story by way of showing how upright his father was, but Anny found it sad that someone would deny himself so many pleasures for the sake of religion and social reform.

One morning, Leslie and Anny took a walk around the grounds. The air retained the dampness of the previous night's rain, and accentuated the sweet smells of spring. The purple iris with their ruffled beards stood staunchly upright along the path, while the lush pink peony blossoms, too heavy for their stems, lay with their cheeks to the ground. A thin layer of damp moss covered the stepping stones, and Anny walked gingerly beside Leslie, careful not to lose her footing.

"I feel so distant from Min here, surrounded by these frivolous gossipy Ritchies," Leslie said. "They aren't interested in ideas. You're the only one I can talk to."

"Oh don't be ridiculous. I'm worse than the lot of them. Where do you think I get ideas for my stories, if not from gossip?"

"I find myself thinking wistfully of my dear little study with its books and comforts," Leslie said. "Can we not go back to London early?"

"Oh, but the visit is doing Min so much good. She needs sunshine as well as rest. I mean the sunshine of people she loves. What a difference it makes. I haven't seen her look so bonny in weeks."

"Yes, but have you seen the doleful way she watches Blanchie and her baby. It must be unbearably painful for her."

Leslie was the one bothered by the happy exchanges between the new mother and her baby. Anny had been so focused on Minny over the past weeks that she had forgotten that Leslie, too, had lost a baby.

They walked through a break in the hedgerow and continued along the edge of the archery field. Her younger cousin Richmond was pulling out arrows from a straw target. He had arrived from Eton the night before, and she had not seen him yet. They waved at each other.

She and Leslie followed the path back to the house. Ivy beds flanked both sides. In some spots, the vines had climbed the trunks of the enormous oaks, reaching the lower branches.

"I've been thinking. I believe a trip to America would do Minny good," he said.

"But she's still so weak," Anny protested.

"We wouldn't go until August. That would give her plenty of time to recuperate."

"But I couldn't bear to be parted from her."

"You must come too, of course. I wouldn't have it any other way. You would find the country much to your liking. I confess that the Americans' uncomplicated honesty shocked me a bit at first, given, as I am, to turning on my heels and laughing when I'm most touched. But the people there remind me of you in their naturalness and open-hearted generosity. You don't exhibit that dreadful reserve that is the curse of Englishmen everywhere."

She feared her sister's vigor was simply not up to the difficult ocean passage and the unknown dangers of a country so soon after the Civil War. "What does Minny think?" she asked.

"I haven't asked her yet. I need to find the right time."

Richmond caught up with them, out of breath from running. He had a quiver of arrows on his back and wore a three-fingered leather glove.

Leslie had been a day student at Eton and shared a few reminiscences with Richmond, but the young man showed little interest. Instead, he turned to Anny.

"What's it like to be a famous writer?" he asked, with a naïve enthusiasm that comes from being fourteen.

"Well, I'm not really famous," Anny said, and glanced nervously at Leslie. She was uncomfortable being the center of attention.

"Of course you are," Richmond forged on. "My friends at school are all impressed. They can't believe I'm related to you and Uncle William."

Anny was clear-headed about her success. She was not a towering talent, but she had a knack for depicting the lives of women in a way that her readers could relate to. She benefitted from a growing number of middle-class women who, freed from housework, had time on their hands and wanted to read about women like themselves.

"Have you seen Leslie's article in the most recent *Saturday Review*?" she said.

"None of my friends read that," he said.

Anny felt Leslie's discomfort as if it were her own. "They should. He gives a clear explanation of the English parliamentary system to Americans. It's fascinating."

"For some people, I'm sure," Richmond said, and adjusted the leather guard he wore to protect his forearm.

Anny cringed. Without knowing it, her young cousin had veered into delicate territory.

She knew Leslie worried about his reputation. Would he win the admiration of his colleagues? Would he receive the recognition he deserved? Would he write something important enough to outlive him, the way her father had? At present, he was hacking out journalism pieces that, while good, would be forgotten as soon as they were set aside.

With three books to her name and a devoted following, she was more well-known than Leslie. She had never been preoccupied with success, which had come to her without really trying, while Leslie, who cared so desperately, found that success eluded him.

She tried to steer her young cousin in another direction, but he blundered on. "To have all those readers clamoring for the next installment, talking about it with their friends. That must be intoxicating," he said.

"I'm afraid my trifles won't last. Luck has played a rather large part in my success."

"You're entirely too modest—isn't she?" He turned to Leslie, who grumbled a response.

It was her curse that she could neither ignore nor accommodate his deep-seated need for praise. "There are more important things than fame," she said.

"Like what?" Richmond said, waiting for her answer with wide eyes. At that moment, Richmond's mother called from across the lawn and he excused himself.

When he was gone, Leslie said, "Well, there's an impudent

young man if ever I saw one. I don't know how he got the reputation for being so clever."

"Oh, Leslie, don't be too hard on him. He's just young. You, I am quite certain, were never guilty of any infelicities when you were his age," she gently teased.

"I sincerely hope not."

She regretted that Richmond had wounded Leslie's pride. She so wanted Leslie to fall in love with the Ritchies, who were important to her and Minny, and the closest family they had.

When they reached the house, she said, "I'm going to join the ladies in the parlor for a rubber of whist."

"Those chattering gossips!" Leslie said. "I shall take myself as far away as possible."

AUGUST ARRIVED, AND LESLIE had not given up on his plans to go to America. Though Minny was much improved, Anny didn't trust him on the subject of her sister's health. While he clearly adored her in his silent Dobbin-like way, he was a bit thick-headed about the hardships travel would pose. Anny suspected that his judgment was colored by his desire to visit the friends he had made on his visit just after the Battle of Gettysburg.

One day Anny found Minny in a dither in the bedroom. An open trunk sat beside the bed. Several dresses were laid out on the coverlet. "I have no idea what to take. It's so hard to pack, when I dread going in the first place. America seems so impossibly far away. How many traveling dresses are you taking?"

Anny ignored the question. She had decided not to go to America and was waiting for the right moment to tell her sister. After mulling over her decision at great length, she had come to the conclusion that Leslie and Minny needed time alone to heal after the loss of a child. She would only be a distraction.

"I just heard the most delicious gossip," Anny said, changing the subject. "This will cheer you up no end."

"Anything to avoid this wretched packing." She moved aside a dress and sat on the bed.

"It's from Cammie's sister, so I know it to be reliable. A young girl's body washed up on the banks of the Thames."

"Oh Anny, how horrid. I thought you said it would cheer me."

"Bear with me. You know, or maybe you don't, but Nelly recently disappeared without a word, leaving unclaimed her husband's support."

"Who?"

"Nelly—Ellen Terry Watts. You know, your favorite painter's child bride." Minny, a very accomplished amateur painter, had never been a fan of George Frederic Watts, finding him altogether too stodgy and traditional. Anny continued: "Nelly's father went to the morgue and identified the body. Her sisters, who were off at boarding school, donned mourning attire. Everyone discouraged the mother from saying goodbye to her daughter, afraid that the sight of the body would distress her. But she insisted. The corpse at the morgue was tall and pale and thin with masses of honey-colored hair, just like Nelly. But her mother noticed that it had no strawberry mark on the left arm, like her daughter. Soon after, Nelly showed up in London. The rumors of her untimely death had reached her. It turns out she had run off with a theatrical designer."

"*Quel scandale!*" Minny said, appearing to forget, for the moment, her quandary over what to take to America. "I wonder what Mr. Watts thinks of this."

"I don't care. I'm just relieved to know the poor child is alive," Anny said.

"You and Papa could always revel in stories of people's foibles without judging."

"You know that canvas Mr. Watts painted a decade or so ago, when Nelly was still in pinafores."

"She was in pinafores when he married her," Minny pointed out.

"True. The painting—you must have seen it at his studio—shows the body of a disgraced woman washed up on the shores of the Thames. It's called *Found Drowned*."

"What a terrible coincidence. I always thought Nelly was ill-used. I would be very distraught if she had committed suicide." She stood up and looked at the frocks arrayed on the bed. "I don't think all of these will fit in the trunk. You are taking the other trunk, are you not?"

Anny took a deep breath. "I've decided to stay in London."

"But how can I manage without you?" Minny said, with a look of alarm. "You know how to jostle me out of my moods. I depend on you for so many things."

The deep furrow in Min's brow caused Anny to waver for a moment, but then she renewed her resolve. "Leslie is convinced a change of scenery will do you good. He will take excellent care of you," she said, though she had her doubts. "I shall miss you dreadfully, but I promise to write every day."

She remained confident of the wisdom of her decision until the day of their departure. After tears and hugs, she watched the carriage piled high with luggage disappear, phantom-like, into the dense fog, with only the clop of hooves to prove it was not a hallucination.

From the first day, Anny missed Min dreadfully. As she walked around the neighborhood, she found herself overcome with nostalgia for the Kensington of their childhood, when sheep grazed in Kensington Gore and cattle drank at the pond by a neighbor's orchard, now hidden by row houses. She remembered how she and Minny had gathered hawthorn branches to make garlands and picked strawberries from the banks now laid with paving stones and coal holes. Kensington Palace was closed to the public in their youth, but she and Min had explored the mossy doorways, gables, and quaint corners of the exterior walls. They took absurd delight in standing motionless in the niches, hoping to fool passersby into thinking they were statues.

Now she found herself at loose ends, barely able to run the household, much less the finances. She was a hopeless manager. The housekeeping was disorganized, the servants poorly instructed, the budget overspent. She befriended the servants, even though she knew Minny would disapprove. She didn't like to admit how dependent she was on her sister.

A month into the trip, Minny's letters began to arrive, and Anny's worst fears were confirmed. Her sister had not weathered the passage well and arrived in New York with a cold that quickly turned into influenza. The contents of her trunk had gotten soaked in a cloudburst, and it was impossible to dry things out in the damp climate. Min wrote of being confined to a bed that was "a horrible bundle of straws." Her illness forced Leslie to cancel a hiking trip in the Adirondacks, and she was overcome with guilt. She was recuperating in Boston at the home of the poet James Russell Lowell, one of Leslie's dearest friends.

From Minny's correspondence, Anny could tell that her sister viewed the New Country from a four-poster bed. Minny told of asking Mr. Lowell about American novels, just to be polite, and suddenly finding a whole stack next to her bed. "How I long for one of your novels to help the days pass quickly. Instead I must make do with stories about ladies named Humility and gentlemen named Kesariah who spend their whole time going to church and singing hymns and then die without marrying anyone."

Minny appreciated the kindness of Mr. Lowell's second wife, who brought her pears and peaches from the orchard and tried to make her sickbed more comfortable. But she identified much more strongly with Mr. Lowell's first wife, a poetic beauty. "I feel her everywhere here at Elmwood, though she's been dead for many years. How could any woman survive the loss of three of her four children? It's beyond comprehension. She had lungs that wouldn't heal, just like mine. If I should die, please don't let Leslie marry the governess, like Mr. Lowell," she wrote. "If I were an intellectual wife in heaven, I should be disgusted."

Yet Minny tried to present a cheerful front. "I wish you could see Leslie," she wrote. "He has a kindred spirit in Mr. Lowell. After dinner they sit in the library puffing their pipes, both wearing red velvet jackets. (When, I ask you, have you ever seen Leslie in a red velvet jacket? I didn't know he owned one. It is all I can do to keep him out of his ratty waistcoat and raveling sweater, just like dear Papa.) The two friends will sit reading for hours in companionable silence. Then one will bring up some point that requires verification, and soon the floor will be covered with barrowloads of opened volumes. Les has a tremendous respect for Mr. Lowell's intellect. Even my scholarly husband cannot claim to have read Dante and Boccaccio in a dead language."

Instead of complaining about being an invalid, Min ranted at Americans for being so beastly virtuous and abstemious. She declared the country to be a great big hideous overrated place. The children looked pinched and careworn; women's dresses were dowdy in the extreme.

She missed pork pies and lobster from Freshwater and was totally perplexed by Americans' love of popped corn, which tasted like the inside of a quill pen. "I expect I shall soon be nibbling at my boots," she wrote, "and Leslie asked me for a packet of gloves this morning in a most suspicious manner."

In London, the post arrived twice daily, and in a single day, Anny received a letter from Minny in the morning decrying the arrogance of Boston's intellectual elite and a letter from Leslie in the afternoon saying he liked America so much he could see himself living there. "Min blows me up for saying so, but I sometimes rather envy this way of life. But in my dreams there is always a London in the background—to say nothing of an Anny in the foreground—so there is no danger of my taking root here or turning my dreams into reality."

Leslie's letters only hinted at his wife's health problems. Anny continued to worry about Min until her mind was set at ease by her father's old friend, Oliver Wendell Holmes, who wrote to thank her for the gift of a paper cutter that she had sent to him by way of Minny. "I hope I shall soon cut the leaves of another story of yours with it as delightful as *The Village on the Cliff*," he wrote. In the letter he mentioned that he had given Minny a prescription for her cold—his early training was as a doctor—but was not satisfied with the results and referred her to a colleague at Harvard, who prescribed a treatment to restore her to health.

Soon afterward, Minny began to improve. "You musn't tell anyone all of the abusive things I said about America—especially Leslie," she pleaded in a letter to Anny. "I've viewed everything through a pocket handkerchief."

As Minny regained her health, she developed an interest in American decoration and was fascinated by central heating and American plumbing—flushing toilets, and water that came out of a spigot with the turn of a screw. She wrote of her ideas for remodeling upon returning to London and vowed to bring back house plans.

"I should so like to be a house builder, and don't see why I shouldn't," she wrote, and then described a stuffy man at a dinner party who believed that women should not have careers, but instead ought to display charming weakness. "I felt much disposed," she wrote, "to throw my soup plate at his head."

Her meek sister was turning into a firebrand, Anny noted with delight. All it took was the least bit of good health. Each day's post brought a new revelation. The opinions that Anny knew Minny possessed were now being expressed with confidence. She weighed in on the Civil War: "I can no more sympathize with people for hacking at each other and blowing out each other's brains for four years than I can sympathize with Queen Mary's religious frolics. I am quite sure that wars must go out with civilization. It is too horrid and when you come to a country like this where people have not yet recovered from killing their neighbors and being killed, you see how brutal it is."

After Boston, she and Leslie traveled to New York. Minny

reveled in the city's glorious chaos and found it to be a jolly, reckless sort of place defined by immigrants from all over. "I quite understand what Papa was talking about when he said walking up Broadway was like a glass of Champagne," she wrote. "It has a bounding sort of go-ahead air and is so shockingly managed, with such a lot of cheating and bribery that nobody ever crams its excellence down your throat like New England and in fact one feels quite at home here."

Leslie loathed New York and found it to be sprawling and ugly, its cabmen dishonest, and everything worth seeing difficult to get to.

Were they on the same trip?, Anny wondered. Did they even talk to one another? They expressed such diametrically opposed views.

With Leslie and Minny out of the house, she had hoped to profit by focusing on her work. But somehow the months slipped by, and she couldn't account for her time, certainly not in pages produced. When she learned of their plans to return to London at the beginning of December, she realized, to her dismay, that she was not ready to resume their unconventional living arrangements. On the other hand, she couldn't imagine getting a place of her own. To avoid a decision, she made plans to spend the winter in Rome.

Her decision provoked a frantic response. Leslie wrote: "Surely it is bad enough that you should be separated from us for four months on end without immediately deserting us again for a couple more. I don't like to feel that I shall be the cause of separating you and Min for four months in one year."

Min's letter was equally strong. "My own dearest darling darling darling. I never never will go away from you again like this. Could Rome not wait until spring?"

Anny canceled her trip and awaited their return in an uncomfortable confusion.

seven

1870

$\mathcal{M}$ORE THAN SIX YEARS HAD passed since Anny last heard her father's voice, but he continued to be a presence in her life. Each Christmas she did her best to celebrate his favorite holiday, though he had forever ruined it for her by dying. When Minny announced that she was with child, two years after the baby that bore his name had died, Anny held a private celebration in her head with her father. He adored children and would be beside himself with joy for Minny.

Anny spent many hours organizing his letters, journals, drafts, and papers, though she kept them private, for he had made his wishes clear: no biography. The ban was having a negative effect on his popularity. The celebrity maw needed constant feeding. By refusing access to biographers, she feared she was conspiring to assure his obscurity.

The reputation of his friend Charles Dickens had soared, even more so after his death that summer. She knew from his daughter Kate, a friend since childhood, that he had authorized a colleague to write his biography to keep him in the public eye. She wished she could do the same for her father, but, always the dutiful daughter, she did not have the confidence to contradict him.

It was remarkable how strongly her father still influenced her life. She couldn't shake the feeling that she was a disappointment to him. He had groomed her for the family business of writing. What would he think of his "man of genius" now, as she floundered with a novel about the Kensington of her childhood.

She remembered as a little girl walking with him in the park after a snowstorm. His feet were unusually large, even for a man of six foot three and wide of girth. She leapt from one footprint to the next and watched the outline of her tiny boot sink into the larger indentation made by his. She made a silly game of challenging herself to never fall outside the impression made by his boots.

Now that she was grown, she wanted the satisfaction of marking the virgin snow with her own prints, however small. But in the past few years, she had produced only bagatelles—a book of adult fairy tales and a collection of short stories and sketches.

At Leslie's goading, she had embarked on a more ambitious novel, and it was not going well. He expressed confidence in her abilities, but still treated her to a reprise of the Jane Austen lecture: she should emulate Austen's graceful style, quick wit, and deep wisdom of human nature. As if, by diligent application, she could *become* Jane Austen. Well, she could tie herself to the chair and write from now to kingdom come, and never become Jane Austen. But that wasn't the point. She wanted to develop into someone who, for better or worse, was indelibly herself.

And if she became that person, would love follow? At age thirty-four, the odds were better that she would become Jane Austen than that she would find someone to share her life with.

But she had not given up hope, unlikely as it was. It was equally unlikely that, as a woman, she had succeeded in earning her living by her pen. And who could have predicted that her work would garner so much acclaim from her devoted female readers, who were less picky than her father's ghost. Life itself was unlikely and took startling turns.

In September, Julia Duckworth, her beautiful friend with the perfect life, lost her husband when she was eight months along with her third child. Anny paid her a visit.

Julia received her in the bedroom. At midday, fog muted the light and the stench of the London air suffused the shadows. The room would have benefited from a lamp, but none was lit. Dressed in black, Julia sat by the window and held a swaddled bundle to her chest.

Even a face as flawless as Julia's could not escape the heavy burden life had cast upon it. Grief had pinched her features into a scowl, and her striking silver eyes, so light they were almost transparent, had acquired a glazed and vacant aspect. She seemed impossibly old and impossibly young at the same time. At age twenty-four, she found herself a widow with three children under the age of three.

Anny pulled back the blanket and looked at the tiny face, with a comma of hair on the top of his head.

"What a precious darling," she said, and rubbed a finger over the soft fuzz. She felt that sparkle of hope all newborns inspired in her.

"Yes, I suppose." Julia stared at the bare branches that scraped against the glass.

It had been a month since her husband's death, and the birth of her son had not lifted her spirits. Anny hadn't known Herbert Duckworth well, but Leslie remembered him from Cambridge as being a simple, straightforward man, wanting in social polish.

The infant chuffled and burrowed, but Julia remained a stone. "This is not what I expected," she said.

"Life rarely is, but we must carry on." Resilience was a quality Anny poorly understood—who had it, who didn't, and why.

"I loved Herbert so." Her voice was wooden, and the bundle in her arms might as well have been, for all the attention she gave it.

"And that was a great gift. 'Better to have loved and lost than not to have loved at all,'" Anny said, quoting their mutual friend Mr. Tennyson, who was so wise in the ways of the heart.

Was profound sadness the price one paid for intense happiness, Anny wondered as she considered her friend, so fulfilled in her marriage and now so devastated.

"Julia, we all feel deeply for your plight, but you must find a way to hasten your recovery. You are too young to accept sorrow as your lifelong partner."

Anny was not presumptuous enough to pass judgment on her friend's grief. But she had a preternatural sensitivity to mothers who ignored their babies because of their own despondency.

"What's the point?" Julia said.

"The point, my dear friend, is gurgling in your arms."

"Oh, you must think me beastly!" She kissed the top of her baby's head, then rubbed the spot, as if to erase any trace of affection. "I don't want to feel this way. Truly I don't. But I'm so bound up in my efforts to hold myself together that I hardly feel anything at all."

"Your friends are here to support you. But you must learn to be yourself again. You owe it to your children—Herbert's children—to replenish yourself."

How she wished that someone had shaken her mother out of her black moods after Minny was born. The repercussions never ended.

Anny held Julia's hand. "Deep as your sorrow may be, it will not permanently injure your capacity for happiness—only deprive it, for a time, of its sustenance."

AT THE BEGINNING OF DECEMBER, Anny received an invitation from Henry Liddell, dean of Christ Church, Oxford, to attend a showing of the works of Julia Margaret Cameron at his home. Anny took an early train so she could explore the narrow cobbled streets, walled gardens, open meadows, sleepy rivers, and hidden passageways of Oxford. Snow was starting to fall when she arrived late to Tom Quad. A thin outline of stone traced side-by-side arches on the four sides of the ground floor, but no cloisters were added. Either the money had run out, or the Court had become preoccupied with the marital imbroglio of Henry the Eighth. She covered her head with a scarf and walked along the uncovered stone platform that jutted out from the building like a quay.

On the way, she ran into a familiar face.

"Mr. Dodgson! I didn't realize you lived on Tom Quad," she said. He did not like to be called Lewis Carroll in Oxford, or ever, really, except on the cover of his books. She had heard that he returned all correspondence that arrived at Christ Church addressed to Lewis Carroll, afraid that a scribbler of whimsical children's tales would not merit respect among his mathematical colleagues.

"Yes, I live right there," he said and pointed to a corner of the quad. The monastic quarters did not seem fitting lodgings for the famous author.

"Are you working on another children's book?"

"There's no such thing as a children's b-b-book. There is a good story, and a not-so-good story, " he said, avoiding the perilous *b*'s that tripped him up. "They each have more to do with the author than the audience. One should never write down to children. They are so much cleverer than adults."

She was reminded once again how poorly she got along with men her own age. She tried to smooth things over. "Adults and children alike identify with your marvelous Alice. What child doesn't see herself as the only sane person in a world of lunatics?"

"I hope the magic holds for Alice Two. I'm almost finished." Snow collected on the brim of his hat. He looked dressed and ready for a party. Then again, he always did, even at the beach.

"Are you going to the showing of Julia Cameron's work?" he said.

He was a long-time friend of the host's family, especially Henry Liddell's middle daughter, Alice, who had served as the muse for *Alice's Adventures in Wonderland*. "I'm looking for the Dean's lodgings," she said. "I understand he lives on Tom Quad."

"Yes, the deanery is in the corner of the Great Quandrangle, which very vulgar people call Tom Quad. You should always be polite, even when speaking to a Quadrangle." He did not smile, and she could not tell if he was being playful or spiteful.

"Mr. Liddell must be accepting vulgar people to the showing of Julia Cameron's work, for I have an invitation in my possession," she said and walked toward the deanery without waiting to see if he would follow.

Inside, over three hundred people had gathered for the event. Tapestries covered the stone walls of the medieval room, and a fire roared in the enormous fireplace. Photographs were displayed on easels around the room. Surrounded by well-wishers, Cammie looked totally at home with the praise and admiration being proffered. She had brought her graying hair to heel and had managed to find a shawl free of burn holes. Photography was a dangerous art. Chemicals seared cloth and skin; burns resulted from holding the glass plate too close to the flame to heat it before the varnish coat. Only someone of Mr. Dodgson's fastidious nature could emerge unscathed.

After years of hard work, Mrs. C. had attracted a devoted following. Unfortunately, money had not kept pace with her reputation, and her art broke even, if that. These days she was hard pressed to find funds to pay bills or finance new work. According to the whispered concern among the Camerons' large circle of friends, Cammie's meager income from her photography was the only thing saving the family from insolvency. Her husband had returned from another unsuccessful trip to Ceylon to revive the family coffee plantation, leaving the estate manager and the distributor in Colombo to squabble over who was to blame for the failure.

But Cammie measured her success not in pounds earned, but in artistic benchmarks met. She had always treated herself like a successful artist, even when she had no public following. "If I don't take myself seriously, who will?" she had told Anny, who now wove her way through the crowd to reach her friend.

"Minny sends her regards and is sorry she could not be here," Anny said, after congratulating Cammie on her new work.

"Poor dear. How is she getting on?" Fame had not diminished her concern for others.

"Not well, I'm afraid. She's had a devilishly hard lying in. We're watching her carefully. She keeps to the sofa all day and has even consented to being carried around. Leslie frequently makes the trek down from his aerie to check up on her."

Minny had another few months to go, but Anny was afraid to leave her for more than a day. She felt a stab of guilt when she remembered how she had been away when Minny lost her first baby, and vowed never to let that happen again.

"Just think. Julia's little Gerald and Minny's baby can grow up together at Freshwater," Cammie said. The thought of a new generation developing close ties to the island had tremendous appeal for Cammie, who was certain the two infants would grow up to be artists.

Cammie continued: "They're practically related, you know. Your father almost married my sister Mia."

Anny paused. Mia was Julia's mother. "What? Why have I never heard of this?" She knew very little about her father's bachelor days. She couldn't wait to share this new piece of information with Minny.

"It's true. He held a flame for Mia, the real beauty in a family of beauties. This was before he met your mother, of course. At the time, our mother was looking for a match for Mia, and adored William Thackeray. She would have loved to have him in the family. But his infatuation with Mia came at the same time the Bank of Bengal failed, and he lost his inheritance."

Anny knew about the bank failure, but had never heard her father mention his feelings for Mia.

Cammie continued: "He wrote our mother a letter explaining that he was ruined, no doubt hoping she would overlook such an impediment, but she was not about to make a bad match for her beautiful daughter."

Someone approached Cammie to congratulate her, and Anny moved on.

How strange to consider what might have been. Had fate not made her father a pauper, he would not have been forced to work for living, and he never would have penned *Vanity Fair*. He also would never have married her mother, and Anny and Minny would not have been born. Tragic as her father's marriage turned out to be, she was grateful life had unscrolled the way it had.

Her father had remained close friends with Cammie, who had become such a role model for Anny. She had stayed with her at Freshwater while she completed her first novel. Their close artistic friendship dated from that time. Anny had dedicated *The Story of Elizabeth* to her. Had she known that her father would be dead a year later, she would have dedicated the book to him, but at the time, she didn't want to be seen as trading on her famous literary lineage.

Anny looked around the crowded room for someone she knew, and spotted Emily Tennyson by the fireplace. Dressed in simple Quaker grays, she was the most unostentatious woman in the room. Painfully shy, she looked relieved when Anny approached. "Isn't it wonderful to see Cammie get the attention she deserves?" Mrs. Tennyson said. She explained that Alfred had chosen to stay behind, but she wanted to show her support for their dear friend. "She is the most generous of souls, even if it's always on her terms," the laureate's wife said.

"Yes, I know. I'm always afraid to admire anything in her house for fear she'll give it to me. Her gift-giving is like an incurable mania," Anny said.

"How well I know," she said and recounted the time Mrs. Cameron presented the Tennysons with thirty rolls of wallpaper to replace the paper she didn't like in *their* house.

"Oh, there's Mr. Dodgson," Anny said. I must go and apologize. On the way over, he insulted me two times in as many minutes, which must be some kind of record."

"Perhaps *he* should apologize to *you*."

"There was no excuse for me to be rude." Mr. Dodgson was so socially awkward that she may have taken offense when none was intended. But she didn't relish speaking to him alone. "Would you like to come with me?

"Goodness no," Mrs. Tennyson said, and pulled her shawl closer to her. "I'm afraid we've had a falling-out."

She told Anny that Mr. Dodgson had somehow received an unpublished poem her husband had written and requested permission to keep it and give away copies to his friends. This insensitivity echoed an earlier time when he came into possession of a poem written in the poet's teens titled "The Lover's Tale."

"A gentleman should understand that when an author chooses to withhold any work from public view, he must have a good reason for doing so," she said. Though timid, Mrs. Tennyson could be fierce in defense of her husband.

As Anny left, Emily Tennyson squeezed her arm and said, "Please know that you are welcome at any time of year at Farringford."

When Anny reached Mr. Dodgson, he said, "I saw you talking to Mrs. Tennyson. Is her husband here? We've had a misunderstanding."

"So I hear."

"What did she say?"

Anny told him.

"I would like to know exactly how I violated even the strictest code of propriety. I acted in compliance with Mr. Tennyson's wishes and destroyed the poem."

"No one is accusing you of ungentlemanly conduct," she assured him, but quickly changed the subject. "I've never met the little girl who served as the inspiration for *Alice's Adventures in Wonderland*. Is she here tonight?"

He shook his head, but pulled her away from the crowd to the front hall where his most recent portrait of Alice was displayed on the wall.

"Children have a disagreeable way of growing up. She's eighteen now, and her mother wanted something that would attract suitors."

The framed photograph showed a young beauty in elegant dress, slumped down in a leather armchair. She had a sullen downcast glance and appeared fatigued by life, the wonder wrung out of her.

"That's the saddest portrait I've ever seen," Anny said, and then corrected herself, afraid he might take it as a criticism of his art. "I mean, her expression."

It was almost impossible to link this spiritless creature with the saucy little sprite in the portrait Mr. Dodgson had shown her at Cammie's before his children's book was published. Mr. Tennyson had pronounced it quite the most beautiful photo he had ever seen. It portrayed a barefoot little girl in beggar's rags leaning against a mossy rock wall. With a hand on her hip, the bob-headed tomboy stared at the camera with a devil-may-care attitude. This was the Alice who had launched the famous book, not the resentful beauty who glowered at the camera.

Mr. Dodgson stared at the image on the wall with a misty, far-off look. "I shall always remember her best as a fascinating seven-year-old girl," he said, and sighed deeply.

What he guarded in his heart, Anny realized, was the secret Alice, the jaunty, inquisitive little girl who made Wonderland come alive. In the magical world he created underground, and in the earlier photograph, he had done what he could not do in life:

stop time. But time had moved on, and that moment of perfect innocence was gone forever. Anny heard all this in his sigh and forgave him everything.

eight

1871

THE HOUSE WAS SILENT WHEN it should have been noisy. The month before, Minny had given birth to a daughter, Laura Makepeace, named after her grandfather and his pet heroine. Born too early, she weighed only three pounds. Anny's finger seemed so enormous when she rubbed it against this precious Thumbelina's cheek. For the first few weeks, the baby's eyes were sealed shut. The veins visible beneath her skin gave her body a purple cast. She was so weak that her tiny arms and legs flopped out, froglike, and had to be bound close to her body with linen strips. Then she was wrapped head to toe in flannel, with a small opening for her mauve face, which emerged from the swaddling clothes like a Reine des Violettes rosebud. The baby made barely audible grunts and bleats. The household silence signaled a terrible truth: a baby too weak to cry.

Anny was equally concerned about Minny, who remained bedridden after a difficult childbirth. She knew her sister would not recover if she lost another child.

The nurse was a stern middle-aged woman with a thick Yorkshire accent who insisted on being called Mrs. Pitkin, though she had never been married. Mrs. Pitkin had strong opinions about caring for weaklings and ran the nursery with an iron fist. "I've never lost a wee one yet," she said with absolute authority, and for some reason everyone believed her.

As a condition of employment Mrs. Pitkin specified that she would not empty slops or trim lamps. Furthermore, she would only concern herself with the cleaning that she considered to be medically necessary, and then only because she didn't trust others to do a proper job.

To begin with, Mrs. Pitkin demanded that the carpets be removed; the pile was a filth trap, she claimed. The clean rags she stuffed in the crevices between the window and the frame prevented drafts and kept out London's fetid air, soiled by smoke, sewer emanations, chunks of unburned fuel, and bits of straw fouled by horse dung. On clear days, she opened the windows to air out the room.

People entering the nursery had to first wash their hands. Leslie, who suffered from the most minor of sniffles, was banned completely until his cold went away. "She fancies herself Florence Nightingale," he grumbled, but he did exactly as he was told, sensing that Mrs. Pitkin was the bulwark between life and death.

The baby slept in a wicker basket stuffed with cotton wool and warmed by a stoneware bed warmer, refilled with hot water every three hours. The fireplace was frequently topped off with coal, making the nursery the warmest room in the house.

Because the baby was too weak to suckle, Mrs. Pitkin fed her a solution of milk, a drop of castor oil, and a pinch of milk sugar. She insisted that the milk be of the purest quality. Everyone knew of the tea scandal, in which merchants toasted used tea leaves and sold them as new. Rumors of watered-down milk were common. Mrs. Pitkin refused to take chances with the milkmaids who came to the door bearing pails on either end of a wooden yolk. Instead, she arranged for a farmer to bring a cow to the house and looked on as he pulled the udders by the front stoop, sending a stream of bluish milk into the crockery she provided.

For the first month Mrs. Pitkin fed Laura every two hours

throughout the night, weighing the infant before and after each feeding. Anny had never seen the woman out of her crisp white hat and starched apron. She had no idea when Mrs. Pitkin slept—she didn't seem to be the kind of woman who required sleep.

With Leslie and Anny, Mrs. Pitkin was a tyrant. She viewed them as infection factories best kept at a distance. But she was tender and loving with the baby. Anny passed by the nursery once as the nurse held the swaddled bundle and cooed, "How's my wee one. You're a stubborn little mite, ye are."

She was also ferociously protective of Minny, and took the infant for short visits, even though Minny was not yet strong enough to sit up in bed. "A babe needs a mother's love as much as she needs food or water," Mrs. Pitkin said, and placed the child face down on Minny's chest, holding her gently in place, since Minny did not have the strength to do so. The tightly-wrapped creature atop Minny's chest put Anny in mind of a cocoon, the life inside inert while it developed into a beautiful butterfly.

Though everyone lived in fear of Mrs. Pitkin, Anny knew that the nurse was the main reason that Laura, against all odds, began to thrive. The downy fuzz that covered the infant's body disappeared, along with the scaliness of her tiny hands and feet. She grew into her loose-fitting skin until, by the end of March, she looked like a normal baby, only smaller.

She was crying all the time now, as if she had saved up all the cries during her early months to release at a later date. The sound was cause for celebration. "There is more poetry in a squalling brat than in a play of Shakespeare," Leslie said, full of pride.

The household talked baby from morning to night. "The emperor of all of the Germanys isn't so important to us as that little mite on Minny's chest," Anny wrote to her Ritchie cousins.

In April, Mrs. Pitkin left their employment. She had made it clear when she took the job that she would stay only until the baby was out of danger. Her replacement was a German girl named Louise, who had Mrs. Pitkin's sternness without her tender heart. Anny guessed that Laura would outgrow Nurse before the year was out. But it didn't matter, since Minny was more involved with her child than most mothers Anny knew.

Min was now strong enough to hold the baby on her own. It warmed Anny's heart to see her leaning over Laura making exaggerated expressions and funny noises, and covering her in little kisses. "Oh, Anny, you can't imagine what it is like to have your own child," she said.

Anny knew that neither Minny nor Laura was out of danger. Janie, born a year after Anny, had been a healthy baby, and then died at eight months of a chest infection. Anny remembered her father saying, "The sweet-tempered lamb learned to say Pa before she died. She reached out her dear little arms to me every time she saw me. I'll never get over her suffering. Never." And he never did. He observed her birthday every year and, at his request, was buried beside her in Kensal Green.

Their mother never recovered from little Janie's death. When Minny was born fourteen months later, her third child in as many years, she was despondent. It didn't help that the new baby looked remarkably like Baby Jane. Even her cry was the same. For the first several months, their mother could not even bring herself to give the newborn a name. Everyone called her Baby.

Laura, on the other hand, had many pet names. Leslie called her Laurekins. Both parents called her Memee or Memekins. Leslie delighted in being a father. When he returned in the evening, Anny could hear the clump, clump, clump of his feet on the stairs as he went straight to the nursery. "How's my Laurekins, my precious Memee?" he said, with his hands behind his back, peering over the basket and staring as if the infant were a rare museum object.

"Look at her oversize head. It contains an amount of brains that would astonish any humble phrenologist," he said to Anny. The shape of her feet would make her a first-rate mountaineer, he predicted, and her hands quite clearly were formed to grasp a pen. "It is true that my Memee is the best of all possible babies," he said to Anny, his face aglow.

WHEN LAURA WAS FIVE MONTHS old, Anny asked Minny's permission to take the baby to visit their mother, who lived with her caretaker in a flat on the outskirts of London.

The birth of a new generation had not softened Minny's feelings toward their mother. She would not hear of the idea.

"Memee will cheer her up," Anny said. "Babies do that to people. Do you despise Mama so much that you would deny her the chance for a little happiness?"

"You're always trying to fix things, and some things can't be fixed." She sat in the parlor with Laura cooing softly in her lap. In the hallway, sun through the stained-glass transom made green squares on the floor.

"I'm not asking *you* to go. I just want to take Laura for the afternoon."

"And I forbid it. Don't ask me again. She's not your baby."

"But Mama is her grandmother. Whether you like it or not, that will never change," she said, still feeling the sting of Min's words.

"Oh for heaven's sake. Have it your way. You always do."

Funny, Anny thought. She would have said the same thing about her sister.

That afternoon, before Minny had the chance to change her mind, Anny took Nurse and the baby to the caretaker's flat and waited in the back garden. An unpruned sweetbriar hedge formed a brambled mass at the end of the property, and grass grew knee-high. Mrs. Bakewell took such good care of their mother that Anny couldn't complain that she let the garden grow wild.

Soon, Mrs. Bakewell guided her mother out by the elbow, as if she were an invalid. Once she got her settled in the wicker chair, she hovered in the background until she was sure things would go smoothly. Anny was surprised by how pretty her mother looked, dressed in an olive green frock that complemented her auburn hair. She always forgot what a beauty her mother was. On her finger she wore the engagement ring their father had given her: a moonstone set in black enamel between two diamonds. Before asking for her hand, he had proudly shown the ring to a friend, who said, with alarm, "But William, see what you have done. This is not an engagement ring. It's a mourning ring!"

Anny kissed her mother's cheek and said, "Mama, it's Anny, your daughter." Her mother was always happy to have visitors, but Anny might as well have been a random stranger. "Look, I've brought you a lovely surprise today." She took Laura from Nurse Louise and turned the baby toward her mother. Laura was a beautiful child with a halo of golden curls.

Delight washed over her mother's face. She reached out her arms. Anny handed the baby to her, but remained vigilant, ready to snatch Laura away at the first sign of danger. The baby lay face up on her lap amidst a froth of pink lace and ruffles, as if emerging from a giant peony.

Her mother smiled at the child. The madness seemed to fall away, replaced by some universal instinct, if not maternal, then at least protective of something so small and defenseless.

"Mama, sing to her. She loves it when people sing."

Her mother began to sing a nonsense song. Her voice was clear and true, her face luminous.

> Lee ma tom kin, hold er ree.
> Have a baby, have a snee.
> Insy woo wa, bool be born
> Hallelujiah, on this morn.

Excited by the music, the baby pumped her legs and flapped her hands in the air. Her grandmother leaned closer and whispered nonsense phrases. Laura struggled to lift her head, smiling and gurgling. Anny wished they could go on like that for the rest of the afternoon, but after a while, the baby began to cry. Anny's mother recoiled, and Anny scooped the child up before she rolled off her lap.

"It's not your fault, Mama. She just needs changing. We'll take care of it." Anny gave the baby to Nurse Louise, who took her inside.

She sat down beside her mother and took her hand. "I'm so glad you could see our precious Laura."

Her mother looked baffled.

"The baby. Minny's baby."

"Minny's my baby." She had not seen Minny since she was an infant.

"Yes, she was. And now she's grown and has a baby of her own. Laura is her name. She is your granddaughter."

A deranged look returned to her eyes and her upper lip began to twitch. Anny was afraid of setting her off. She stood up and kissed the top of her head.

"I'll be back in a month. Can I bring you anything?"

"A baby," she said.

"I'll try to bring Laura back for a visit," Anny said, though she was fairly certain that Minny would not grant her permission again.

"No, I want my own baby. To keep."

"I was your baby once. A long time ago."

Her mother tilted her head and frowned, as if such a thing were inconceivable.

"You?"

"Yes, truly. You sang to me. Do you remember the organ grinder in Paris? In the street?"

Anny stubbornly held on to the hope that the right image,

the right story, the right memory would awaken something long dormant within her mother, and miraculously the door would fly open, and the doting mother she had once been would step over the threshold and into the light. But the door remained stubbornly shut.

"Don't worry about it, Mama. I'm glad you enjoyed Laura," she said, and left before her mother could see her tears.

BY SUMMER, MINNY AND LAURA were strong enough for a visit to Freshwater. Anny proposed that they rent The Porch.

"That's ridiculous," Leslie complained, when Anny suggested a sum to pay Cammie. "We've always stayed there for free."

"We both have steady incomes. It's not a hardship for us."

She knew the Camerons were facing financial difficulties.

"Your profligacy is misguided," Leslie said.

"On this point, I won't be countermanded. Cammie needs the money. It's as simple as that. And there's no reason to injure her pride by making a point of it. Just pay her the rent. It's the least we can do."

Leslie had not spent summers at Freshwater and had not fallen under Cammie's spell. Now Cammie's friends rallied around her, helping out where they could, in an effort to preserve an endangered way of life—a respect for beauty and art and conversation.

Even dear Mr. Tennyson had come to the aid of his neighbor. Much as he complained about the blood-sucking autograph seekers who gathered at his gate to catch a glimpse of the famous poet, he nevertheless signed scores of the photographic portrait she had taken of him. "Now the innkeepers recognize me and charge me double," he groused, but his fame brought Cammie both sitters and buyers.

Arrangements settled, Anny and the Stephen family took the

ferry to the Isle of Wight, where Cammie had carriages waiting to transport them to the house.

At Dimbola, she came out to greet them, more disheveled than usual. Gray strands escaped from the ivory combs that held back her hair. Her mismatched blouse and skirt had a slept-in look. Even by the island's relaxed standard of dress, the outfit was shabby.

Minny took Laura from Nurse Louise so she could show her off to Mrs. C. The servants and luggage in the second carriage continued on to The Porch.

"Oh look at this sweet, darling child. What a tiny chick she is." Cammie chucked the infant's chin with a finger stained black. Minny deftly pulled the baby out of reach.

Leslie said, "She does not weigh as much as some babies, but she is a baby to be proud of, as anyone who has an eye for the best qualities of babies can see."

"To be sure," Cammie said, covering her mouth to cough. She had a nasty chest rattle brought on, no doubt, by excessive exposure to the ether and potassium cyanide used in the photographic process. "And Leslie. I understand you're the new editor of the *Cornhill*," she said.

He was following in the footsteps of William Thackeray, who had founded the magazine and edited it at the end of his life. Leslie's ordered mind, intellectual rigor, and dislike of false sentiment made him a natural editor. He had some reservations in accepting the job—why take on a magazine that forbade discussion of politics and religion, the only two topics people were interested in?—but he overcame them in favor of an income of 500 pounds a year, for he now had an expanded family to support.

"I'm afraid my writers think I've gone over to the enemy's side. They're convinced that my sole mission in life is to suppress their genius," he said.

"Someday soon you'll be able to add photographs to your magazine. That will widen its appeal," Cammie said.

"What! And put our engravers and artists out of work? Never!"

"The camera is changing everything. In the future it will be photographs, rather than drawings, that define how people view the world."

"I seriously doubt it. Look at poor Matthew Brady. He took thousands of images of the Civil War and now he can't even give the glass plates away. I understand from my American friends that some have been sold to gardeners to make greenhouses."

She held her hand to her mouth in horror. "What a terrible loss to history."

"Perhaps," Leslie said, with a patronizing nod. Anny knew he didn't believe photography to be an art. Because of Mrs. Cameron's discombobulated style, he vastly underrated her talent.

"You must be exhausted from the journey," Cammie said. "Some tea will fortify you."

They followed her into the parlor. When Leslie sat on the brocade settee, a pouf of dust rose from the pillows. Cobwebs sheathed the ivory elephants on the mantle. Every surface was covered with books, photographs, and mementos from Ceylon and India haphazardly placed about. Anny saw Min survey the room with disgust.

Orderliness and household management were not among Cammie's many endearing traits. She had allowed the parlor maid Mary Hillier to neglect her duties in favor of posing for portraits. For Cammie, beauty eradicated class. The maid's luxurious Pre-Raphaelite curls had been immortalized in some of her most successful photographs. Anny had seen sepia-tinted images of Mary as Psyche, Saint Agnes, the Greek poet Sappho, the muse Clio, and a frankly wanton-looking angel. She had posed for so many versions of the Madonna that villagers had taken to calling her Mary Madonna. It was no wonder the maid had little time or inclination to clean house.

The baby started to cry and Minny said, "If you'll excuse

me, I'm going to get Laura settled and take a rest myself. Anny, will you come with me?"

"We'll be in the garden, Anny. Join us later if you'd like," Cammie said.

Min and Anny walked along the lane to the cottage.

"That place is filthy. It's an outrage," Minny fumed.

"Not everyone is as gifted as you at running a household," Anny said, grateful that they had their own cottage to stay in.

"How could anyone be oblivious to that mess? She's from a good family. What's wrong with her?"

"Depends on who you ask," Anny said. Cammie had too many things on her mind to worry about cleaning.

"Well, I won't allow my Memekins near that pit of sloth," Minny said.

Anny helped her get Laura settled in the cottage and then returned to Dimbola by the back path. In contrast to the house, the garden was in perfect order. Cammie was an avid gardener and had planted all the beds herself. Flowers provided an artistic outlet for her.

Anny followed the footpath under the arbor. Climbing roses arched above her. Red in the bud stage, the roses opened up to be light pink. Through the lattice, she saw Cammie and Leslie seated at a table covered with a white cloth and silver tea service. Anny heard her name mentioned and paused to listen.

"It's high time we matched our Anny up with a suitable man, don't you think?" Mrs. C. was saying.

"Anny?" Leslie said. "Do you really think she'd be interested?"

"My dear fellow, women are always interested. I'm quite experienced in these matters."

"What about her writing?" Anny could hear the clink of a silver spoon against china.

"There's no reason married women can't write. Look at George Eliot and Elizabeth Gaskell."

"But Anny's special," Leslie said. "She's such a beautiful

mixture of talent and simple kindness. She's a jewel that demands to be properly set. I can't endure to think of her throwing herself away on a man who is unworthy of her."

Anny moved in closer and snagged her sleeve on a thorn.

"Robert Browning is the man I had in mind," Cammie said.

"That crochety old poet? He's old enough to be her father!"

"You must admit he's worthy. He's been a widower for ten years, and the man is lonely."

"One genius per family is enough."

Anny blushed. She wasn't aware that Leslie held her in such regard.

He continued: "Anny is so good and charming that she would do her duty to her husband till her heart broke from it. I'm quite certain she would stop writing."

"Elizabeth Barrett spent her most productive years when she was married to him," Cammie pointed out.

"But he's an old man now. Anny would end up taking care of him."

"My, you are negative."

"Only realistic."

Anny emerged from her hiding place and approached them. "Are you two scheming behind my back?"

"Did you hear our conversation?" Leslie said, taken aback.

"Some of it. It appears that Cammie has offered to exercise her well-honed skills as a matchmaker."

"I would be delighted, but only if I have your blessing."

"I should like Mr. Somebody to turn up one day. Dear me! How nice that would be. But Mr. Browning was my father's friend. I could never think of him in any other way."

Cammie sighed. "Well, I shan't give up."

"You may be the only one," Anny said. "I fear I am too old for love."

"My dear, one is never too old for love," Cammie said, with certainty.

AFTER SETTLING INTO THE PORCH, the Stephens quickly established their island routines. Laura was tolerating the local milk well. Minny found one particular cow that suited her perfectly and arranged to have the animal milked twice a day.

She took the baby out every morning for a short stroll while Leslie hiked for ten miles. He was getting in shape for a trip to the Alps in July. With his alpenstock and funny-looking green hat, given to him by his favorite Swiss guide, he strode off every morning as if the devil himself were in pursuit.

Anny's friend Julia Duckworth was staying on the island with her three children. Cammie no longer sought out her niece for the camera. Unhappiness of this depth was not something she wanted to preserve on a glass plate.

"Happy people don't like to be around unhappy people," the widow said.

"How well I know," replied Anny, who often felt like an intruder on Min and Les's domestic happiness following Laura's birth.

Anny was glad to have more time to spend with her friend and requested her help with *Old Kensington*. She was working every morning on the final rewrite and manuscript preparation. Julia was an ardent reader of Anny's novels and had a keen literary instinct.

Julia devoured the novel in two days and brought back the pages to The Porch wrapped in brown paper and string.

"You've inherited your father's quick eye for all kinds of delicate shades and touches," she said. "When I'm reading the novel, I feel as if you're speaking to me personally. No one else writing today does that. But I must say, at times, the story seems hard to follow."

"Oh my goodness, you're right," Anny burst out. "I live my

life with the demon of disorder nipping at my heels, and I write as I live!" Structure was her weakness. Despite dominant female characters and many brilliant fragments, the string did not always connect the pearls. "You must help me craft this muddle into better shape. You're so much more organized than I."

"I'm afraid I can't be of much use to anyone in my current state."

"Oh, but you can. You must!"

"Why would you want me when you have such an esteemed editor living under the same roof? One of the brightest literary minds in London."

"Leslie reads with his mind. You read with your heart. You are my ideal reader."

"Well, I suppose I could use a distraction," Julia said.

They met at the cottage every morning. Julia had an instinctive feel for which paragraphs and descriptions should be cut, and which could be rearranged for greater impact. When they worked together, she seemed engaged and lively. But when she was not working, her melancholy returned.

"After Papa died, I found it beneficial to take long walks alone by the sea. We're going to the lighthouse with Cam today. Let the children come with us and you can take some time for yourself," Anny offered.

At noon, the picnickers trooped across High Down and set up camp on a rocky stretch of shore with a view of the red-and-white striped lighthouse at the westernmost tip of the island.

Minny put Laura on her back on a blanket while Julia's nurse settled Gerald in a wicker basket. He wore a white dress with a black mourning ribbon tied at the shoulder. Julia's two older children, George and Stella, amused themselves by digging a hole and lining it with oyster shells.

After lunch, Cammie picked up the children's red ball and held it in front of Laura, who nestled in her mother's arms.

"This is a ball. Can you say ball?" Cammie said.

Laura stared out in the distance and gave no indication that she heard Cammie.

"The glare from the sea bothers her," Minny said. "She's used to the dim London light."

Cammie held the ball directly in front of the child's face. "Where is the ball? Can you show me the ball?"

Pointing was not something Laura did. Ever. She stared beyond the ball with an unfocused gaze as if it were beneath her to even look at the ball, much less repeat the word, simply because some batty old woman was thrusting a toy in her face.

At six months, Laura had said "Papa," to Leslie's delight, and "bow wow" a few days later. But in the following five weeks, she had added no new words to her vocabulary.

"What about this. Who is this?" Cammie said, pointing to Minny. "Can you say Mama?"

Laura looked straight through Cammie as if she were glass.

Minny bristled. "My little darling was tiny when she came into the world. She's got some catching up to do." She pulled the baby's head to her and covered it with kisses.

There was a certain dignity in refusing to perform like a circus animal on demand, Anny thought. Laura was going to talk when she was good and ready.

"I'll leave you to enjoy the fresh air. I need to tidy up my studio for the rehearsal this afternoon," Cammie said, getting ready to leave.

Minny suppressed a smile, and Anny knew what she was thinking: Their friend Cammie, tidy up? Unlikely.

Her son Henry had written a Roman drama and friends had agreed to act in it. The dress rehearsal was later that afternoon. Henry was living at home after having dropped out of Oxford—for inability to pay tuition, it was rumored, though he was also lazy and had a weakness for billiards.

Anny and the two young mothers had declined to act in the play. That left an all-male cast—"Just like in Shakespeare's time,"

Cammie had said. Anny wanted to support her hostess, so she had offered to help the actors rehearse their lines and to make fair copies of the play. She never traveled anywhere without her writing slope.

"You will come to the play tonight, won't you Minny?" Cammie said. "Alfred has graciously offered his ballroom but he's requested that everyone enter by the back door."

"What! Like the knife grinder?" Leslie said.

"He doesn't want anyone at the gate to see who comes and goes," Cammie said. "Don't tarry. We have much to rehearse before tonight," she said.

"Wave bye-bye," Minny said.

Laura turned her palm to face her forehead and wiggling her chubby fingers, as if bidding goodbye to herself. The child's palms always seemed to be in the wrong place: Facing out when she covered her ears, facing in when she waved goodbye.

"Tennyson is the queerest old bloke I've ever met," Leslie said after Cammie left. "I find him absurdly obsessive, not to mention unkempt. Does the man not wash his hands? Minny, you would never let me out of the house with dirt under my fingernails, would you, darling?"

"Certainly not," she said.

"Don't be harsh," said Anny. "He's gruff on the outside, but soft on the inside, once you get to know him."

"He fancies his damned Cockneys are lurking about. Frankly, I wouldn't be surprised if they lived only in his imagination."

"He just wants to be left alone," Anny said. "He's someone who experiences life more deeply than other people. You can tell by his poems."

"You have a refreshing talent for looking at people's faults in a way that makes them excusable," Leslie said. "Well, that tragic, woebegone pose may work for some, but I wouldn't give tuppence for it."

Anny happened to know that the act of memorizing reams

of Tennyson's poems as a child had put Leslie into such an emotional state that the family doctor ordered him to stop.

"You are no stranger to a gloomy countenance," she chided gently.

"That's how you view me?" he said.

"I'm only pointing out that there's not that much difference between the two of you."

"Only genius," he said glumly.

ANNY GATHERED HER THINGS and called out for Cammie to wait up for her. They hiked together across the Down.

"It's wonderful to see Minny in better health," Cammie said. Furze bushes seemed to slide precipitously over the sheer cliffs.

"It does my heart good to see her so happy. But I worry about Memee. Is she . . . does she seem . . . quite normal to you?" Anny asked, gingerly. Laura had an ethereal vagueness about her that troubled Anny, but she knew so little about babies. Cammie had raised eleven children—five of her own, five orphaned relatives, and an Irish beggar girl. She should know.

"It's difficult to see progress when you are watching her every hour. I am quite sure that no one can tell what capricious powers are folded up in her."

"You're right. It's just that Julia's baby seems so . . . I don't know how to describe it . . . so completely present, so responsive."

One day, Anny had happened upon Julia in the garden. She sat lifeless as a scarecrow, while her baby squirmed in her arms, hungry to take in the world. He pumped his chubby arms and legs and grabbed at everything in reach—his mother's black collar, her sleeve, her ear. Laura was only a month younger than Gerald, but for her, the world failed to fascinate.

"Don't compare, don't judge. Life will be much easier," Cammie advised.

"Gerald seems almost more than Julia can handle," Anny observed.

"Much as I adore my darling niece, I'm afraid she has made a luxury of mourning. It's time for her to pick herself up and carry on. My other nieces would never wallow in pity like that," Cammie said, freely ignoring the advice she had just dispensed.

IT WAS LATE BY THE TIME LESLIE reached the former chicken coop converted to a photography studio. Members of the cast were already selecting their costumes from the vast array of props and clothing.

Cammie had a wide range of friends willing to do anything for her because of all she had done for them. They were less supportive of her youngest son Henry, a rather pallid young man with delicate features and a weak chin who, having failed at Oxford, now fancied himself a playwright. His mother was eager to help him, unconcerned about the faint stink of impropriety associated with the stage. Now she gathered the amateur actors around her as the afternoon sun bore down through the squares of the glass house.

"Gentlemen, you should be able to find anything you need in these trunks. I will happily bring tea to anyone who desires it. Anny is here to help you with your lines, and Henry can help with interpretation."

Alfred Tennyson's son Lionel rifled through the trunk in search of a dress that would fit. He had agreed to play the part of the shopkeeper's daughter, who is wooed by the wealthy merchant's son. That role was played by his Eton classmate Richmond Ritchie, who was spending the weekend with the Tennysons. Lionel held up several dresses to his waist for size, but could not find one large enough.

"You don't have to button it all the way," Richmond offered.

He had already draped himself in a toga which showed to advantage his lithe figure. Now seventeen, he was tall and athletic.

The other men were sifting through the costumes in the trunks, though, in truth, they could have been easily provisioned from the contents of the linen closet. Leslie came from behind a carved teak screen in a toga, his thin legs covered in red hair. Cammie helped him adjust the garment's drape.

Alfred Tennyson emerged in a long robe with gold braid down the front, more befitting a wizard than a lower class Roman shopkeeper. His hair stuck out in all directions and crumbs had taken up permanent residence in his beard. Anny willed herself not to look at his fingernails.

"I refuse to wrap myself in a silly bedsheet," he announced.

"But your outfit is not historically accurate," Leslie pointed out.

"If you want authenticity, then I suggest we send the togas to a fuller's shop, where they can be cleaned with stale urine. Would you like to volunteer to collect the chamber pots, pour the contents into a vat, and then stomp on the togas? In the interest of authenticity, of course," Mr. Tennyson said to Leslie.

"We're honored to have Alfred play his part in any costume he chooses," Cammie said, in an effort to soothe both men's pride. "And Leslie, you look so handsome in that toga. It shows off the results of your mountaineering training."

"I ought to be at home working on my own lines instead of memorizing someone else's," the poet grumbled.

"Now Alfred, I know someone with your prodigious memory should have no trouble with a few simple lines," she cajoled him.

The thespians spilled out into the garden and broke off in groups to practice.

In a rare appearance, Mrs. Cameron's husband, Charles Hay, sat beneath the rose arbor to watch the rehearsal. He was a dignified, reclusive man with a long white beard that Tennyson had once described as being dipped in moonlight. His humble manner served as the perfect foil for his wife's exuberance. More a scholar than a businessman, he mostly studied Classics in his room at Dimbola and rarely took part in the dinner parties, theatricals, balls, and pantomimes that his wife loved to organize.

Anny adored Mr. Cameron, who was like a grandfather to her. Poor health and the prospect of financial ruin had aged him considerably. She sat beside him and held his hand. The perfume of the garden mingled with the salty air.

"My heart will always be in Ceylon," he said, in response to Anny's inquiries. His eyes misted over, as if remembering the sparkling waterfalls, verdant forests, and dramatic vistas that he had so vividly described to her in the past.

"Do you ever think of moving there permanently?" On this beautiful island, surrounded by the endless sky and the sea, she could not conceive of wanting to be anywhere else.

"I don't know. It is so dispiriting to discover, this late in life, that the thing you love most is the thing you're not particularly good at," he said wistfully. "Dear Cam has found what she's good at. Henry, I'm afraid, has not. Have you?"

"Writing, I suppose. It's the only thing that, when I'm doing it, I don't feel I should be doing anything else."

"You are among the fortunate few. Count your blessings."

Anny looked out over the ragtag assemblage of Romans cavorting barefoot on the lawn wielding India rubber clubs, scepters, sabers, and swords. Being in costume gave them license to discard their inhibitions.

Out by the lilac hedge Richmond was on one knee, extolling the beauty and virtues of Lionel, who stood stiffly in an ill-fitting dress that had been expanded in the back with corset-like strings.

"Oh, heavens, Richmond! Do you call that lovemaking? I know you can do better than that," Mrs. C. chided.

"But it's Lionel, my cricket teammate," Richmond complained.

"You don't find me comely," Lionel put a hand to his shoulder and struck a pose reminiscent of Michelangelo's David.

Under the rose arbor, Mr. Cameron said to Anny, "Cam *does* get involved, doesn't she?" He smiled, as if he were still smitten after all these years of marriage.

Anny excused herself to help Leslie rehearse his lines. He was playing the part of a Roman guard.

"Intellectuals in togas. It always warms the heart," she said, as she flipped through the pages of the play to find his part. "Now, let's start at the top of page five."

"I'm not going to say 'Harketh.' No one says 'Harketh,'" he complained.

"Your character does. Henry has written it right here: 'Harketh. The master approaches.'"

She had to admit that, judging from what she had read, the theater was not an obvious pathway to success for dear Henry.

"Well, I refuse to say something so patently inauthentic."

"And the alpenstock?" she said, looking at the tall alpine staff he had brought from London for his daily walks. "I don't remember that as being part of the traditional Roman attire. Of course, it might come in handy for stirring the cleaning vats of togas." She could not resist a sly smile, enjoying a dalliance in the scatological, if only to scandalize her prudish brother-in-law.

"Aunt Anny, can you help with my lines?" Richmond called from the lilac hedge.

She joined him on the wooden bench by the gate. Lionel was escaping along the garden path, the hem of his dress scattering wood chips as he went.

"Please don't call me Aunt. It makes me feel so old," she said. In fact, they were second cousins.

"Can you read the part of the shopkeeper's daughter," he said. "You must help me learn to make love convincingly," he said.

"I'm afraid I have scant experience in that," she laughed.

"What about the characters in your novels? How can you write about love without feeling it?"

"I can only suggest ways you might think about your character. You are a wealthy merchant's son, in love with a lower-class girl. Everyone around you is profoundly opposed to the match, yet something about her makes you oblivious to the objections of others—some spark, some place in your heart makes you willing to risk everything for her. Love is a wild thing. Try to harness some of that wildness," she counseled, hoping she knew more than he, at least.

They practiced his part together. Memorization was not a problem for him. As part of his education, he had committed an enormous number of poems to memory, as had the others. But he was the only one trying to put real feeling into the melodrama that Cammie's son had penned. Richmond was used to being the best at everything he did, and now he was determined to be a good actor. There was no arrogance in his effort, just an intense desire to give everything, no matter how trivial, the full measure of his attention.

Such sincerity made Anny feel tarnished and slightly ashamed. She had allowed cynicism to creep up on her at the age of thirty-four. She wanted desperately to regain the freshness and naïveté he embodied. Was that not, after all, what love awakened?

After they had run through the part several times, she excused herself and wandered alone beyond the garden to the hill leading to High Down. The afternoon sun turned the vertical face of the chalk cliffs gold. How she loved this island. Yet she felt a despondency creep over her. She had much to be grateful for—a successful career, a loving family, a close circle of friends. She was William Thackeray's daughter, Minny's sister, Laura's aunt, and Leslie's sister-in-law. Why then did she feel so alone?

She could hear her friends soldiering through their parts with good humor. (Except for Leslie, who resisted having fun in any situation). Where did she fit in? She was the prompter, feeding other people their lines.

A light breeze pushed gently against her face. She stared at the moon, already visible in the afternoon sky. It was a chalky smear, the mere suggestion of itself, not strong enough to cast light on the water, but offering a hint of what was to come.

nine

1873

LONDON WAS BURSTING AT THE seams, with new houses springing up in the muddy streets beyond Kensington with alarming dispatch. The bucolic neighborhood that Anny had so tenderly rendered in *Old Kensington* was only a memory.

Anny, Minny, and Leslie purchased one of the houses being built on Southwell Gardens, scheduled for completion in the spring. Anny preferred the genteel shabbiness of their home on Onslow Square to the soulless uniformity of new construction, but she was in no position to object, not after the conversation she had overheard by chance the previous fall.

Anny had been adjusting her hat in the hall mirror when she heard talking in the parlor.

"It's high time we had our own house. Just you, me, and Memee."

Anny recognized her sister's voice and dawdled a moment before putting on her cloak.

"What about Anny? Where will she go?" Leslie said.

"She's resourceful. She'll find a way."

"But our darling Laurekins is so fond of her."

"She'll still visit, of course." Her sister's tone was brittle and unforgiving. Anny clasped her kid gloves in her hands and felt the leather press against her damp palms.

"I feel bad for her. Can she really manage on her own? You know how she is," Leslie said.

"Why are you always thinking of her above me? We need our privacy, now that we have our own family."

A housemaid passed through the hall, and Anny moved on before she heard the conclusion. She felt crushed, knowing that Minny didn't want her. When her sister became excited about buying one of the new houses being built less than a quarter of a mile from their present home, Anny voiced no objection, lest she give Minny an excuse to toss her out like an old slipper.

That winter, Minny pored over drawings and rearranged rooms, fulfilling her lifelong dream of designing a house. She insisted on the latest plumbing and heating, as well as a skylight and a special ventilator for Leslie's pipe in the attic study. As a surprise, she painted and fired tiles to surround his fireplace. One tile depicted Laura with Troy, the adored and mistreated dog who endured Laura's fur pulling, ear cuffing, and tail tugging with remarkable equanimity.

Minny had a strong artistic eye and excellent taste and was never happier than when picking out wallpaper, tiles, light fixtures, and hardware. Anny restricted herself to one modest request: please, for the dining room wallpaper, something plain, preferably without cabbages.

Minny, who was a tyrant when it came to cleanliness, unaccountably loved to visit the construction site, with its plaster dust, loose nails, scattered tools, and drop cloths. An exacting taskmaster, she had no trouble expressing her opinions to the workmen with fairness and precision.

Visiting the house in progress sent Anny into fits of despair. Gasmen in one room, carpenters in another, tap, screw, grind, creak. The floor was covered with mud from the daily drizzle. Her hem sopped up the sludge.

During construction, banknotes flew out the window and vanished like a startled flock of starlings. Anny worried about Leslie. Under financial stress, he became like a cornered animal. "Oh, the carpenters, the fendersmiths, the looking glass people. Their bills! Their bills!" he complained to Anny. But they were both eager to please Minny. Anny secretly suspected that Minny had agreed to keep living with her because she needed the money to finance her exquisite taste.

Laura remained at the heart of the household, but she was a mystery to Anny. How could this changeling with a pixie nose and rosy cheeks, act in such an incomprehensible fashion? When she fell and whacked her forehead, she didn't emit a peep. Yet a draft from the window would cause her to erupt into a mind-piercing screech. She could be giggling and filled with mirth one moment and then go blank the next. When she was the one who initiated the contact, she could be generous with her hugs and kisses. But if Anny made the first move, the child would retreat into an interior walled fortress.

Prone to unpredictable outbursts, she would go into fizzy spins of excitement as she danced and spewed forth a torrent of gibberish, with a few recognizable English and German words thrown in. The German she picked up from Nurse Louise. The English words she learned one day and forgot the next. She was almost two and a half, yet she knew fewer than a hundred words. One of her words was "more."

Her favorite poem was "Jabberwocky." Lewis Carroll's sequel *Through the Looking Glass and What Alice Found There* was a rollicking success from the moment it was published. Anny wanted to kiss that fussy Oxford logician for the magical way he had with children. Laura adored that nonsense poem from the book and made Anny recite it a mind-numbing number of times. The rhythm and the sounds soothed her. After the last line, as Anny caught her breath, Laura would pat the air with her hands and say, "More."

But when Anny tried to read *Through the Looking Glass*, or the other poems about the Walrus and the Carpenter or Tweedledum and Tweedledee, the child quickly lost interest. This saddened Anny. Her warmest childhood memories were of being read to by her father. When she and Minny lived with their grandmother in Paris, his visits from London were special and most special of all was when he read his girls to sleep. His rich baritone could climb the register for female voices, or drop to a bass for threatening monsters. He was particularly good at creating sounds—a creaking door, a screeching owl, a whinnying horse. During the bedtime stories, Minny was always the first to nod off, but Anny struggled to keep her eyes open, knowing that the following morning, he might be gone.

One evening, she asked him, "Why are there no fairies in fairy tales?" Minny was cuddled under one arm and she under the other. "Oh, but there are fairies in other tales," he said, and the following evening produced a charming volume called *The Book of Fairies*, filled with rough woodcuts of gnomes and sprites. "The Irish call fairies the Good People," he said, reminding the girls that their mother was Irish. "They have human shape, but no human heart, so they don't grow old like you and me."

That book had survived many moves and jumble sales. It had been read so many times that the cardboard poked through the corners and the cover peeled away at the spine, exposing the threads and mustard-colored glue of the binding. One day Anny brought the volume to the nursery. She found Laura on the floor, emptying wooden animals from a toy ark. Anny pulled up a rocking chair and said, "Come sit with me and I'll read you a special story."

Laura looked up from her ark and said, "Jaba-Woga."

"Yes, my little Jub Jub bird, I'll recite the poem later, but first I want to share a book that is very special to your Aunt Anny."

She put Laura in her lap, but the child squirmed down and returned to her spot on the floor.

"You can play while I read a story," Anny said.

Laura gave no indication she heard, but Anny bravely carried on. "Did you know that the fairies of Irish legend were hidden in everything? They gave color to the grass, gaiety to the hearth, and grace to the rags the poor children wore."

Anny embellished the written story by adding a little girl named Laura who wore white stockings and a navy blue sailor dress and loved to organize the animals in her wooden menagerie. Laura did not perk up at the sound of her name or the description the clothes she was wearing. She was absorbed with arranging the brightly painted lions, giraffes, zebras, and bears from the toy ark, each one the height of a tea cup. If one animal appeared to be a fraction of an inch out of position, she adjusted it. The child had Leslie's uncanny ability to concentrate on one task to the exclusion of everything else.

Anny continued with the story, introducing a tiger and a monkey. When she looked up from the book, she found herself surrounded by the wooden animals that Laura had placed, two by two, in a semi-circle around the rocker, as if to create an audience.

Anny skipped several pages to see if Laura would notice. She did not. Apparently, she had not heard a word. "Well, my Frumious Bandersnatch. We'll do it your way." She set the book of fairies on the floor and began to recite "Jabberwocky." At the end, Laura said, "More."

While she listened, the child roughly flipped the pages of the fairy book without looking at the illustrations. Anny, lulled into a stupor by the endless repetitions, did not catch Laura at first when she attacked the pages with a pencil, stabbing the woodcuts that had meant so much to Anny as a child. "What are you doing? Bad girl," she shouted when she realized with horror what was happening.

Laura looked up, surprised, and then resumed her destruction.

"Laura. No! Stop this minute."

As Anny swooped in to rescue the book, the hem of her skirt brushed against the wooden animals and scattered them about on the floor.

Laura took one look at the wreckage and put her hands over her ears, palms out, fingertips down, and emitted a heart-shattering screech.

"Oh, Baby, I'm sorry. I didn't mean to hurt your animals." Anny crouched down and put her arms around Laura to comfort her but the child pushed off with her feet and shouted, "Bad!" then curled up in a ball.

Anny collected the wooden figures and tried to put them back in a semicircle, but made a hash of it. Laura had placed them in a particular order that Anny could not replicate.

Lip out, the child scooped up the animals and hurled them at Anny with astonishing force for such a mite. Bears and lions and giraffes shot through the air and ricocheted off Anny's body.

"Shssh. My darling Laurekins. Calm down," she said, feeling out of her depth, alone with this wild creature. She knew she had badly mishandled the situation, but didn't know how to contain it.

"Louise. Help. Come quickly," she called out for Nurse, who rushed in immediately. "I'm afraid I've made a mess of things. Can you take over?" she pleaded.

She left Laura in Louise's care and went downstairs. She found Minny at her desk poring over expenses for the new house.

Anny explained what had happened. "Any other book, and I could have kept my temper, but that precious volume. It still has the oil from Papa's fingers."

"Anny, she didn't mean any harm," Minny said. "She's too young to know better."

"I know, I know. But it worries me, the way she overreacts. I can't tell what's bothering her because her language is so limited."

"Memee may be a little behind, but she's surrounded by three doting adults who do everything for her. She doesn't need to talk."

Anny thought of how slow Minny had been to develop. When they were children, Minny knew if she failed to do something, Anny was always there to take up the slack.

"I can see your point," Anny said.

"You're the one who acted badly. Don't go blaming the poor little chick."

"I'm not blaming her. I'm just . . . It's just . . . I wonder if she might . . ."

"Might what?"

"Never be able to read." It slipped out.

"How dare you. Not even a little genius like you could read at two. You have no right!"

Why did their arguments ignite in a flash, out of the same combustible material? What bothered Anny was not that Laura couldn't read, but apparently the child did not understand what a book was *for*. Like someone using a fork as a hair ornament, without knowing it was intended as an eating utensil.

"There's nothing wrong with my darling that a little extra attention can't correct. I don't need for my child to be perfect," Minny said. "I only need her to know she's loved."

"I adore her. You know that," Anny said. "It's just that she can be very trying, and I'm not sure I have the patience."

"That's why God made me her mother, and not you!"

AFTER TAKING A REST TO CALM HER nerves, Anny climbed the stairs to check on Laura. She found the child alone, her tears dried, the nurse gone. The wooden animals were restored to their rightful place. They stood in an orderly semicircle on the floor, outside the reach of the sunlight, which fell in neat squares on the wide wood planks where the shadows from the window muntins formed a grid. In the middle of the room Laura straddled the bright squares. The sun brushed her cheek and illuminated her curls before falling to the floor. With outstretched arms, she turned slowly, very slowly, humming as she moved. She took one step at a time, careful never to touch the lines. She was in a trance, lost in a mysterious world of interior delight.

Could this serene child possibly be the same one who, less than an hour before, had sparked such anger in Anny? This airy, impish being who, like the fairies of Anny's mother's Irish culture, did not follow the rules of men. If the child was unable to return the warmth that Anny showered on her, it was not an intentional cruelty.

Anny watched in silence and felt her soul fill with light. So what if the child remained elusive; she would love her all the same.

THE NEWLY OPENED Brighton Aquarium drew crowds from all over England with its exhibits of exotic sea life displayed under arched cathedral ceilings. Tanks displayed starfish, seahorses, anemones, jellyfish, crabs, lobsters, and many species of fish. But it was the devil-fish octopus that was all the rage. Shortly after entertaining hordes of holiday-goers at Christmas, the octopus went missing, and foul play was suspected. Then one astute attendant noticed a spotted dogfish in the tank that was looking quite bloated and lethargic. When he cut into its stomach, he found the expired octopus in its entirety, all eight tentacles intact. Newspapers nationwide covered the loss of the cephalopod celebrity and the octopus mania dissipated somewhat, but the replacement octopus remained a big draw. Anny and the Stephens arranged a trip to Brighton with the Ritchie cousins.

Laura came down with a cold, so Anny agreed to visit the aquarium with Richmond and his Eton classmate Lionel Tennyson. Anny was secretly glad to be going on the outing with the boys, and not Laura, who could act unpredictably in crowds.

At the aquarium, Richmond and Anny got separated from

Lionel early on. They decided to view the tabletop tanks first, hoping that the crowd in front of the octopus tank would thin out. When that didn't happen, they joined the elbow-to-elbow spectators keeping watch for any signs of the shy octopus. Algae, seaweed, and coral provided ample hiding spots. After an hour, Richmond suggested they have luncheon.

"Excellent idea," Anny said. She had heard so much about the new restaurant, which boasted an indoor waterfall. "Do you suppose Lionel will find us?"

"He's clever. Waiting around for the octopus is a capital bore. He's probably in the reading room making up a poem for the chaps at school to disguise the fact he never saw the temperamental creature." Lionel stayed clear of serious poetry because of his famous father, but specialized in doggerel. Richmond began to recite his own:

> "Two octopi meet and embrace,
>   Gingerly hugging in case
>   Their suckers attach
>   And they can't unlatch,
>   And must untwist their arms in disgrace."

"What an image," Anny said, laughing. "Sixteen tentacles, all entangled. I love it. You didn't just make that up, did you?"

"Actually, I was amusing myself while we were waiting in front of the tank. Needs a little work, but it never hurts to stay a step ahead of Lionel."

The elegant restaurant featured tables with white cloths beneath a high glass ceiling held up by Corinthian columns. Marble statues stood in niches along the wall. Richmond let Anny have the seat with the view of the waterfall, tumbling over rocks several stories high.

"It was worth coming to Brighton just for this restaurant," Anny said. "To tell the truth, I'd rather look at a lion for ten hours than an octopus for five minutes. But it appears as if we may not even get our five minutes."

After they ordered, they caught up on family news, and then the conversation turned to writing, as it often did with Richmond. No one she knew delved as fearlessly into the creative process as he did. He had reached the age where he was hungry to know everything, not to add a feather to his cap, but to burnish his own understanding of the world and what made people tick.

"Critics are always complaining that the clever characters in my novels are rascals and my good people are idiots," Anny said.

"Perhaps you have a touch of wickedness you're not willing to acknowledge," he said, with the hint of a smile.

He unfolded his starched napkin to make room for the waiter to serve the first course.

"I do admit that villains are infinitely more interesting to me. But you don't think I am like them, do you?"

"Certainly not."

"Then I must be an idiot. Or a bore. But I couldn't be more boring than that ridiculous octopus!"

He turned serious. "What are you working on now?"

"I'm thinking about writing a novel on the life of Angelica Kauffman."

"The eighteenth-century artist who painted the ceilings at Somerset House?"

She nodded. The breadth of his knowledge astounded her. There was a reason his family nickname was Whizz. She lacked his public school training. Her father had done his best to expose her to the great art and literature of the day, but she would never have Richmond's strong foundation.

"I feel a real connection to her. She was prey to her own whims and didn't have the best judgment in love, but she found her salvation in art."

"I've always been in awe of creative people."

She assumed he meant Miss Angel, the title she was considering for her fictional treatment of the artist.

"Are you interested in writing fiction?" She could think of no other reason for his intense interest.

"Good God, no! I haven't a creative bone in my body. Facts, logic, and analysis come easily to me. But you—you deal with people's tender core that would remain inaccessible, were it not for our writers. What could be more important?"

She felt the color rise to her cheeks. He made her feel that what she did was worthy, and, more importantly, that she was worthy for doing it. This past year, her soul had felt parched, and the compliment quenched her, even coming from her young cousin.

She was sorry when Lionel waved from across the room and approached their table. "Where have you b-b-been?" he asked. "I've been looking all over for you."

"We stood like a couple of dunces in front of the tank for the better part of an hour, waiting for that damn cephalopod to show himself, but he refused to oblige us. So we wised up and came here. Please join us. For dessert, at least," Richmond said.

"I'm not coming this far to miss the main attraction," Lionel said.

"Why do you care?"

"B-b-bragging rights. The chaps at school will be so jealous. Everyone's talking about the octopus."

"Suit yourself," Richmond said. They made arrangements to meet later for dinner.

He and Anny finished a leisurely luncheon and then made one more futile pass by the octopus tank before returning to the hotel.

Anny found Minny in front of an open window, taking in the salt air. "I had the most marvelous time," Anny said, taking a seat beside her. "Richmond and Lionel are so fascinating. They have turned into such handsome young men."

"How was the octopus?"

"We didn't see it."

"What were you doing all day?"

"We had luncheon and walked back. Frankly, I think the whole octopus craze is overrated."

"Leslie and I are meeting Blanchie and her husband for dinner at eight. Would you like to join us?"

"Oh, let's see if Richmond and Lionel want to come too. They make every outing so much fun."

"You do gush on about those boys," Minny said in that way she had of making a statement sound like a criticism.

THE VANS ARRIVED ONE DAY IN early spring as Minny and Anny were having tea in the parlor. The movers took the tea cups out of their hands and transferred them, along with all of their belongings, to Southwell Gardens. Anny took private leave of the place where she and Minny had lived since their father's death, and then went to their new home to help Minny, who, in the chaos of dust, packing paper, and boxes, directed each piece of furniture to its resting place.

One day, shortly after they were installed but not completely unpacked, Anny said to Minny, "I received a telegram from Julia Duckworth this morning with an urgent request for me to come over."

"You haven't even finished putting your books on the shelves. You can't rush out every time a friend has some need, particularly Julia, the Widow Martyr." Behind Minny's façade of sweetness lay a barbed tongue. "Leslie and I have no power to keep people off you. You must learn to say no. Don't you see Julia quite enough?"

Minny kept her distance from Julia, even though they went through major life events in tandem. They were married within a month of each other. Minny's first child, who died, was born a month before Julia's first child. Julia's Gerald was born a month before Laura. Despite shadowing each other, they had never developed the close friendship that she and Anny shared.

"I'm concerned about her. Left alone, she tends to fall into black moods," Anny said.

"I don't mean to sound heartless, but her husband has been dead—what?—close to three years now, and she hasn't mitigated her weeds. Her mourning is none of my business, but I do care how she saps your energy with her worries."

"Actually, the problem is Cammie. She's laid up at Julia's house with a frightful cold. You know how demanding she can be. Julia is feeling overwhelmed. It will only take me a few minutes to walk over."

Anny went directly to Julia's house in the thick fog. Street signs and the tops of row houses were lost in gauzy swirls and the gas lamps, which remained lit during the day, glowed like ghostly orbs.

"I'm so glad you came," Julia said, greeting her in the hall. "Cammie's been impossible—conferring dozens of charges on me between fits of sneezing and coughing. She came to London to talk to the South Kensington Museum, but caught a chill on her first day. I've ignored the children to cater to her every whim."

"I'm here to relieve you," Anny said.

"You're a saint. You're much better at dealing with her."

Anny climbed the stairs to the sick chamber and found Cammie propped up on pillows, wrapped in India shawls. Gray hair escaped from her poufy nightcap and her nose was bright red. Tiny glass bottles with cork stoppers cluttered the bedside table. The medicine labels were tied to the necks with string.

"Oh, my dear, darling Anny, how lovely to see you. Achoo! Hand me a handkerchief, if you please. Oh, this is dreadful. I have so much to do, and I so hate imposing on Julia." She blew her nose into a clean lace handkerchief and tossed it aside with the other crumpled wads that lay about her like bruised camellia blossoms.

"Julia has nothing but these dainty hankies and this is not a dainty cold. It's a man-size cold, but she has no men in her life to provide larger handkerchiefs. Perhaps Leslie could help. How is he, and lovely Minny?"

Without pausing for an answer, she was on to the next request. "Would you mind dashing off a note to your father's dear friend Henry Cole? He's such a gem. I've applied for space to exhibit my photographs. All I need is a small corner of the museum. I must get back to work. This has been my *annus horribilis*." She was referring to the death of her daughter, which she had taken very hard. Anny wanted to offer words of comfort, but there was no break in the torrent of Cammie's complaints. "If I only had a deadline, I would be motivated. To make matters worse, my life's work is disintegrating before my eyes. My precious original negatives are developing this insidious honeycomb tracery. I have no power over the chemicals supplied me. The manufacturing formula for the collodion must have changed. It's the only explanation I can come up with. The men in the Photographic Society all have different explanations—everything from the salt air on the island to my own incompetence. But that doesn't explain why the negatives from my first four years are as perfect as the day they were created."

She covered her mouth and coughed. "This air is suffocating me. How does anyone breathe in this city? How I long for the sweet breath of my island, but I am too weak to travel."

Anny dipped the pen into the inkpot and started taking dictation from Cammie. Unable to keep up, she said, "Slow down. You're getting ahead of me." She wished she had followed Minny's advice several years earlier and taken the Pitman shorthand classes that were all the rage. Minny and Leslie's mother corresponded in shorthand, which made the task so much quicker.

Another fit of coughing interrupted Cammie's train of thought.

"Perhaps we should wait until you feel better to continue," Anny suggested.

"I'll be fine. Just give me another tincture of laudanum. It's the only thing that helps."

Anny poured the reddish brown liquid into the silver teaspoon and held it to Cammie's lips.

"Yes. That will hold me for the moment."

The coughing stopped. Cammie launched into a rambling letter to Alfred Tennyson. At the end, she tendered her greetings to his son Lionel.

"Just between you and me—don't write this—Lionel's speech has not improved since Charles Dodgson wrote to recommend a system to treat his stammer. Though I can't say that our Lewis Carroll has benefited from the therapy either. But how can Lionel improve if he won't do the exercises, and his parents won't make him? I always thought they spoiled that boy. They are still distraught over that unpleasantness at Eton."

Anny put the pen down. "What unpleasantness?"

"Richmond didn't mention it? That whelp is so starry-eyed over you. I thought he'd tell you for sure."

Richmond was not one to gossip. "Are you saying there was some scandal involving Lionel?" Anny said.

"It was nonsense. A storm in a teacup. The whole thing proved to be a lie. Could you be a dear and hand me another handkerchief? This abominable cold. It is ridiculous to keep a house so drafty. Julia really must talk to the servants. I've watched that boy grow up. Perhaps he's a touch too dramatic, but with a poet for a father, who can blame him? But that's neither here nor there. Now, where was I? Oh yes, could you add a postscript?"

"Wait a minute. What happened with Lionel?"

"Forget I mentioned it. This cold has clouded my head. It's not important. Ugly rumors. Nothing more. Something about one of the younger boys. Eton suspended Lionel. Imagine that. The son of England's poet laureate. Lionel assured his parents that there was nothing to the rumors. Such a distasteful business. I feel so sorry for Emily and Alfred. Thank goodness it all turned out to be rubbish. Now what was it I was going to tell Alfred? Oh yes, I remember now."

Cammie gave detailed instructions for Alfred to visit her husband and engage him in a discussion of Latin poetry to improve his spirits until she got back. Anny faithfully transcribed her words. At the end, she folded and sealed the letter.

"You're fortunate Alfred will do your bidding," Anny observed.

"I bully the poor man, but I have a large corner of worship for him in my heart," she said. "I know that my immortality is bound up with his. Oh, I just thought of something I need to add."

"I'm afraid it will have to wait. I've already sealed the letter," Anny said, and slipped out before she could be charged with another commission.

THAT SPRING, ANNY'S NOVEL *Old Kensington* finished its serial run in the *Cornhill* and shortly after came out in book form. She dedicated it in part to "Our Laura, who measures the present with her soft little fingers as she beats time upon her mother's hand to her own vague music."

As Laura's father and editor of the *Cornhill*, Leslie felt a special connection to the novel. "It's a smashing success. You should feel so good," he told her. But she didn't. Instead, she felt superfluous, like a sixth finger—not an impediment to grasping things, but not needed, either, and unsightly to boot. Her presence in the household was being tolerated out of duty.

One day in late spring, Leslie proposed a family outing to

the zoological gardens at the north end of Regent's Park. A brass band played from an open pavilion and the sound of the instruments could be heard above the cries of monkeys. The gardens were crowded with visitors who wanted to take advantage of the perfect spring day, with the grounds bursting with blossoms.

Laura skipped along beside her parents as they toured the elephant house and the seal pond. At the lion's den, the keeper fed a cub in his lap beside a fire. Laura was particularly intrigued by the hippo, curled up like a huge ball of India rubber. The animal lumbered into its pond, splashing everyone within five yards.

They stopped to look at a squinty-eyed rhinoceros tied to a stake. Minny lifted Laura so she could see over the low stone wall that supported the bars.

"When Anny was a little girl, she declared that the rhino's skin must be tied on because it was so loose," Minny said to Leslie. "Papa couldn't get over how precocious she was."

"I don't remember that," Anny said.

"How could you forget? He told the story over and over. Just in case anyone happened to miss the fact that you were a little genius."

"Your Mama's being a silly willy nilly," Anny said, and rubbed her nose against Laura's, eliciting a laugh.

The child wore a dress of white pleats and red piping, more sophisticated than the frilly concoctions favored by most children her age. Minny loved dressing her up in exquisitely tailored frocks.

A young couple stopped and smiled at the child in Minny's arms. "What a beautiful little girl," the woman said. Laura gave them a radiant smile, then looked down, suddenly shy. With her striking curls and blue eyes, she often attracted comments.

Leslie thanked the strangers, beaming with pride. He had a weakness for beauty and a fathomless need for praise, and that day, Laura filled both needs.

On the way to the bird enclosure, they passed a row of lilac bushes in full bloom. The overpowering scent unsettled Anny's stomach and revived childhood memories of watching her mother, overcome by a black madness, yank out fistfuls of her beautiful auburn hair.

Outside the monkey house, they stopped to watch an orangutan climb a tall pole. A chain ran from its ankle to the pole. Bystanders threw cakes and fruit in its direction. From the other side of the enclosure, another orangutan loped along the fence, dragging a chain from its ankle. The enormous animal had somehow gotten loose. It stopped directly in front of Laura, bared its teeth, and reached its wrinkled gray fingers between the bars, perilously close to the child's face. She did not flinch. She did not even appear to be aware of the shaggy ape pressing its chest against the bars less than three feet from her.

Minny quickly grabbed Laura and pulled her back, but not before the beast let out a screech.

"Oh my little darling. Are you all right? Were you scared?" Minny said, pulling her close. Laura stared blankly at her mother, as if in a trance. She did not appear to understand what all the commotion was about. Moments later, the keeper dragged the orangutan away by its chain.

Anny's heart continued to race, even though the danger was over. She was perplexed at how Laura, within arm's length of the animal, could be so oblivious. Once again, Anny wondered if perhaps there was something wrong with the child's eyesight or hearing.

On the way to the bear pit, the wind lifted Laura's skirt. Startled, she stopped in the middle of the crowd and refused to go forward.

Minny pulled her gently by the hand, but did not succeed in dislodging her.

"What's wrong? Did that big old ape back there scare you?" Minny asked.

Laura did not respond. Her feet remained firmly planted. The words "yes" and "no" were not in the child's vocabulary. This made it hard to ascertain what she was thinking.

Minny tried to coax her forward. "Come on, Sweetheart. Let's go see the bears. Don't you want to see the bears? Like the ones in the fairy tale."

When gentle persuasion didn't work, Min tried bribery. "There's an ice cream cart by the bandstand. Would you like some?" Despite her sweet tooth, the child was unmoved by the offer. She curled up her tiny hands and refused to budge. Closed fists meant a closed mind, Anny had observed.

Losing patience, Leslie said sternly. "You will move forward, right this minute."

"Listen to your Papa," Minny said hopefully.

Leslie took his daughter's hand and pulled her. After dragging her a few paces, he let go.

Anny knew that if Leslie made this into a contest of wills, he would lose. She tried to lighten the mood.

"I think Memee's feet are set in concrete. Are your feet set in concrete? I don't think you can move them. When the sun sets, and the wolves start to howl and the lions roar, you'll still be here and before bed we'll say, 'I miss our precious Memekins. Do you think she's sleeping with the monkeys?'"

Anny's approach was equally ineffective.

Leslie was not amused. His face had taken on a deep red hue. "All right, if you won't move on your own, I'll help you." He set down the wicker picnic hamper and picked her up.

This six-foot-four inches of red-bearded fury was no match for the tiny child, who let out a feral screech that, even at a zoo, was notable for its savagery. She thrashed her arms and legs violently. The monkeys shrieked as if in response.

Visitors cut them a wide berth and looked on disapprovingly. Some averted their eyes. Anny had never seen a child misbehave in public. Ever. It just didn't happen, and here was the status-conscious Leslie at the center of a scene that publicly called his authority and his manhood into question.

When he set Laura down, she threw herself face down and pounded her little fists in the dirt.

"Minny, do something," he demanded.

"The poor little dear. She can't help it," said Minny, who seemed to know instinctively that the outbursts were beyond the child's control.

"You must learn to calm your child," he said.

Anny winced at "your child."

Without warning, Laura put her arms over her head and started to roll, turning and turning like a log on a downhill slant. Her pristine white dress collected bits of straw, crumbs, and manure. The crowd parted to make room for the revolving child. Leslie ran and planted his feet in her path, and she landed up against his boot.

"That's quite enough Laura," he said, humiliated and bent on reasserting his authority.

Minny crouched beside Laura and spoke in low tones.

"Get me the tablecloth. Quick," Minny commanded. Anny took the flowered cloth from the hamper and Minny wound it tightly around Laura, binding her arms to her side. It always soothed her to be tightly wrapped.

"Minny will have better luck calming her if we leave them alone," Anny said, eager to extract Leslie from the situation. "Let's wait by the bandstand."

Anny took Leslie's arm and steered him away from the scene to a nearby bench. His breath was uneven and his face was red.

"Where in the dastardly hell is Louise when we need her?" Leslie said.

"It's her day off." Anny vowed never to leave on a family outing again without the nurse.

"Well I should think that three adults would be able to

handle a two-and-a half-year-old. What could possibly make a child act like that?

Anny felt protective of both her sister and Laura. "The poor little dove gets overwrought when she's tired, and then the world is too much for her."

"That's no excuse to act like a beast. I must institute stricter rules."

"No, no. That's not the solution," Anny said. She and Minny had been raised in an atmosphere of loving chaos, with few rules but an overabundance of warmth and humor. Laura did not respond to rules either, but it was unclear if she didn't understand them, or simply refused to follow them.

"Well then, Minny must find a way to discipline her more effectively. She's entirely too lenient."

"It's not Min's fault."

"Then exactly whose fault is it? Will you tell me that?"

"Blame is not what's called for," she said, sensing that a bout of finger pointing would result in no beneficial end.

"Why me? Why must I have a child who acts like a savage? I sometimes wonder . . . I've never met your mother but . . ."

"Shh. Stop this minute," Anny said, placing the pads of her fingertips against his lips to quiet him before he said something that made her permanently hate him.

Before long, Minny returned with the exhausted child wrapped in the tablecloth. They secured a private cab home. Laura immediately fell asleep in her mother's lap. Her angelic face, luminous in the late afternoon light, seemed utterly incapable of creating any disruption. She was still young enough and beautiful enough to be excused for her outbursts. Part of Anny wished that, like the fairies she resembled, she would never grow old.

1874

NNY TOOK A VOLUME FROM the ornamental bookshelves at the cottage in Freshwater and, to her dismay, discovered that lice had found their way into the George Sands. She didn't have the heart to complain to Cammie, who was leasing The Porch to her for several months and depended on the meager income.

"Have you noticed any lice at the cottage?" Anny asked Mary Madonna, the parlor maid who had served as the model for so many of Mrs. Cameron's photographs.

"Oh lord yes, mum, the place is reeking with 'em. I tried to ketch one yesterday, but it ran too fast for me—them as run fast is quite harmless."

Anny had the rooms treated with Keating's Powder.

That spring, she was immersed in a new novel and hoped to spend long hours at her desk. *Old Kensington* had gone through numerous printings, and she found herself, for the first time in her career, an undeniable success, with money at her disposal. Minny had suggested that she buy land near Cammie. "Otherwise," she said, "the money will fly out of your hands and you'll have nothing to show for it. Property, at least, will increase in value, or so one hopes."

Anny wanted to build a house of her own, and what better

place than on her island, where so many lanes, cliffs, meadows, and downs had meaning for her.

The Porch served as her base while she searched for property. She felt at home on the island and never longed for companionship as she had at the Henley cottage she rented after her sister's marriage, or in London, where, against all reason, she felt lonelier surrounded by people than she did when she was alone. She welcomed the separation from Minny and Leslie.

Her writing was going exceedingly well. For the first time ever, she established a routine and worked from morning until mid-afternoon, commencing each day with a walk on High Down. Before the residents at Dimbola arose, she climbed the steep path past grazing sheep until she reached High Down, mystical in the morning light.

Here, on the roof of the island, she felt close to heaven. The walk put her in the meditative state that she needed to write. Sometimes she met a shepherd or a fisherman or a soldier from the fort. On rare occasions she crossed paths with Mr. Tennyson, in his flowing black cape and distinctive velvet squash hat. The sea was his tonic as well, and he understood perfectly when she waved and passed by without stopping, lest she break the spell.

Often, she worked into the evening. She felt such delicious forward momentum in her writing that she neglected her property search. She was grateful when Jeanie Senior, a friend of her father's, set up a meeting with her brother Hastings Hughes, a London solicitor who made frequent trips to the island on business. Anny knew Jeanie well—they were active in many of the same charities—but she had only met the brother once. A recent widower, he had four small children.

On the appointed day, he came to pick her up in a carriage, carrying a list of properties he had procured from a local agent. He was a pleasant-looking man, with a high forehead, crinkled eyes, bushy eyebrows, and a full brown beard salted with gray.

It was early spring, and the island was awash in color. The

paths were strewn with the pink and white petals of fallen magnolia and tulip tree blossoms. Fields of daffodils glowed in the sun and wands of blazing forsythia brightened the verges.

The carriage turned onto a narrow lane and drove beneath overhanging boughs with the new beginnings of leaves pushing out. Anny asked after his children. The eldest boy was thirteen.

"It's been difficult for us all," he said. "I get by as best I can, but I worry about the little ones, growing up without a mother."

"My father raised me and my sister by himself, and we got on capitally," Anny said. "Ours was essentially a bachelor's establishment. The home arrangements varied between a certain fastidiousness and the roughest simplicity. We didn't mind the mismatched cups and saucers and the chipped spout on the teapot."

"That's not at all how I would have imagined it," Mr. Hughes said.

"This was before Papa wrote *Vanity Fair*, and we were living on a pittance. One day our butler, whom we called Jeames de la Pluche after one of Papa's characters, found a hamper by the door filled with a beautiful set of breakfast china, including a teapot with Papa's initials in gold amidst a trellis of roses. My sister and I amused ourselves by speculating about who could have secretly sent over such lovely things. It wasn't until Jeames moved to Australia several years later that he admitted to being our benefactor."

"I certainly hope I can be a better provider than that," Mr. Hughes said.

"But you don't understand. Ours was a happy household and I have such warm memories, and so shall your children. Do not lose heart. What you are doing is eminently worthwhile."

"Thank you," he said. "I need the encouragement."

"Spend as much time with your children as you can. That's my advice. Good memories, not matched china."

They stopped by the woods just beyond a sheep meadow.

A creek ran through the property. The low stone wall along the road was covered with bright green moss, and snails clustered at the base like barnacles. The rain-drenched air intensified every smell. The ground was too spongy to walk on, so she stood by a roadside fringe of weeds and looked over the wall, imagining a house there.

"This parcel is significantly below market value," he said.

It was a handsome location, but much as she tried, she could not visualize a house there.

"An excellent investment," he continued.

"But I don't want an investment. I want a home," she burst out. "I had my heart set on something with a sea view."

"You can get twice the land here."

"But if it's land I'm unhappy with, why would I want twice as much of it?"

He looked disappointed.

"I prefer the other side of the island, closer to Mrs. Cameron and Mr. Tennyson. Are you acquainted with them?"

"I know of Mr. Tennyson, of course."

"Are you fond of his poetry?"

"Oh, I find poetry a waste of time."

"I see." She wondered if he was aware of her work. The fact would be hard to escape, since the second line of any description of her designated her as a novelist, the first being that she was William Thackeray's daughter.

"And do you know Mrs. Cameron?" she asked.

He nodded. "An odd sort, don't you think?"

"Her quirkiness is perhaps an acquired taste. But that is part of what makes her so original."

"She's from a distinguished family. Why does she dress like a beggar?"

Anny knew it would be futile to try to enlist him into Cammie's circle of admirers.

They visited another inland piece of wooded property with

a simple farmer's house and a couple of dilapidated outbuildings. She knew immediately that she was not interested, and didn't get out of the carriage.

"It feels claustrophobic here," she said. Everything she loved about the island—the sea and the sky—was not accessible to her here.

"But there is a tenant who would provide income while you build," he said. "It would be a very sound use of your funds."

"I want something with a sea view, or I want nothing." She was afraid of being rude, but truly, the man did not seem to understand her wishes.

"Of course, that would augment the price considerably," he said.

"I understand. I'm willing to sacrifice acreage for a view. If I cannot afford what I want, then I shall wait until I can."

To her, the sea was everything. She loved the placid mornings when glassy waves came from far past the horizon. She loved the stormy afternoons when the waves churned and frothed. She loved the nights when the moonlight illuminated the surf's ruffled edges, and she fell asleep to the tranquilizing rhythm of the waves.

"The upkeep on a seaside house would be unsustainable. The daily salt spray eats away at any exposed metal, and when squalls blow in, one risks damage to the roof or the porch. You will spend all of your time dealing with maintenance."

"Perhaps, but that is what I want."

"I've found that women tend to be emotional in their decisions."

She knew that it was his job, as legal counsel, to steer her in a practical direction, but she resisted any hint of being dominated, something he could have guessed had he read *Old Kensington*. In the novel, the main character Dolly rejects the advances of her suitor Robert because, though he loves her, she knows in the future he would try to rule her. "In her life, so free hitherto, there would be this secret rule to be obeyed, this secret sign," Dolly reflects. Anny remembered writing that sentence and wondering if such a sentiment might be too daring for the English public. Her worries were unfounded. Women read the novel in great numbers and passed it along to their daughters, mothers, and friends.

"Do you think your future husband would be pleased if you built a house that required constant maintenance?" Mr. Hughes asked.

"You are the solicitor. It is my understanding that a woman who never marries maintains complete control over her property and inheritance. Is this correct?"

"Yes."

"Then I would take that as a perfectly good reason to never get married."

They rode to back in silence.

As he handed her out of the carriage, she said, "I'm sorry to have been such a troublesome client. I do so very much appreciate your taking time out of your schedule to help me."

"Not at all. I fear I have offended you. I didn't mean to."

"No, no. You haven't offended me. I just think we approach matters differently."

"I come to the island often on business. I would be honored if you would allow me to take you around to view more properties."

Cursed by the habit of civility, she acquiesced.

MINNY BROUGHT LAURA TO THE island for a visit. Anny was delighted to see her niece looking so bonny, with rosy cheeks and a healthy glow. Now three going on four, she acted much younger. She referred to herself in third person and had her own private fashion of communicating that often involved sounds rather than words.

One day Minny set up an easel and was painting a seascape while Anny sat by the front door and bounced Laura on her knee.

> Ride a cock-horse to Banbury Cross,
> To see a fine lady upon a white horse;
> Rings on her fingers and bells on her toes
> And she shall have music wherever she goes.

Laura had not outgrown her love of rhyme. She begged Anny to repeat the poem.

"A gentleman is coming to pick me up soon, and I fear I may become too weary," Anny said.

Minny held the brush in mid-air and said, "Hastings Hughes? I shall be glad to meet him."

Laura was in Anny's lap when Mr. Hughes drove up in his carriage. Anny set the child down and introduced him to Minny.

"My sister speaks so highly of your family," he said.

Laura tugged at Anny's skirt and said, "More."

"I don't have time now, Baby."

"Nooooo."

Afraid the child would throw one of her tantrums, Anny relented.

"One more time, and then I really must go," she said, and bounced Laura on her knee in time to the nursery rhyme. Then she joined Mr. Hughes in the carriage.

"You're very good with children," he observed as the horse trotted down the lane.

"Only if they are not my own," she said.

They spent the afternoon looking at a few parcels on the southern coast. Anny found the process tiresome, but she didn't know how to refuse his generous assistance.

When they returned, he helped her out of the carriage, then continued on. Minny was still at work on her watercolor. Anny looked at the emerging seascape. "Papa always said you had an artistic eye," she said.

"It's nothing, but it pleases me immensely." Minny set down her brush. "If you fancy it, perhaps I'll give it to you for a house-warming present. Did you find any property you liked?"

"I'm losing heart. I haven't been able to find anything."

"You keep looking for perfection. Sometimes good enough is good enough." Minny gave her a long look. "And Hastings Hughes?"

"He means well, but he doesn't listen. He always thinks he has a better idea."

"Maybe he does," Minny said.

"It's intolerable. He thinks I have no right to my opinion. Well, it's *my* money."

"Anny, don't be so pigheaded. You're apt to make an ill-advised purchase."

"I intend to make my own decision, with or without his advice."

"You're perfectly capable."

"Of making my own decision, or making an ill-advised investment?"

"Both, really." She swished her brush in the jar. "He has four children, does he not?"

"Yes, poor man. He's under a great deal of stress."

"Mmm," Minny said, meaningfully. She closed up her box of paints.

"Surely you're not thinking . . ."

"Certainly not. An eligible man with a good job and good standing in society. The thought has never ever crossed my mind."

"And I'm sure it's never crossed his either!" Anny said.

"Well, perhaps it might, if you don't go alienating him."

"I will not pretend to be someone I am not."

"Be yourself," Minny advised, "only less so."

THE FOLLOWING DAY, THEY TOOK a picnic to the shore. It was still too cold to swim, and the beach was empty, except for a bathing machine abandoned and turned on its side like a tossed-off tinker caravan. The faded advertisement painted on the wood was still legible: Beecham's Pills! A cure for Bilious and Nervous Disorders, Headaches, Giddiness, Swelling after Meals, Dizziness, Drowsiness, Cold Chills, Loss of Appetite, Shortness of Breath, Costiveness, Scurvy, Disturbed Sleep, and Frightful Dreams.

"I wonder if Beecham's pills also cure gullibility," Anny said.

The day was windy and bright. Nurse Louise had set up chairs on the sand, close to the water's edge, then returned to the house for the picnic provisions. Minny got out her sketchbook, but kept the pencil box closed, preferring, for the moment, to watch her daughter poke between the rocks with a stick. "Look at my precious Duckling. She so loves to explore."

The sea was choppy, with white dotting the surface where waves broke far from shore.

"How is Leslie getting on?" asked Anny, enjoying the warmth of the sun. She had brought her inkpot, but the wind made writing difficult.

"He's rather in the mopes, I'm afraid. We rarely see him, and when we do, he's short-tempered and exhausted for want of a holiday. The situation has made me exquisitely irritable just now."

Minny did look pinched and sallow, though the salt air was bringing color back to her cheeks.

"I've been thinking," Minny said, watching her daughter spear a piece of seaweed on the end of a stick. "Now that you're building a cottage here, we don't really need such a big house and all those servants."

Anny started. They had only been in the new house for a year.

"I hate to see Leslie toil for eleven months of the year,

staying up late every night editing—a thankless task, I can tell you. His writers are a whiny lot. All they do is complain. And on top of that, he's expected to entertain them. We had a perfectly dreadful dinner for his newest discovery, Thomas Hardy, who was in town to go over the proofs of *Far from the Madding Crowd*. He is an exceedingly damp young man, and dampness I abominate."

"Was the dinner a success?"

"It was chaos. I drowned my cares in drink but it only affected my feet. The ice was too warm and the hot viands too cold. I had an expensive dish of peas which came up like so many hard little pills and about as digestible."

"You could have no doubt cured a world of woes, had you substituted Mr. Beecham's pills," Anny suggested.

Minny scowled. "This was no laughing matter. I will never attempt such a thing again without an augmented service, and Leslie can't expect it!"

Minny had alluded several times to money woes and she was genuinely upset.

"I have funds that could be tapped," Anny volunteered.

"Certainly not. Leslie is too proud. He would never hear of it."

"He would not need to know."

"We keep nothing from each other. Besides, there are a hundred things in civilized life that one could so perfectly do without," Minny said. "Starting with dinner parties."

Strange, Anny thought, how they never seemed to be in equilibrium. When things were going well in her life, Minny was in the dumps.

Anny looked up and saw Laura marching toward them. She held the stick on her shoulder, as an infantryman would his rifle. A mop of green seaweed dangled at the tip.

Minny called out to her. The child didn't look right or left, but soldiered on, passing so close they could have touched her.

"Oh, let her go. She's not hurting anyone," Minny said, as if there were nothing strange in Laura's behavior. Anny thought of the Irish myth in which the real child was snatched away at birth and replaced by a fairy child, who looked identical to the human one, but was missing a heart.

Laura threw her stick at a group of seagulls squabbling over a dead fish. The birds rose into the air with a flutter and she passed under them, continuing her journey.

Anny and Minny watched her silhouette get smaller and smaller until she was a tiny dot.

"Sometimes I think she's making progress, and other times I wonder why she doesn't pick up more."

"You didn't talk until you were three, and then you started conversing in whole sentences," Anny pointed out. She still held out hope that Laura would surprise them all.

"It worries me that I don't understand her better. Sometimes when she doesn't want to be held and pushes me away, I wonder: does she see some darkness in me that repels her?"

"Oh Minny, darling, you mustn't think such a thing," she said, rejecting any reference to the chaotic forces that lurked in their heredity.

The child was approaching the end of the beach. Minny called out to her, but she did not turn around. The only way forward was into the sea, toward the giant Stag Rock, separated from the cliff by a narrow channel.

Knowing Minny was too weak to chase after the child, Anny trotted down the beach, calling out to her.

Laura turned around. A sheer wall of white chalk rose behind her.

Suddenly an image came to Anny again, as uninvited as it had been ten years before, shortly after her father's death, when she found herself alone on this same stretch of beach. It was of herself as a child of three, flailing about underwater, held down by her mother until, in a profusion of froth and bubbles, she was pulled up, sputtering and gasping for the one thing that connected her to life—not her mother's hands, but air. Sweet air. Was her mother trying to drown her or save her? She would never know. But in this cove, the thought came to her that family was an odd mixture of dark and light. Minny's daughter was part of a larger vessel containing their mother and father, and their mothers and fathers, and on and on, each one adding particular ingredients to the mix—a touch of madness, a dollop of genius, a great measure of love.

She reached Laura out of breath. "Are you trying to swim off to Ireland, or do you want to come back to your mama?"

Laura looked straight through her, as if she were transparent.

"Laurekins, my precious. Are you with us?" she said, knowing if she initiated the first touch, things would go badly.

Something switched on inside the child, and a radiant smile spread over her face. "Dat mees Anntee."

She wasn't sure if the child said Auntie or Anny. "There. That's more like it," she said, and tried to take her hand, but was rejected. She walked ahead, looking back to make sure Laura was following.

After a while, the child said, "Memeee tired. Do tarry Memee, Annee." She held her arms out wide.

Anny picked up the child and carried her as long as she could manage, then set her down. "I'm afraid your Auntie is getting old. I need to rest." She sat down.

Laura crawled in her lap and put her arms around Anny's neck. "Memee love Annee very much."

Anny felt her tears drop onto the child's hair, already damp with sea mist. How could she have ever thought of Memee as a fairy child without a heart when this very real child nestled against her breast made her own heart nearly burst.

ANNY SPENT THE SPRING AND summer commuting between Freshwater and London. She suspended her efforts to find land, mostly because she did not wish to spend time with Hastings Hughes and didn't know how to gracefully decline his assistance, other than by abandoning the project entirely.

Her novel based on the artist Angelica Kaufman continued to go well, but she felt that the early chapters on the artist's life in Venice lacked authenticity and concrete details. She was delighted, then, when the Ritchie cousins invited her to accompany them to Venice that fall.

In addition to Anny, the party consisted of Richmond, his mother, two of his sisters and their husbands, three other Ritchie relatives, and an entourage of maids. Anny shared a room with her father's elderly unmarried cousin Charlotte, who lived in Paris. She carried more ivory in her mouth than a harpsichord, often complained of aching joints, and chose to sit out many of the sightseeing excursions.

In Venice, Anny took notes madly. She experienced a place differently when she was writing about it. The sights, sounds, and smells seemed more real to her, knowing she had to translate them into description. She wrote Minny every day, using the correspondence as a first draft for the visual and olfactory details of Venice. The sumptuous city she remembered from earlier visits took on a special significance since she experienced it four different ways: as memory, as present encounter, as details in her letters to Minny, and finally, as reworked description for the novel.

One day, after a morning visiting churches, a leisurely lunch, and an afternoon looking at pictures, the group took a rest at the outdoor tables on St. Mark's Square. Pigeons swirled about the vast expanse.

"Looking at the Van Dykes and Tintorettos is like pouring wine into one's veins," said Richmond, who was in his final year at Eton.

"Yes, but it does tire one out so," his mother said. "I'm grateful for a seat."

Anny announced that she was going in search of a present for Laura. "Something other than those idiotic wooden gondolas."

Richmond in tow, she strolled along the arcade, past shops selling crucifixes, old lace, buckles, and glass beads.

"It's shopping, not museums, that exhausts me," she said. "I have a limited tolerance for this."

They followed a side street and found themselves at the fish market along the Grand Canal. With cats underfoot, they wandered through stalls selling scallops, baskets of sea urchins, and silver fish arranged in a star formation.

"Dear stinking gorgeous Venice," she said. "I much prefer this to shopping."

They continued walking across bridges and through the tangle of sun-starved streets that zigzagged through the city.

"I think we're lost," she finally said. "What shall we do about your sisters and mother?"

"They'll return to the hotel for a rest. I can't give up an afternoon in Venice. There's too much to see."

They wandered through the alleys. "Teach me to see like a writer. What do you do? Show me," Richmond said.

"All right," she said, flattered to have a pupil. "Close your eyes and I will lead you."

She took his elbow and he opened his eyes.

"You're cheating."

"Apologies."

"The pavement is uneven. Go up a step. There's a curb. Now we're going to climb a series of steps."

She led him onto a cambered footbridge that spanned a canal and stopped in the middle.

"Now. Open your eyes."

The canal was lined with palaces, each with differently styled windows—mullioned, Moorish, lancet, stained glass.

"Imagine that it is a hundred years ago. How would things be different?" she asked.

"Well, the pigeons would not change," he answered.

"Progress or no, pigeons are forever. What else?"

Boats glided under the bridge. People called to one another across the canal.

"I don't know. It doesn't seem as if that much is altered. Let's see. A hundred years. Napoleon hasn't yet conquered the city, but people would still be plying the water in boats. Were the gondolas the same?"

"More or less. In the sixteenth century it was decreed that they must be black."

"I guess there wouldn't have been a railroad station, but that shouldn't affect the city's core," he said.

"Fair enough. So, you might see pretty much what we see now. Close your eyes again. Imagine you are an artist like Angelica Kaufman. Now open your eyes and look. What do you notice?"

"I don't know." He seemed bothered, unaccustomed to not knowing the answer.

"Light. It is everything—you notice every nuance, the way it burnishes the walls, plays off the water, throws shadows, alters the colors."

"I see what you mean. If you look at the same thing for long enough, you start to notice different things," he said.

"Now imagine that you are of a lower class. The treasures of the city's churches are accessible to you, but not the grand interiors of the city's aristocrats. And then an English ambassador's wife latches onto you and brings you into her opulent marble palace with frescoes on the ceiling, tapestries on the walls, marble sculptures in niches, and paintings by masters you have studied and copied. It's a visual feast for an artist, but intimidating for someone from the lower classes. Still, the light is free and available to everyone, and, most certainly, you. And because you are an artist, you can capture it with a speck of white to create a shimmer, a dot of purple to suggest shadow."

"Fascinating," Richmond said.

"Eventually, the English ambassador's wife took Angelica with her back to London, away from her beloved Venetian light. I can't imagine being an artist in London. Everything gray, gray, relentlessly so. How she must have been bereft."

They stood quietly and looked at the palazzos along the canal. From a nearby square came the sound of bells. The smell of rosemary wafted from a hidden garden.

"Venice is not about what you see, but what you feel when you see it," she said.

They continued standing in silence. Then Richmond said, "Now it's my turn to teach you. You may find me a congenitally inept youth in the giddy vortex of discovery, but I have a few tricks to offer."

He hired a gondola, and a man in a white jacket and flat straw hat untethered the boat and pushed off. "Take us where tourists don't go," Richmond instructed him. "I want to be a Venetian."

They progressed languidly through a dizzying maze of canals, away from the grand palazzos, past modest houses with rotting doors and laundry hanging from windows. Moss marked the high tide mark and walls showed patchwork repair and spots where huge swaths of stucco had fallen away from crumbling brick.

They passed a boat-making shop, a warehouse with saffron and crimson dyes piled inside, and a barge selling eggplants, tomatoes, and squash.

At sunset, Richmond instructed the gondolier to take them to the lagoon. Light slid down the walls of the marble palazzos along the Grand Canal, turning them into crimson waterfalls. As the gondola entered the lagoon, the close tangle of canals gave way to an expanse of water and sky.

The gondolier floated aimlessly about. Seated on a tufted cushion, Anny watched her cousin, who stood with his elbow against a wooden balustrade and looked up at the sky. Did he, too, have the feeling of being suspended in a rose-colored dream between water and sky?

"You know what you said about seeing being a bridge to feeling?" Richmond said. "I think I shall always remember this feeling."

Along the shore, monks were out on a monastery terrace looking at the horizon. Out from behind a plum-colored cloud came a flash of light, and then a silver wreath of stars. Anny gave a little gasp.

"A sign," Richmond exclaimed.

Of what? she wished to say, but the moment fell away, and the gondolier turned into the Grand Canal. They glided past the palazzos at that magical moment before shutters were closed against the night, and the windows behind the long stone balconies of the *piano nobile* revealed luxurious interiors to anyone who passed by.

She settled against the cushion and the boatman said, "Now I sing you love song."

"Oh, you don't understand. We're not . . . no, we are cousins. Distant cousins," she said, her face as rosy as the sunset.

"No, *you* no understand. We Italian," he said, beating his heart with a fist. "We know love," and he serenaded them, maintaining rhythm with each pull of the oar.

Light was gone from the sky when they decamped near their hotel, and Richmond handed her from the boat. "I am in love," she said. "With Italy. With Italians."

She couldn't wait to get to her inkpot to write down all the details she could remember before she met the Ritchies for dinner—at the fashionable Venetian hour of ten.

In the room, her cousin Chattie was waiting for her. "Where have you been?" she said. The elderly Chattie was perpetually out of sorts.

"With Richmond. We took a gondola on the back canals."

"What about the others? Where were they?"

"I assume they came back to the hotel to rest."

"You must not monopolize Richmond," she said.

Anny laughed. "Surely you're not serious. He's a capital escorter."

"It's not a wise idea to go off alone, just the two of you."

"Oh, Chattie. We just wanted a little adventure. He had a chaperone—his old-maid cousin." She wished to document the day's details before they burst into a thousand fragments and vanished.

"You don't know what others might say."

"What do I care? They'll never see me again." She reprimanded herself for making foolish economies by sharing a room, as if five francs a day would ruin her.

"I'm talking about the family."

"Oh, for heaven's sake. Next time, you must join us."

"My poor stomach can't abide the rocking. And my knees are creaky."

"You're not so old. Come with us, or stop complaining."

She resented being supervised. Chattie had not always been like this. The summer after their father's death, she and Minny had traveled to the Pyrenees with the four Ritchie cousins. The villagers didn't know what to make of the seven ladies in full mourning dress, moving along the cobbled streets in voluminous crinolines, like so many floating black umbrellas. It was Chattie's idea to hire a pony cart and driver to take the grieving sisters for a picnic luncheon on the Col d'Aspin, near the Spanish border. Anny remembered the rapt expression on Chattie's face as she watched the feral pigs scour the hills blooming with wild thyme, the air fragrant with the smell of umbrella pines.

What had happened to that adventurous soul? Was this what years of spinsterhood did to one's spirits? At thirty-seven, she felt herself on the downward slope toward Chattiedom.

Early the next morning, Anny returned to her desk to write

Minny. "O darling I'm almost too thrilled to write. At six the sun rose and a thousand bells began to laugh and sing and all the soldiers woke up at the barracks next door and began to sing too. Here everyone sings. You can't imagine how wonderful it is." She ended the letter with "Give a kiss to my darling Laurekins."

SHORTLY AFTER ANNY RETURNED from Italy, she was out walking in the park with Laura and Minny when they ran into Charles Dodgson.

"Laura, this is Lewis Carroll, the man who wrote 'Jabberwocky.'" She turned to Mr. Dodgson. "I hope you don't mind my using Lewis Carroll. 'Jabberwocky' is her favorite poem. No matter how many times she hears it, she wants to hear more."

It was odd to have the spheres of Charles Dodgson and Lewis Carroll intersect when he did his best to keep them separate.

"I shall send her an autographed copy of the book," he said. "Would you like that?" he addressed Laura. She hid behind her mother's skirts.

"Ah, you have a shy one," he said.

Minny pulled Laura closer.

"What a graceful, pretty child. So perfectly simple and unselfconscious," he said.

Anny thanked him. Minny was strangely silent. Laura peeked out from behind Minny's skirt like an actress pulling back the curtain to survey the audience.

"Have you ever seen a man blow himself up like a balloon?" Mr. Dodgson said.

The child didn't answer.

He took off his gloves, put them inside his hat and set it on the bench. He was a tall man with long legs, but he crouched down to Laura's level. "Watch this."

He held the thumbs and index fingers of his two hands to his lips, forming a diamond shaped hole that he began to blow through. With each exaggerated exhale of breath, he rose incrementally, making himself larger and larger, until he was upright, with his chest puffed out, fully inflated. Standing straight, he took in one last loud breath and held it, like someone smoking a hookah. In a funny, air-filled voice, he said to Laura, "Now take your finger and poke me."

Laura covered her eyes with Minny's skirt.

Mr. Dodgson said to Anny, "Show her. Anny obliged, and pressed her finger into his stomach.

"Now you try," Mr. Dodgson said to Laura, holding his breath.

The child came out from behind Minny's skirts and tentatively poked her index finger into his trouser leg.

"Harder" Mr. Dodgson said.

She tried again, and he made a popping sound and with great theatricality, released air loudly through his fluttering lips, as he melted down to his knees like a punctured balloon.

Laura flapped her hands wildly and said, "More," giggling with delight.

He picked himself up and turned to Minny, quite out of breath, for it was a prodigious effort to move around that much air.

"I should love to photograph Laura. She is an angelic child, the epitome of perfection." He turned to Laura and said, "Would you like to pose for a portrait?"

"Why, that would be lovely," Anny said.

Minny glowered at her. "I'm sorry, but I am very busy in the coming weeks."

"It would not be necessary to come yourself."

"Thank you, but the camera would scare her."

"I have any number of games and tricks to make my child-friends relax and act naturally in front of the lens."

"That was a firm no. We do not need a photograph of this child."

Anny was taken aback by Minny's abruptness and tried to smooth things over.

"Mr. Dodgson, it was very kind of you to offer."

"Well. Enjoy the rest of your walk. Good day."

After he left, Anny said, "Minny, what got into you? I've never seen you be so rude."

"I will trundle us all off to the city jail before I will allow that man alone with my child."

"Why so strident? It was a generous offer."

"Mother's instinct," she said, and would not be swayed.

THAT FALL, ANNY WAS BRIMMING with optimism and worked as hard as she had ever worked before. Words and images came quickly, and she recorded them almost as if she were taking dictation. She was carried away by the flow that most people thought came naturally to writers, but had never before happened to her.

In November, Leslie told her that the serialization of Thomas Hardy's *Far from the Madding Crowd* was ending early, and there was an available spot in the magazine.

"I don't suppose there is any way you could be done with *Miss Angel* by the end of the year."

"There's a very good possibility," she said. "The book has been going exceedingly well."

"I've never seen you work with such purpose," he observed.

The novel was not the only form of writing she pursued with such exuberance. She and Richmond were now writing to each other regularly and meeting each other when they could. One day, the maid brought her a letter, just as Minny came into her study. Anny slipped the envelope into the desk drawer.

"Who is that from?" asked Minny.

"It's not important," Anny said.

"It's from Richmond, isn't it?"

She did not say anything.

"Anny, you must stop this silliness."

"What's the matter?" Anny said.

"It appears improper."

"Richmond will always be someone close to my heart. Is there anything wrong with that?"

"Of course not. He's family. But you are not behaving correctly. He's seventeen years your junior. You ought to make a little joke of things instead of taking them so seriously."

"Is there any reason I can't have a little harmless amusement in my life?"

"You have set off a whirlwind of chatter. I've heard separately from Chattie and two of Richmond's sisters. Even Mrs. Ritchie expressed concern and she is one of your biggest admirers. I don't know what went on in Italy, but it was enough to ignite a storm of speculation."

"He's a close friend with whom I feel totally comfortable. He sees me as I am. Everybody else sees an idea of me."

"Anny! Surely you are not falling in love with him."

"I'm just asking you respectfully not to meddle."

"Granted, he's idealistic, passionate, and smart. But he's practically a child."

"He may be young in years, but he's the wisest person I know."

"Have you lost all probity and proportion? This is worse than I thought."

"I don't understand why everyone thinks it's their prerogative to involve themselves in my life."

"You're a mature woman, Anny." She paused. "It's undignified and, quite frankly, embarrassing."

"I will not be lectured by you on what is embarrassing."

"Darling, you're setting yourself up for disappointment, and I can't bear to see you hurt."

"My feelings are my own and nobody can take that away from me!"

"What would Leslie say?" Minny said.

"I'd appreciate it if you wouldn't take it up with him. This does not concern him."

"He would be horrified. You know he would."

"He's never liked the Ritchie cousins and has made no secret of it."

"Yet he cares deeply about your welfare."

"Am I not entitled to happiness? You've had everything you've ever wished for—a husband, a child, a home. Who are you to deny me?"

"I always thought you were happy, but apparently not, before this . . . this . . ." She struggled to articulate the thought.

"Ours is a friendship, nothing more. Whether anyone likes it or not, I intend to continue his company."

"By all means, do. But without all this unseemly emotion!" Minny cautioned.

SEVERAL WEEKS AFTER THE conversation, Anny went to Eton. From the train station, she crossed over the bridge and walked through the town. It was a gray drizzly day. A profusion of swans offered the only bright spot on the Thames. She had arranged to meet Richmond by the stone wall surrounding the Chapel cemetery. Lichen and moss obscured the names and dates of ancient dignitaries buried beneath august monuments.

A bell from a nearby clock chimed the hour. She knew Richmond would not be tardy. It was not in his nature. For that reason, she had made a concerted effort to be punctual.

Why was everyone in a dither over what was a familial friendship? Rumors had even made their way to Freshwater, and Cammie found cause to mention Richmond in one of her letters. Anny felt worn down by all the fuss. She was never judgmental about others' affairs. Why was she not afforded the same courtesy?

Richmond's attentions were nothing more than adulation of an older cousin with a famous literary lineage. They enjoyed each other's company, nothing more. It was not worth causing a fracture in the family. She planned to tell him straightaway that they should stop seeing each other, and then return to London on the next train.

But her resolve wavered when she saw him coming toward her in the drizzle, his top hat beaded with rain, and his dark hair curling around his ears. He was tall and walked with a confident spring in his step. When he saw her, he broke into a smile.

They went into town and installed themselves in the walnut-paneled coziness of the inn.

"How are your preparations for exams?" she asked, glad they had chosen a table by the fire.

"I feel remarkably calm. All my rivals are pale and hurting with facts." He told her about one student who went in five minutes early to write his name and page numbers on about ten pages to save time.

"Lionel asked me to send his regards," he said.

"I shall miss both of you, since I shan't be coming anymore."

"Pardon?" He leaned forward.

"You have to sit for your exams and I have to finish my novel. It's time our visits stopped."

"I don't understand," he said, looking hurt. "Do you not enjoy my company?"

"You know I do. I always feel invigorated by our conversations."

"So why on God's earth would you want to throw that off? You have no idea how I look forward to your visits. When I know you're coming, I can get through the most dreary day, and when you do come, I know I can pass the week in peace. You would deny me that?"

"I think it's better for everyone," she said, adopting a detached tone.

"Everyone?"

"The family."

"Ah, now I understand," he said. "My sisters' tongues have been wagging."

She nodded. "Min's and Cammie's as well."

He leapt up and did a turn in place, as there was no room to pace. "Wretched gossip."

"I didn't mean to upset you," she said.

He sat down and leaned toward her. "They have no idea what our friendship means."

She wanted to ask: *What does it mean?* But she was wary of making a fool of herself. Oh, but how Venice was fading.

"Anny, we're different, you and me. We're not afraid of living, truly. They're stuffed full of stupid rules and ideas about what is proper. Blast it all!"

His youthful passion intoxicated her. Yet, she was the mature one. Her duty was to act responsibly.

"We must keep peace in the family," she said.

"Surely you're not so conventional as that. I thought you had more spirit."

The accusation crushed her. She couldn't bear the thought of disappointing him. "I must leave now if I expect to make the 4:22," she said, rising abruptly. In her hurry, she left her gloves behind on the table.

In the weeks that followed, she anxiously awaited each day's mail, but no letter arrived from Eton. One night, when she returned from the theater, Leslie said, "Richmond came calling for you."

"Really?" she said, making an effort to sound nonchalant.

"He brought by the gloves you left. He asked me to give you his kind regards."

She took the gloves, went to her room, and wept.

eleven

1875

J ANUARY WAS BLEAKER THIS YEAR than most. London's relentless, smog-choked skies fouled the air inside and out. Anny had given up on buying island property. With nothing to look forward to, she felt the stench of the city permeate her soul.

One gray morning, Minny appeared at breakfast and said, "I had such a lovely dream last night."

In a dark mood, Anny did not want to hear about it, but Minny continued: "An angel was guiding me around heaven on a sort of tour. We went to this great green park where all manner of wild animals and their cubs were rolling about on the grass. They were on the most amiable terms—lions and panthers and bears. They pawed me and rubbed their noses against my legs. I said to the Angel, 'But aren't they carnivorous?' The Angel pointed up at the large red, pear-shaped fruits hanging from the branches above. 'That,' the Angel said, 'is meaty fruit that the monkeys throw down to the lions and tigers to satisfy their appetites. Now,' the Angel said, 'I will take you to the heaven of flowers.' But I awoke and never got further than the heaven of beasts."

"What was the angel like?" Anny said.

"You know how dreams are. I don't even know if it was male or female. But the angel was very kind and loving. My only regret was that I never got to visit the heaven of flowers. I have the feeling it must be such an enchanting place, filled with roses and iris and delphinium and all kinds of heavenly scents, just like Cammie's garden. I think I shall like it very much."

"Can't we talk about something more pleasant?" Anny said, shivering.

"But don't you see, it *was* pleasant. I woke up surrounded by the most delicious feeling. Then a horrible thought came to me: If I'm not here to take care of Laura, who will?"

"No need to be digging your grave just yet."

"If something were to happen to me, will you promise to take care of my precious Memee? I fear she would be too much for poor Leslie. It's the one thing that keeps me up at night."

"Don't be silly. You know I will."

IN MARCH, JULIA DUCKWORTH gave a party for her aunt Julia Cameron to celebrate the publication of her book of photographs illustrating Alfred Tennyson's *Idylls of the King*.

The younger Julia was dressed in black silk and greeted guests in the front hall of the house on Hyde Park Gate. After four and a half years, she had not allowed gray or lavender into her wardrobe or any other half-mourning measures. Anny knew the exact length of her bereavement because Laura was born two months after her husband had died.

Anny had encouraged her to go out into society more, but she chose to prolong her mourning. She did, however, work quietly behind the scenes to support friends and family in their artistic pursuits. She had been so helpful in making story suggestions and preparing *Miss Angel* for publication that Anny had dedicated the novel to her. Julia was also an ardent supporter of her aunt's photography.

Cammie had devoted her usual passion and exacting standards to creating the photographs that illustrated *Idylls of the King*. She had produced close to 245 glass plates before deciding on the twelve that would go into the first volume. She then individually printed multiple copies from the wet print collodion negatives, many of which she discarded as unacceptable. The original photographs that passed muster were pasted into the bound volumes by hand, interspersed with lithographs of Tennyson's poetry in her handwriting. At six guineas a copy, the price barely covered her costs.

"Dear Cammie. She's constitutionally ill-equipped to ever make money from her photography," Julia confided to Anny. She was animated as she talked, and Anny could see hints of the great beauty she had once been.

"It's so like her to refuse to economize in any way on her work," Anny said.

"You know her. She insisted on the highest quality paper and the most expensive chemicals. For this project, she hired models for King Arthur, Guinevere, and Lancelot, to get the precise look she wanted. She also had to rent armor and costumes. And alas, there's her lamentable luck."

Though the book was published in mid-December, the reviews didn't come out until January, too late for the Christmas gift season.

"You are a dear to help promote her work," Anny said.

"I wish I could do more," said Julia. "It seems so unfair. She can't even manage to make money from her association with Alfred Tennyson."

"History will be kinder to her," Anny said.

"History will not pay the bills."

Anny saw Cammie sitting at a table in the parlor, a shawl drooping off her shoulder and her hair falling in every direction but the correct one. She had mastered the art of signing books and talking at the same time. Her inscriptions, like her letters, were voluminous.

She had already signed Anny's copy, but Anny brought it

along for Alfred Tennyson to sign. Each volume was, in essence, a portfolio of original prints. One of the photographs in Anny's book had a hair embedded between the paper and the albumen silver emulsion. Another had raised dots that looked like specks of sand. Others had scratches in the patina or crackled areas from the poorly distributed collodion on the glass plate.

Cammie was not after the perfection of machinery, though she often talked with enthusiasm about the day when technology would allow the mass production of photographs in newspapers and magazines. Rather, she was in the thrall of some higher calling, always reaching to express something that was beyond expression. Her work had a directness and a vivid reality. Anny's father's work had that quality, as did Alfred Tennyson's poetry. In fact, she had never met a really great artist without it.

She knew Mr. Tennyson could not have been easy to work with, but Cammie had a disarming way about her and knew how to get what she wanted without being intimidated. Anny couldn't begin to guess how she had wheedled him into letting her use, as the frontispiece, an earlier photograph he had dubbed the "Dirty Monk." The portrait showed him in profile, wearing a cowl-necked robe and holding a book. His indeterminate gaze and wispy hair flying in all directions called to mind either a deeply reflective spirit or an escapee from a lunatic asylum. Mr. Tennyson's vanity, however, had always been focused on his work, not his looks. Cammie understood this and used it to her advantage.

Anny went into the next room to get her book autographed by the Dirty Monk himself. People were crowded around the signing table. The book measured two feet high and was awkward to hold. When she reached the laureate, she told him how perfectly the photographs illustrated the spirit of his poetry. He muttered a brusque response, signed the title page, and turned to the next person in line.

She left the table feeling abandoned. She thought of him as her own personal poet and a close family friend, yet he had signed her book "Alfred Tennyson"—as curt as Cammie was expansive. He did not belong to her here in London the way he did on the Isle of Wight.

She set her book aside and looked around the room for people she knew. Charles Dodgson, who was estranged from the Tennysons, was, not surprisingly, absent. Cammie's husband stood by the velvet drapes. With his ethereal waist-length beard, and wispy white hair falling to his shoulders, he was the quintessential Merlin. Even in mufti, he looked like an aging wizard.

Cammie's son Henry, the aspiring playwright, stood next to the grand piano. He was talking to a group of handsome men she didn't know, possibly actors.

Across the room she recognized Charles Darwin, an old family friend. When he had rented a cottage from Cammie several years before, she had cajoled him into sitting for a portrait. At the end of their visit, Darwin's son told her, "You have left eight people deeply in love with you." These were the encomiums that Cammie treasured and was not shy about sharing with her friends.

Anny made her way to speak to Mr. Darwin but stopped short when she noticed Lionel and Richmond standing on the other side of him. She had not seen them come in.

Flustered, she looked for an exit. It was too cold to go to the garden, so she lost herself among the guests who were crowding into the room.

Both Richmond and Lionel were now at Cambridge. How stupid of her not to have guessed that Lionel would invite Richmond to London to celebrate his father's book. Over Christmas she had visited the Ritchies fully expecting to see Richmond. She had rehearsed what she would say, only to find that he was away visiting friends. Today she was caught off guard.

She felt all eyes on her, though, in truth, the only people who cared in the slightest were Richmond's sisters, who were in the next room, and Cammie, who was busy signing books. She was quite alone.

She conversed pleasantly with various guests, acutely aware of Richmond's location at every moment. Once, she stole a glance across the room and their eyes met. She looked away, as if caught in a shameful act, and turned back to her companion, who was holding forth in a pedantic way about London's craze for all things medieval.

She hoped to escape without encountering Richmond, but found herself in proximity to Lionel at the refreshment table.

"I saw my first daffodils the other day, and a vivid fit of Freshwater sickness came over me," she said. "You must miss the island."

While Lionel answered, Richmond joined them. Struggling to compose herself, she attended with great care to Lionel's words. There was much she wanted to say, but could not. Instead, she blathered on inanely to Lionel about his father's poem, fully aware how unworthy her conversation was.

Richmond inquired after Leslie and Minny, and she responded factually. She noted that his unease seemed equal to hers.

"And what about our little Laurekins?" he said.

"We have a little game we play these days. I blow Laura a kiss, and she runs across the room and takes it to Minny. She adores this little frolic, as long as it doesn't involve lips to cheek—only air kisses. She wants to continue long after she has exhausted everyone's patience," she said, relaxing a bit.

Lionel was pulled away, leaving Anny alone with Richmond. She panicked, realizing that they had exhausted all neutral topics of conversation. An awkward silence fell between them.

"I've often wondered how you were getting on," Richmond said, after an interminable period. "It does seem pointless that we should not write each other once in a while."

"Yes, I suppose it does."

"So why wouldn't you write?"

"I guess there's no harm in the occasional letter," she said.

"Then I have your permission?" he said, brightening. "Good.

You need not answer if you don't wish. I think people should look on letters as gifts, not debts."

She was relieved when someone else engaged Richmond, and she was able to slip away.

She left the party in high spirits. She had not disappointed him so profoundly that he no longer harbored any affection for her.

At home, she arranged with the maid to put any letters that arrived from Cambridge in the lacquer box in the front hall. Though the necessity of secrecy had not come up, she felt it best.

On the days a letter arrived, the maid agreed to place an ivory letter opener on the silver salver with the day's mail. This would be a sign that a special letter was waiting for her in the box in the hall, hidden in plain sight.

She did not have to wait long. Two days after the book signing, the maid brought the morning mail, and, on top, was the letter opener with an elephant's trunk entwined around the handle, a gift from Cammie. She rushed downstairs to retrieve the letter and replied the same day: "Dearest, I said some idiotic things at Cammie's party, and I'm afraid I bored you, but I hope you can find it in your heart to forgive me. I have quite cheered up again now and feel as if you have too and I am so glad of your dear little letter. It is all nonsense about not writing if we feel so inclined. That was my doing, and I take full credit for that impoverished idea, as you should take credit for the disposing of it. It takes but a few sentences to feel that I have regained my old self. This feels like the correct thing to do, and I am too old not to behave correctly."

She continued the letter, filling him in on family news. Taking up her role as his mentor, she ended the letter with some advice: "Do read Carlyle's Johnson and Goethe and you have to work too and do read books and see people and know the world and God bless you."

IN APRIL, SHE RECEIVED A LETTER from the solicitor Hastings Hughes: "I know you said that you were no longer interested in purchasing land near Freshwater, but I believe I have identified a property that meets your specifications. I hope you will allow me to show it to you. Please do me the favor of letting me know when you are going to be on the island."

The letter happened to coincide with her plans to visit Julia Cameron, so she arranged to meet the solicitor.

He took her to a high spot overlooking Colwell Bay, a short drive from Freshwater. That day, the sea was the rich blue of forget-me-nots. The late afternoon light bathed the daisy-filled meadows and washed over the chalk cliffs, highlighting hints of purple, dusky maroon, and yellow. The new moon, a mere swipe of the painter's brush, hung in the afternoon sky. From where they stood, she could hear the waves churning the pebbles on the shore.

"Oh, Mr. Hughes," she said, placing her hand on his arm. "I don't know what to say. It is perfect."

The solicitor seemed pleased with himself.

"I realized that I was not taking proper account of your wishes, and when I learned of this property, I felt I had to let you see it, even though you said you were no longer looking."

"I am quite speechless. I don't know how to thank you."

She returned to London in a state of high excitement and found Leslie in a state of grumble and growl.

"I thought you'd be happy," she said after she told him of her good fortune. "It's the view I've always dreamed of."

"You have enough money to buy the property, but not enough to build," he pointed out.

"Well, I can easily take on more writing. I will set to work immediately."

"Your work will suffer if it is driven by the checkbook," he said. "You musn't put out second-rate material. You have a reputation to consider."

"I wasn't aware I had a reputation to maintain," she said, considerably flattered.

"There are not half a dozen people who have your genius in all of England."

She felt the Jane Austen lecture coming on: She was no Jane Austen. She perhaps had the talent, but not the discipline. If she spent more time rewriting, she might etc., etc. She felt her back stiffen as she waited. But Jane Austen failed to ensue. Leslie took a different tack.

"You are making yourself into a pump instead of a spring, and if you go on at that rate, you will end by pumping yourself dry. That would be such a pity."

He made her feel like a writer, and not some spinster hobbyist. You crusty old curmudgeon, she thought to herself. I have such affection for you!

A few days later, Mr. Hughes stopped by the house unannounced. She was eager to sign the papers and went directly downstairs.

"I am so happy to see you," she said, with a smile.

He handed her a jar of daisies. "I picked these from your meadow," he said.

"Oh, how I love the ring of that. My meadow." She led him into the parlor and put the flowers on a side table. "You have made me the happiest of human beings. Never would I have dreamed that I could come into possession of a piece of ground so perfect in every way. Since I returned, I have thought of nothing but the view, the bay, the sunset, the sky. All soon to be my very own. To think that I looked and looked, and the perfect property arose virtually from nowhere."

"Actually, I was able to pull a few strings," said the solicitor.

"So this is your doing?" She was surprised.

"I knew what you wanted. I heard of a farmer who was considering selling. He just needed a little incentive."

"How exceptionally thoughtful of you. I am truly grateful," she said, thinking that she had underestimated him. "Did you bring papers for me to sign?"

"They are not ready yet," he said, coloring slightly.

"There's no problem, I hope," she said, feeling a let-down.

"Oh, no. Everything is in order. My office is drawing up the documents."

She sighed in relief, but was perplexed by the awkward moment of silence.

"No, I came here on a more important matter."

She felt the need to stall him. "Forgive me. I'm afraid I'm not a good hostess. I haven't even offered you tea." She went toward the bell to call the servant, but he took her hand.

"Please hear me out."

She withdrew her hand. "I beg you, don't continue." But he would not listen.

"Ever since I met you, I knew you would make the perfect wife for me."

"I pray you, please." He was a kind man and she did not want to cast away his feelings unappreciated. "I am deeply grateful for what you've done, really, I am. But it must stop there. We shall both be happier if we terminate this conversation right this moment."

"I insist on having my say. I have given this a great deal of thought."

"Mr. Hughes, I am extremely flattered. Truly I am. But I cannot hear any more of this nonsense. If I have given encouragement without meaning to, I offer you my sincere apologies. But we must proceed no further."

"You would make a wonderful mother," he continued. "I knew it when I saw you with your sister's daughter. My children would benefit from your spirit and your generosity. I think to-gether we could create a happy family."

"Mr. Hughes, I am indeed grateful to you and I wish you and your children the very best, but you must trust me. I am not the right person. It would be a misfortune for all concerned."

"I am aware that you consider me somewhat deficient in imagination, but I am willing to reform myself under your steady hand."

At that moment, Leslie came in and greeted Mr. Hughes, whom he had known at Cambridge.

"I'm sure you two have much to talk of," she said, commencing her retreat.

"The papers will be ready in a few days. I will send you a letter about the other matter we discussed," said Mr. Hughes.

She fled to her room.

That night she slept little. Mr. Hughes was a good man who had made every effort to please her, though she had been exceedingly fractious. But did that make him the right man for her? She was angry that he had presented her with this dilemma.

Her best hope was that he would come to his senses. Who could proceed after such discouragement? Surely his pride would prevent him from exposing himself further.

But the next day's post brought a letter. The maid delivered it on the silver salver. Anny's heart quickened, not at his return address, but at the ivory letter opener on top of it. She rushed downstairs to retrieve Richmond's letter from the lacquer box in the hall. It was filled with the minutiae of his day: a butterfly at the window, a bad meal, a walk through the forest while the moonlight made deeper and deeper shadows. Every detail was filtered through his eyes, and she cherished every word.

She returned to her study and finished the day's work before opening the letter from the solicitor, as if the act of waiting would alter its contents. He laid out in a practical, business-like way his proposal of marriage. He said that she could take as much time as she wished to come to a decision.

She needed to discuss this with someone, but whom? Leslie was out of the question. She knew what her sister would say and she didn't want to hear it. Instead, she turned to Julia Duckworth. She could count on Julia to give her opinion without judgment. Julia could also be trusted to keep her confidence. She was the only person Anny had confided in about Richmond.

"You are calculated to make a man so very happy and to be so very happy yourself," Julia said, after Anny had explained her dilemma. "I can't bear that you should let your affection for Richmond stand in the way of your marrying a man of your own age and standing who would make your life blessed."

"But how can I accept the hand of one man when all I can think of is another?" Anny replied.

"I want to honor the confidence you have placed in me. But truthfully, I cannot see the situation with Richmond ending well. I know this is not what you want to hear, but you have come to me for an honest opinion, and I feel it incumbent upon myself to provide you with it."

"But I am certain Richmond has a strong affection for me."

"Has he declared his feelings?"

"He has not."

"So you are not certain. He's young and impetuous. That's part of his charm. But consider the disparity of your situations. He can retract his love at any moment, with little discomfort to himself, and devastating consequences to you."

She saw the wisdom of Julia's advice. She could be abandoning her last chance for marital happiness. And yet . . .

"The best gift you could give Richmond would be to rid yourself of this discomforting love that torments you—and him too. I'm sure it would do his heart good to see you calm and fulfilled in a suitable marriage. He would not lose you. You would not lose him. You both would gain and he would have a chance of setting his heart on a woman of his own age."

"You were so deeply in love with your husband. I thought you, of all people, would think love to be important above all else," Anny said.

"You will find no more enthusiastic proponent of love than me. But love changes over time. Richmond may discover that his youthful passion is not a lasting one. And then where will you be?"

"Are you suggesting that I marry someone I do not love? You did not." Anny thought of the famous artists of the day who had fallen hard for Julia and wanted to marry her.

"With Herbert, I cannot say I was smitten absolutely when we married. But we grew together and developed a profound bond. He became the center of my life. I cannot imagine marrying someone else, nor will I settle for someone lesser."

"Then you must understand my hesitation."

"Yes, but I have my Stella, Gerald, and George. Had I been childless, who is to say my affection would have expressed itself differently?"

Anny did what she did with all advice she did not want to hear: she ignored it. She decided, instead, to go to Cambridge and see Richmond. She needed to talk to him in person.

Luck bestowed its blessing. Minny and Leslie took Memee to Brighton for the weekend, and she was able to slip away for the day.

She took the train to Cambridge and waited for Richmond by the fountain in the Great Court at Trinity College. The boys milling about looked impossibly young. She was loath to admit that they were all Richmond's age or older.

He met her at the appointed hour, and they walked toward the river. This was the first time they had seen each other since Cammie's book signing. There was so much she wanted to tell him but she didn't know how or where to start. The result was a stilted conversation, unsatisfying to both.

Finally, he said, "I can tell something is wrong. Why did you come here?"

She blurted out her news.

"I'm relieved. I was afraid you were going to tell me we had to stop writing each other."

His reaction threw her into a state of confusion.

"You do understand that Mr. Hughes has asked me to be his wife?" Perhaps she had been so overwrought she had not made herself clear.

"Yes, but surely you are not going to accept," he said.

"I am seriously considering it. He is the nicest of men with many admirable qualities."

His face altered. "Have you lost your senses? This will not do." He raised his voice a notch. "No, this most certainly will not do. I do not want to come between you and your happiness, but, really, is he the person to provide it?"

"He is very steady," she said. "And most responsible."

"And a royal bore to boot."

"So you know him?"

"Indeed I do not. I know the type. He would smother you like a candle snuffer. Does he appreciate your talent? The merriment that you bring to everything you do? Mark my words, he will demand that you give up your writing to raise his children." He picked up a stick and hurled it in the river. The current caught it and carried it away.

He raked his hand through his hair and continued: "You are making a terrible mistake. He is no match for you. Will he really let you be who you are? Do you want to spend your life being told what to think and how to behave? I beg of you. Do not do it."

"And why not?" She did not want an assessment of Mr. Hughes's character or a recitation of her many fine qualities. She wished for some greater indication of his affection toward her.

"It will be the biggest mistake of your life. If you marry, it must be to someone worthy of you, one who will be a real companion and appreciate your originality."

And who might that be? she wished to ask but lacked the courage.

"I am too stunned," he said. "I can't collect my thoughts. I wish I didn't have an appointment now. Promise me you will not do anything rash," he said.

"I cannot promise anyone anything," she said.

With that, they parted.

THE TRAIN RIDE HOME WAS TORTURE. One unequivocal word from him, and the affair would be settled. But he had not stepped forth. She was in emotional tatters. She had worked herself up into a foolish state and needed to set right her life. Richmond's affection, most likely, was a fanciful conjecture. Why sacrifice her remaining years to a chimera of youth?

He would never intentionally play with her feelings; that she knew. But his youthful exuberance might be misleading her. Clearly he adored her, but for what did that count? As a relative? A close friend? A mentor? Were his feelings merely the adulation of a successful older cousin? He was so terribly, terribly young. She now saw that clearly.

It would be foolish to pass up a suitable offer of marriage with matters so ambiguous with Richmond. Surely she could find happiness—if not passionate love, then at least equilibrium and welcome protection—in a steady man like Hastings Hughes. He was of proper age, perfectly agreeable, and had four children. At thirty-eight years old, she was getting too old to have children of her own. Would it be so bad to marry for the sake of comfort?

The following day when Leslie and Minny returned from Brighton, she took up the matter with them. Enough people knew about Hastings Hughes's offer that she did not want them to hear about it from someone other than herself.

"What are your feelings about him?" Minny said, searching her face. Anny had not slept for three days, and the strain showed in her eyes.

"I vacillate." She spoke hesitantly, careful not to let anything slip out about Richmond. Neither Leslie nor Minny was aware that she and Richmond had resumed their correspondence.

"Do you remember the time, before Min and I were married, when I left you both in Switzerland without a word and went hiking in Transylvania?" Leslie said. "I was confused about my feelings and when I returned to London, you grabbed onto me like a terrier and wouldn't let go."

He turned to Minny. "She gave me a good thrashing and told me I was making the biggest mistake of my life if I let you slip away."

"She did that?" Min said. "Truly?"

"Indeed, your sister was full of fire. It was a frightening thing to behold. I remember thinking, I better not run afoul of such passion or I will be tossed straight to Hades by this woman."

Anny smiled at the memory.

"You made me realize my doubts were unfounded," Leslie said, "and I was being a fool, and if I hesitated, I risked losing Minny and I would never forgive myself if that happened. I shudder to think what might have become of me if I hadn't listened to you. I would be a pathetic old crank rattling around to avoid funeral expenses."

"No one ever told me," Minny said.

"The best thing I ever did in my life was to marry Min, for she has made the last seven years a time of happier relations with my family, with my work, and with myself," Leslie went on. "I do not wish you to wake up when you are older and look back on this moment and reproach yourself for giving up what might well be your final opportunity. He's a nice enough fellow."

"Well, I think he's a capital bore!" Min blurted.

Anny's jaw dropped. "I was under the impression you thought he was a good prospect."

"Well, I've changed. The man is in a marriageable humor, and will be wed in six months—if not to you, then to another."

"And why not to Anny?" Leslie wondered.

"Because he is a controlling humorless prig. She would wither in such an arrangement!"

Mr. Hughes's offer had nothing to do with Richmond, Anny realized, suddenly gaining focus. Even if Richmond didn't exist, she would not accept the proposal. He was not right for her and could never be. Minny made her see that. Better to be an honest, dreary old maid than to go against her instinct.

She threw her arms around her sister who was, after all, the one person in the world who knew her best.

IN MAY, MINNY ANNOUNCED SHE was expecting another child. Leslie was elated, but Anny's happiness was tempered by concern. Minny had had difficulty in the past, and it was the birth of their mother's third child that had tipped her over into madness.

Minny was weak from the beginning. "I sometimes feel more like a torpid animal than anything else," she confessed. "And I do so like to be able to snooze over a book without having to think about anything else."

"There's no reason for you to exert yourself," Anny said. "Leslie and I are here to pamper you."

When Minny did not improve, the doctor recommended a trip to Switzerland. Leslie did not need prodding. The Alps were in his blood, and when he was away too long, a part of him went hungry. In July, the household relocated to the small mountain town that had served as the starting point for many of Leslie's alpine expeditions.

Upon recovering from the arduous journey, Minny became more lively, and was able to go out daily with her favorite coachman for a ten-minute ride—no more. She improved daily, and Leslie commended the doctor's good judgment in sending her here, away from misery.

One day Leslie took Laura and Anny into the mountains on horseback. They rode through pine forests, fields of wild strawberries, and valleys of wild flowers with thousands of glittering spider webs. Anny wished she could wrap up some of the beauty and send it home to Richmond. They were now writing to each other every day.

Laura zigzagged up the mountain path, chattering with the guide. She paused to say "Bowwow. How do?" to a border collie that had Troy's black and white markings. By early afternoon they reached a chalet surrounded by cows cropping the alpine grass. Nurse Louise took Laura to play while Anny and Leslie ate bread and honey on the porch that looked over the distant lakes. Billowing waves of snow-crested mountains were partially hidden behind a curtain of clouds which, at moments, parted to reveal the great White Monk and Monte Rosa, shining like glazed icing in the scraps of sun. Anny looked over at Laura, frolicking amidst the alpine flowers, and felt a flood of well-being. The only thing missing for complete happiness was Richmond.

"I got a letter yesterday from a Cambridge classmate," Leslie said, passing Anny some honey. "He told me that Hastings Hughes was engaged. I wanted you to hear the news from me."

"Well, he went to work in short order. It's only been three months since his offer," she said, in mild irritation.

"Are you upset?" he said, observing her closely.

"Quite the contrary. I'm delighted. Perhaps a tad chagrined that I did not break his heart just a little."

"Are you sure? Because if I thought he hurt you, I would . . ."

"What?" she teased.

"Give him a few whacks with the old collegial cane."

The image amused her. "At the time, I was stirred up because everyone was pushing me toward a decision that I intuitively resisted." She paused and looked at him, for he had been one of those people. "But I knew what my response should be the moment I read his letter of proposal, which had all the precision of a 'Situation Vacant' advert: 'Wife-wanted. Middle aged. Excellent character. No widows. Must be good with children. Apply today between one and three.'"

Leslie added: "'Proficiency in needlework not required.'"

"Oh, no, that's too many words. The good solicitor would never pay a tuppence over the word limit." They laughed.

Laura and Nurse returned, and the child dumped a handful of wilted wildflowers in Anny's lap.

"Aren't these lovely. Thank you," Anny said.

"No. For mees Mama. She sad."

"She's not sad, my little duckling. She doesn't feel well."

"Memee make Mama angry?"

"No, no sweetheart. She doesn't smile because she's sick."

"Why?"

Anny looked at Leslie, hoping he would chime in. If anyone was going to tell Laura that she was soon to have a new brother or sister, it should be him. But he kept silent. He seemed to enjoy his daughter more in her absence. His letters were always affectionate: "Hug my darling Laurekins," or "Kiss my little pet." But when he was actually with the child, he appeared embarrassed by her.

Anny tried to explain. "It's hard to smile when you don't feel well. Remember when you had that summer cold last month? You went around with a great big frown on your face. This is what our Memekins looked like. . . ." Anny hooked her index fingers in the corners of her mouth and pulled them down.

Laura giggled.

"But if anything can make your Mama smile, these flowers will. Let's see if we can get a wet cloth to wrap them in, so they'll survive the trip back."

They returned home after dark to find the hotel lit up by Chinese lanterns. Music came through the open windows. Anny chose to skip the festivities and went directly to her desk to write to Richmond. Their correspondence was still a secret, and that added the excitement of being slightly illicit. She chose not to mention the solicitor's engagement, but she did report that her sister was improving. "I overheard the doctor talking to Leslie about Minny," Anny wrote. "He said medicines are a mere accident but that people are certainly medicinal—some are sedatives, some are irritants, and some are tonics. So with that, My Dearest Tonic, I will take your leave, for I am most frightfully tired after scrambling feebly after our horses' tails through the dark. But now all the stars are rushing in a stream between the mountain and my window, and I can hear a waltz in the background. I will fall asleep thinking of you."

WHEN THEY RETURNED TO London in August, Minny quickly lost the gains she had made in Switzerland. "It's very odd. I got almost well before Laura was born but I am not well now. I do not understand," she confided to Anny. Her face was arsenic-pale.

"Is there any possible way you could save up enough strength to go to the theater with me?" Anny asked one morning when Minny seemed to be having a good day.

"Oh, Anny, I'd love to, but I just don't feel up to it," Minny sighed.

"I was passing by the Lyceum Theater and saw the playbill for the upcoming *Merchant of Venice* and you'll never guess who is starring."

Minny was too weary to show an interest, but Anny continued on.

"Our own Nelly Watts. She's now going by Ellen Terry."

"Isn't she still married to Mr. Watts?"

"Officially, yes, but I don't think they've seen each other since the separation."

It had been eleven years since Anny had befriended the child bride in Freshwater, and during that time, Nelly had created a scandal by running off with a theatrical designer and having two illegitimate children. Rather than allowing her outrageous behavior to destroy her, she had cocked a snook at society and emerged triumphant, now appearing on stage in a distinguished Shakespeare production. Anny had to admire her spirit. Who would have guessed the naïve, moon-faced muse would develop such mettle?

But she could see that Minny was not strong enough for a theater outing, and did not press her. She was strong enough, however, to receive Lionel, who came calling to announce his engagement.

Anny immediately wrote to the Tennysons: "Lionel came yesterday and made Minny and me both behave like two gooses when he told us his news—God bless him and make him happy happy happy! I think Eleanor is the most most happy maiden to have won such a dear and noble heart. Minny declared she only cried because she had so hoped he might have waited for Laura."

Anny kept private the real reason for her euphoria. Lionel and Richmond were the same age. If Lionel was old enough to marry . . . she dared not think further, but her spirits leapt.

AT THE END OF OCTOBER CAME the sad news that Cammie and her husband were moving to Ceylon. It was not completely un-expected. Nonetheless, Anny felt heavy-hearted. She couldn't imagine the island without her. Cammie was the glue that held together the odd assortment of writers, poets, painters, and scholars that gravitated to Freshwater. She created an egalitarian ambiance and included, in her warm embrace, everyone from Alfred Tennyson in his mansion to struggling artists in their garrets.

Anny understood Cammie's decision. Despite the appearance of flightiness, her friend had a strong practical streak. Faced with a struggling photography business, tattered finances, and an elderly husband who yearned to return to Ceylon before he died, it was the only sensible course. In addition, her sons had moved there to salvage what was left of the coffee business. "Where your heart is, there is your treasure also," Cammie said, accepting the move with her typical optimism.

Anny and Julia Duckworth traveled to Southampton to see the Camerons off. There was a festive atmosphere at the wharf as crowds of well-wishers gathered by the four-masted steamer *Pekin'*, which had banners flapping from the flag hoist. Cammie's husband wandered along the quay with an ivory-handled cane in one hand and a white rose in the other. The Tennysons had given him the rose when they bade farewell on the island. Looking more spry than she had seen him in years, he directed the porters to lead a live cow into the hold. Cammie was convinced that milk from their own cow would ward off tuberculosis.

Other porters carried two wooden coffins up the gangplank. Mrs. Cameron never went anywhere without something to be buried in, given what happened to her father. The story of the exploding cask, like Cammie herself, was larger than life, and may, or may not have been one hundred percent factual, but contained a large element of truth.

The Camerons had spent their last guinea on the way over, and Cammie was handing out copies of her photographs to the astonished porters in lieu of tips. "Save these. They'll be worth a lot of money one day," she said.

True to form, Cammie was dispensing advice until the last possible moment. When it was Julia's turn to bid adieu, Cammie said, "My dear, it's way past time to give up these wretched weeds and remarry. Such gloomy frocks can ruin the most persistent beauty." Julia was wise enough not to contradict her.

"Please write the moment you get there to let us know you're safe," Anny begged, when it was her turn. They all knew the voyage was dangerous.

"The Suez canal will cut two weeks from our journey," Cammie said.

Anny had trouble imagining a creature as social as Cammie thriving on a remote coffee plantation that was an eight-hour donkey ride over narrow dirt paths from the nearest town. But Cammie was amazingly resilient and had always taken in stride what she called the little frets and insect stings of life.

"Please, promise not to give up your photography," Anny begged her dear friend.

"Oh, my child, it's as much a part of me as the air I breathe. There's a whole native culture there, waiting to be immortalized." She walked up the plank and turned to wave at friends and family.

A brass band played as the steamer pulled away, and with it, Anny's not-quite mother, not-quite mentor, not-quite muse.

THROUGHOUT NOVEMBER, ANNY experienced a gathering sense of gloom. Losing Cammie marked the end of an era at Freshwater, and Anny's enthusiasm for building a house there dwindled, yet she still felt the pressure to earn more money. Lionel's engagement had elicited from Richmond hearty avowals of joy at his friend's good fortune, but nothing more. The thrill of their clandestine letter writing had worn off, and now Anny yearned for their friendship to be public. She felt guilty about keeping such a secret from her sister.

Toward the end of the month, she experienced a strange sort of fright—a certitude that wherever she went, sorrow would follow. Haunted by the sensation, she went to a nearby church, but found no solace in the stony emptiness of the sanctuary. Afterwards, she called on the elderly Valentine Smiths, friends of her father's, but they could not see her, so she returned home.

When she told Minny about her terrors, her sister laughed and said, "You went to the Valentine Smiths because you thought them so old and so ill, nothing would much matter." In the comfort and warmth of Minny's sitting room, Anny's outlook improved. "Now if you would be so good as to bring my precious Memekins down to me. She will cheer us both up."

That weekend, Anny went to visit the writer Margaret Oliphant in Windsor. She knew the train station well; Eton and Windsor shared the same stop. But Richmond was no longer there, and the ghost of sorrow trailed her.

The first morning in Windsor, Anny received an urgent telegram calling her home. She was on the next train. Leslie's brother Fritzy met her at the station.

"Tell me. Don't make me wait," she commanded.

"I'm so sorry. Minny went into premature labor. The child did not survive."

"Yes, yes, that I can bear. It's my Minny. Tell me quick. My Min?"

He shook his head and looked down.

On the carriage ride home, Fritzy told her that Minny had not felt well the night before and moved into a room where the maid could be on call. At midnight, she went into labor, followed by violent convulsions. She blacked out immediately. The doctor came at once, but she never regained consciousness. She passed away early that morning.

Everything seemed so familiar to Anny. The difficult birth. Minny, alone. Anny gone when her sister needed her most. Same plot, different ending.

"How is Les?"

"Poor fellow. He's inconsolable. You will be better at comforting him than I. It's his birthday today, you know."

When she got to the front hall, she was met by Nurse Louise and Laura. Louise's eyes were swollen but Laura was jolly.

Before she could take off her cloak, the child was tugging at her skirt. "Come see Memee's drawing."

"I will darling, but first I have to go to your mother." Anny mouthed the words "Does she know?" to Louise, and the nurse nodded yes.

"She's back," Laura said.

"What do you mean?"

"Papa says she go to heaven, but she back now. Memee sees her. She sleeping." Anny cast a desperate look at Louise, who looked equally baffled.

Anny took the child to Minny's room, where the body was laid out on the bed. She thought of the heaven of flowers that Minny had not reached in her dream. She only hoped her sister was there now.

"I wake her," Laura said, and before Anny could stop her, she was tickling Minny under the chin. Laura waited. Minny did not move. The child tickled her again.

"Dearest, she's not going to wake up. She's dead." Anny struggled to think of a way to describe death to a child who understood so little.

Without warning, Laura slapped her mother across the cheek, making her head roll to one side. "Wake up," the child yelled.

Jolted into action, Anny pulled her back. She knew Memee didn't understand the situation, but the slap was so shocking.

"Darling, your Mama can't respond. She's not with us anymore. She's dead and she's not coming back," she said, avoiding a mention of heaven, which had confused the child before.

"Who will take care of Memee?" she asked.

"You have many people who love you and will take care of you. Your papa, me, Nurse Louise. Many, many people."

"But I want my Mama," Laura said.

"I know you do, dearest. We all do, but we have to learn to live without her."

"Nooooo." She started beating Anny's skirt with her fists. She was surprisingly strong. Soon, she was in a full-blown tantrum, screeching, then gulping for breath. Anny called out desperately for Leslie or Louise, but no one came.

Alone with the wild child, she had no idea how to comfort her. She knew that Laura was simply acting the way Anny would like to act—raging at the tragedy of it all.

In desperation, she yanked the cover from the bed and wound it around Laura, binding her arms and legs so she could no longer thrash. It always calmed her to be swaddled. The child would turn five the following week, and even though she was small for her age, she was too heavy to pick up, so Anny sank to the floor and pulled the bundle close to her chest. The body of her sister was stretched out above them on the bed. "Calm down, my little Dumpling," Anny said, and made soothing nonsense sounds. Soon, the child stopped shaking and the whimpering tapered off.

When she was sure the child had calmed down, she said, "Now I want you to tell your mother goodbye. Can you do that?"

Laura nodded solemnly. Anny unwrapped her and the child moved to the bed, cupped her hands, and whispered something into her mother's ear.

"What did you tell her?" Anny asked.

"A secret," Laura whispered, as if someone might overhear.

"Did you tell her you loved her?"

Laura put her hand on her hip and gave Anny a pitiable look, as if she were such a simpleton. "*That's* not a secret," she said.

twelve

1876

HOME WITHOUT MINNY WAS A dreary place. Gloom hung about, as foul as London's air. Anny lost all interest in the greater world. Writing was out of the question; visiting or receiving friends was a chore. Going out was taxing; staying in, worse. Since Minny's death, she thought much about their father. Mourning, like a strong wind, uncovered buried sadness. She had never considered how much grief felt like influenza. No one part of her hurt; she just ached all over.

Leslie gave up his clubs and only left the house to go to the office or the bookstore. He pottered about, trailing the sickeningly sweet smell of pipe tobacco. His stooped posture, imploring glances, and moans made it impossible to ignore his misery. As if he were not already needy, self-regarding, and cantankerous, grief made him more so. Anny and Leslie lived together in shared solitude, each alone in pain.

No one felt Minny's absence more than Laura. Leslie couldn't bear to listen to her howls in the night, and acted as if the child were personally trying to torture him.

Every meal was a battle of wills. Nurse Louise was convinced that Laura needed meat, even though she was accustomed to the vegetarian diet Minny had fed her of goat's milk and fruit.

When Nurse forced meat into the child's mouth, she spat it out and screeched.

Sometimes a torrent of unintelligible words exploded from her tiny mouth. She tried to control the outbursts by spinning—not the gentle turning that had once served to comfort her, but a maniacal whirling where, bent at the waist, she went faster and faster until she collapsed.

When she wasn't spinning herself, she found other things to spin. Minny had loved dolls and collected them, even though Laura showed little interest. Minny's favorite was Missy, a doll with a kid leather body and bisque head. She had dressed the doll with the same exquisite care that she devoted to Laura's outfits, instructing the seamstress to add piping and smocking to miniature versions of Laura's frocks. Laura developed the habit of violently twirling Missy by the arm. One day, the stitching pulled away at the shoulder and the doll flew across the room, leaving Laura holding its soft leather arm.

Anny picked up the doll. Its nose was shattered and a glass eye sprung from the socket. "Poor Missy. Look. She's hurt," Anny said, cradling the doll in her arms.

The child stared at the doll blankly, still holding its severed arm. Stuffing dribbled onto the floor. She tossed the arm across the room, then plopped herself on the floor and retreated to that remote place where she was unreachable.

She had an infuriating habit of repeating the same question over and over. Answering her did not stop the question. It was the repetition itself that seemed to comfort her.

One day she was mooning about on the landing when Anny returned from a walk. The child fit her tiny face between the rungs of the bannister and said to Anny in a plaintive voice, "Why does not my Mommee come?"

It broke Anny's heart. She removed her cloak and said, "Your Mommee loves you very much."

Laura said, "Then why does not my Mommee come?"

Anny sat on the landing beside the child. "When your Mama was a little baby, her eyes were always sore so she had to wear a long green veil," she told Laura.

"Mommee was a baby like Memee?" the child asked.

"Yes, once, long ago." Anny realized that she had inadvertently stumbled upon a way to stop Laura's questions: diversion. "One day, our governess let me attach your mother's green veil onto my hat, and I ran through a field of buttercups with the veil floating behind me. When I reached the lake, I hid the veil behind a rock. I told the governess I had lost it, but that wasn't true. I didn't want your Mommee to have it."

"That's naughty," the child said, with a pout.

"I'm afraid I was a very naughty little girl. One night I dreamed that someone cut off Baby's two little feet. That's what we called your Mommee when she was a wee thing. Baby. I climbed out of bed and peered into the crib. There was Baby, warm and fast asleep. That was the first time I really loved her. Before that, she was just a bother for me."

Laura listened in rapt attention.

From then on, whenever Laura said, "Why does not my Mommee come?" Anny said, "She's dead and she's not coming back, but let me tell you a story." She told her about how Minny hated rhubarb, vegetables, and pudding, but loved to dig deep holes in the garden to reach the center of the earth. She told her about the time in Paris when their father came for a visit and had grown a funny little moustache. Minny cried and cried and would only kiss him through the newspaper. He immediately went to his room, shaved off his moustache, came back and gave her a big kiss.

She told her about the time Minny disappeared and they thought someone had stolen her. Their father galloped off to the park to search for her. The governess cried and cried and started packing her box, certain she would be sent to jail. Then Anny heard a tiny voice calling from the cupboard. "It was your very own Mommee. She had hidden there for a lark, and when everyone made such a fuss, she was afraid to come out."

ANNY HAD MANY FRIENDS, AND following Minny's death, they all offered to help. She accepted the goodwill with which such offers were made, but the burden was on her to ask. Julia Duckworth didn't ask; she just acted. She saw a need and quietly filled it, recognizing that often, the need could be as simple as unassuming companionship.

Julia stopped by the house often, sometimes with her children, sometimes alone. She was the only one of Anny's friends that Leslie could tolerate. He felt she understood his grief, having gone through the loss of a spouse herself. She was content to sit silently in the parlor doing needlework while Leslie and Anny read by the fire.

One evening Julia stopped by with her nurse and Gerald, a confident five-year-old who was already reading. Julia's nurse took him up to the nursery to play with Laura.

"If Gerald ever falls in love with Laura, he will have a hard time of it," Leslie said to Julia. "The little mite can be such a coquette, the way she cocks her head to one side like a mischievous magpie and makes completely irrelevant remarks with the most provoking good temper."

Julia smiled and said, "She's quite impish, I'll admit."

They gathered around the table for a game of cribbage. Anny barely knew the rules, and pulled her chair next to Julia so she could watch.

Julia sat with her back perfectly straight, her chin high, expertly shuffling and dealing the cards. For someone so accommodating, she loved to win, and gleefully moved her red pegs along the holes in the wooden board.

After they had played several matches, the game was interrupted by a shriek from the nursery. Leslie turned to Anny in a panic. Julia stood up. "Some misfortune has befallen the children. I'll go and see."

"I'll be there shortly," Anny said, as Julia rushed upstairs. Leslie made no effort to follow. She could feel his mortification.

"Another of Laura's superficial tantrums. Can the child not behave herself for one evening?" He put his head in his hands. "I have spared no expense on any aspect of her care, and this is what I get in return? I always imagined that I would have a daughter that I could share books with—*Arabian Nights*, *Grimm's Fairy Tales*. I admired the reading bond you and Min had with your father. I always assumed that fatherhood would be like that. And what do I get? An imbecile."

"Leslie!" she cried out in horror. His harshness, under the guise of honesty, made her shudder.

"Minny was willfully blind; I can see that now. The child is backward. She has no moral fiber."

"How can you talk about moral fiber when the poor mite just lost the one person in the world who loved her more than life? It's only natural that she should backslide."

The child's behavior Anny could excuse. Leslie's, she could not. "Whatever she is, and whatever she becomes, she will always be your daughter," she said, trembling.

"And you will always be your mother's daughter."

Anny scooped up a handful of scoring pegs and threw them at him. The wooden pieces ricocheted off his waistcoat and scattered on the Turkish carpet. She put her hand over her mouth, so astonished was she by her own actions. Then she crouched on the floor and swept up the pieces with her hand.

She was on all fours when Julia came in with her son and his nurse. Gerald's eyes were red and puffy. The nurse made no effort to hide her displeasure.

"I think it will be easier to calm Laura without us," Julia said, glancing at the floor. Anny stood up, but made no explanation. Leslie stood rigidly as he watched the guests leave.

"She will not be back. With Gerald, at least," he said, full of self-pity.

Anny loathed him.

"You do not know her if you think that," she said, and went upstairs.

Laura had changed into her bedclothes. Anny sat beside her on the bed and tried to hug her, but she stiffened.

"Don't reward her," Nurse Louise said with a jaw clenched so tight the cords in her neck protruded.

"I'll do as I see fit," Anny said. She did not ask what the child had done. It was irrelevant.

"As you wish, ma'am," the nurse said, and left.

Laura pulled the blanket over her mouth and nose so only her eyes were visible.

"Are you sad?" Anny asked, afraid to touch her and upset her even more.

She stared at Anny with no expression.

"There's nothing wrong with being sad," Anny said.

Still she said nothing.

Then she lowered the blanket below her chin. "Promise you won't die," she said.

"I'll be around long after you've turned old and gray."

The answer seemed to satisfy the child, and she rolled over and closed her eyes.

ANNY AWOKE THE FOLLOWING morning full of regret. She was horrified by how she had reacted when Leslie linked her mother's madness to Laura. But she had no inclination to apologize.

A month before, she had visited her mother to let her know about Minny. Her mother clearly understood that someone close to her had died, but reacted with confusion. She had not seen Minny since she was a baby. It saddened Anny to think that two of the females closest to Minny each, for different reasons, could not mourn for her. That job was left to Anny and Leslie, and they were making a hash of it.

One morning, a week after her row with Leslie, Anny heard shrieking coming from the nursery. She went upstairs. Laura stood in a white chemise and knickers, her fist balled up, her lower lip out.

"She refuses to get dressed," Louise said, holding the black mourning frock in her hand.

Anny remembered how Minny had hated the scratchy black crepe she was forced to wear after their father's death.

"Will you wear another dress?" she asked Laura. "The soft blue velvet with black trim? That's one of your favorites and you look so pretty in it."

Laura stared blankly and didn't answer.

"It's disrespectful to her mother," Louise said firmly.

"Minny would much prefer that she be happy."

"No, I won't allow it. The child must wear black."

Louise pinned Laura down and tried to force the dress on her amidst a blur of thrashing limbs and ear-piercing screeches.

"Stop it. Stop it this minute," Anny said, pulling Louise off the child.

Laura whimpered and rolled herself into a ball.

"Mr. Stephen says I do not have to take orders from you," Louise said, panting from the exertion.

"What?" Anny said, furious. "When did he say that?"

"Two days ago. Ask him yourself, ma'am," she said in her thickly accented voice.

Anny flushed crimson. She suspected Louise might be manipulating her.

When Leslie returned from work, she met him in the front hall. Without so much as a greeting, she said, "Louise said that you told her that she did not have to follow my orders."

"That is correct."

"How could you do such a thing?"

"You're too lenient with Laura. The child needs a firmer hand. Louise is a better disciplinarian."

"The outbursts aren't Memee's fault. You can't blame her. She needs gentle guidance, not iron discipline."

"I am her father. I will make the decisions."

Anny stared at him in disbelief. Trembling with anger, she reached for her cloak and left.

It was cold outside, but she took a brisk walk to collect her thoughts. She stopped by Julia's house and told her about the situation. Julia suggested that she stay with her until she found other lodgings. "You and Leslie will work things out," she predicted. "You always do."

Anny returned from her walk and announced to Leslie her decision to move out. She felt she could not stay under the same roof with him for one more night.

"You can't leave me," he cried in anguish.

"I can, and I will," she said.

"But I can't be alone! Not now. It would be a catastrophe!"

What right did he have to proclaim the supremacy of his suffering, as if mourning were some kind of competition, and he had an insurmountable lead?

"I drive you to distraction. That much is clear," Anny said. "We are no good for one another. Surely you can see that. We make each other miserable. It's like a scab you shouldn't pick at, but can't help yourself."

"You may think you are doing me a favor by leaving, but I can assure you, you are not. I would become totally isolated on my own. I implore you not to leave. I really couldn't bear it."

She was surprised by how upset he was. "I cannot live in a house where one of the servants has been authorized to disobey me," she said.

"I made a terrible mistake. I see that now, and I'm truly sorry. But you must not leave me. That would really make me feel as if I were not fulfilling my duty to Minny."

Instinctively he had found her weakness. She felt a personal responsibility to make Leslie and Laura happy, for her sister's sake. And she had failed miserably with both. She hesitated.

"Sorrow tries my temper," he continued. "I am fretful and irritable by disposition, as you know, and sometimes I bully you shamefully, but I need you desperately. I may not express myself properly or make you feel appreciated, but it would really hurt my feelings if you were to leave."

"You will speak to Louise?"

"At once. And I promise to behave better. The problem of making sorrow ennobling is a terribly hard one, and I'm a royal flop in that department, I'm afraid."

"Grief is not meant to be ennobling. It's meant to be endured," Anny said, with tears in her eyes. "How I wish Minny were here."

He put his arms around her and they held each other.

THROUGH THE FIRST SIX MONTHS of mourning, Anny and Richmond continued to correspond, but their letters were less frequent and less intimate. She still felt a catch in her chest when she saw the ivory letter opener that signaled his waiting letter in the downstairs hall. But his words, so full of tender concern, did not seem as crucial to her new life.

By May, Anny's grief had dissipated somewhat, and she had whole days where she didn't think about Minny at all. Then the smallest detail would plunge her back into despair—when she smelled Minny's beloved hyacinths in the garden, or a feral cat, with a remarkably human cry, awakened her in the night, as if contesting Minny's departure.

One afternoon in late spring, Richmond came to London, and Julia invited him and Anny to tea. Julia had proved to be a stalwart friend. Anny felt, on a deep level, that Julia truly wished the best for her. After having advised her to marry Mr. Hughes, she did not act hurt when Anny ignored her advice. With admirable flexibility, Julia quickly turned her support to Richmond and offered Anny an uncritical ear. Anny's trust in her had been rewarded. Julia never said a word to Leslie, or anyone else, about Richmond.

When he arrived for tea, Julia deftly absented herself. The maid set out the tea service and then left them alone.

They exchanged pleasantries about school and family. Anny tried to keep the conversation light. She didn't want to scare him off with her misery.

Her heart still lurched, and perhaps always would, when she saw him. Life had handed him a wealth of blessings. But as she looked across at his shining face—so innocent and hopeful—she realized, in a way she had not before, what an enormous gulf separated them—a gulf of years, experience, and, most of all, loss.

What could he know of misfortune? He had led a carefree life, untouched by shadows. She in no way blamed him for that. It was the purview of youth.

She, on the other hand, had lost her entire family, except for her mother, who would probably outlast them all. She couldn't bear one more loss.

She and Leslie were united in gloom, but at least they were united. With Leslie, she could express her feelings forthrightly. With Richmond, she held back. She was always protecting him, fearful of him, confused by him. She cared too desperately about the outcome to say what she truly thought.

It was a mistake to have agreed to meet with him. She should end the conversation and send him on his way.

Gathering her nerve, she refilled his cup. The tea quivered as it poured from the spout.

"I'm afraid I'm grim company. I won't apologize," she said, though she was doing just that. "It can't be otherwise. There's no possible way you could understand. Nor would I wish you to."

"You underestimate me," he said, moving his cup to the side and leaning forward. "I *can* understand, or at least, I want to. What I lack in experience, I can fill in with my imagination and my heart," he continued, with his usual eagerness and sincerity. "All the good will and sympathy in the world are ineffectual. I know that. I can see that you are enveloped in a sort of invisible cloud and nothing I can say or do can pass through. It frightens me terribly to see you suffer like this and to feel so helpless," he said. "But even if I don't understand first-hand what you are going through, I can stand by, quietly, until the time when you are ready to join the world again."

His words were wise beyond his twenty-one years. In fact, that's exactly what she needed: For him to wait and not pressure her.

"That gives me more comfort than you will ever know," she said.

"In the meantime, can I still be your Dearest Tonic? I miss that," he said.

She smiled—a real smile, not the false one that never reached her eyes. "No matter what happens, you will always be that to me."

After he returned to Cambridge, a letter arrived without delay. "We drove back through the sunset and the stars blazed and a little crescent moon hung ever so high up; and I had only just time to rush to my school; and after that I thought of you and went to bed and to a sound, sound sleep," he wrote.

With Richmond's visit, she felt a veil had been lifted. She needed reassurance, and even if he understood imperfectly her state of mind, the mere act of trying to see things through her eyes was comforting.

Now the letters came with more frequency, and more ardor. "I have solemnly sat down to inaugurate a splendid and economical piece of furniture which I fished out of a pawnbroker's for three pounds," he wrote. "It is a high bureau with little drawers which I've filled with the contents of one desperately untidy

Augean Stable of a drawer—all your letters are comfortably in-stalled in an absurdly small receptacle which has a special key and if you are alarmed, you may have it in your keeping."

Richmond was on her mind continually, and judging from his letters, the same was true for him: "Sweetheart, I would have sent you a goodnight last night but Lionel appeared just as I was beginning so I couldn't, but you know I wished you one?" he wrote.

Like someone involved in an illicit affair, her secret life be-came her principal one.

TO MARK THE END OF MOURNING, Anny took Laura to the mil-liners to buy them both spring hats. Minny had always loved to see her daughter adorned in beautiful outfits, and Anny felt that a new hat would lift her own spirits as well.

The shop was crammed with cubbyholes containing feath-ers, crêpe flowers, ribbon, netting, lace, and fur. Several adjustable wooden head forms held hats in various stages of completion. Anny and Laura both picked out the trimmings for their hats and the following week returned to the shop when the hats were completed.

The outing was fraught with potential disaster. Laura was very particular about how things felt against her skin. The straw hat might scratch her head; the quill end of a feather could prick her. A stiff taffeta flower might annoy her, or a dangling ribbon tickle. In retrospect, Anny wondered why she had ever gone through with the idea in the first place.

In the shop, the milliner put Anny's hat on her head and af-fixed it with a pin. "No pins for Laura," Anny warned. The child made no objection when the milliner cocked the hat on her head at a jaunty angle. Anny and Laura stood side by side and gazed into the mirror.

"Oh, look at you! You're adorable!" Anny said, exclaiming

at the sight of the gorgeous child, her thick curls falling to her shoulders beneath a pink hat piled high with feathers and lace.

"Anny pooty too," Laura beamed.

The moment was completely unremarkable—two females in a shop, preening in front of the mirror, delighting in a new purchase. The milliner had witnessed the same scene countless times. But to Anny, it felt like a miracle.

NOW THAT ANNY WAS IN BETTER spirits, Julia stopped by less often. Anny called on her friend and said, "We miss you. I wish you'd visit more."

"You both seem to be doing better," she said. When people were happy again, Julia moved on to those more in need.

"We'd prefer to think of you as our friend, not a savior," Anny said.

"I'm afraid I'll bore Leslie. I don't possess the intellectual breadth that he is accustomed to."

"Oh don't be ridiculous. He loves your visits. Don't let him scare you. His sarcasm and sharp tongue hide a deep shyness."

"Well, I do enjoy his company."

"And he yours. Just the other day he said, 'I sincerely hope we don't have to be abjectly miserable to merit the benefit Julia's company. She always makes the day brighter.'"

"He said that? He was just being charitable."

"Charity is not in his character. Trust me. He can be hurtful, but he is invariably honest."

WHEN CHARLOTTE RITCHIE VISITED London from Paris, she invited Anny to luncheon at her hotel. Anny had not seen her since Minny's death, and her elderly cousin offered her sympathy. "I know what love and tender trust Minny had in her older sister. I've watched you girls since you were born," Chattie said. Long ago, when Anny and Minny lived in Paris, they had been frequent visitors to Chattie's apartment.

"I know Minny and I can no longer be together, but I like to think that we are somehow still heart to heart," said Anny. "I miss her so."

"We all miss her. But you need to get on with life. You must find someone to marry."

"Who would want a plain old spinster like me?" Anny said.

"Darling Anny, your father was my favorite cousin, but I always thought he did you a terrible disservice, making you think you were plain. I used to cringe every time he called you 'My Dear Old Fat Anny.' I know he meant well, dear man. No one loved you more than he did. But you are not nearly as unattractive as you think you are and you would make some man a wonderful wife."

Anny knew that Chattie would regret her comments if she were aware of her deepening friendship with Richmond. She was tired of keeping her feelings hidden. She wanted to broadcast them to the great world, even to one as vehemently opposed as Chattie had been in Venice. The secrecy felt demeaning.

But Anny sensed that Richmond was not ready to come out of hiding. He was worried that their letters would be discovered and had recently burned a stack. "The ashes are still reproaching me in the little grate with sparks running about like fairy good wishes," he wrote.

Anny listened politely as Chattie held forth on the subject of finding a husband, and then moved on to another topic.

ANNY HAD NOT WRITTEN A NOVEL since *Miss Angel*, and now her bank account was dangerously depleted. One day when she was complaining about her lack of funds, Leslie said, "You should write a biography of your father. It would secure his legacy and your financial security."

"I am not the person to do it," she said.

"Charles Dickens was not two years in the grave before a biography was published about him. That champion self-promoter knew exactly what he was about, leaving his friend John Forster an account of his early life to work from."

"Mr. Dickens was Minny's favorite writer," Anny reminded him. "After Papa, that is."

"I cannot abide a man who tosses out the mother of his ten children for a young hussy. You can be sure THAT was not covered in the biography."

"You are confusing the man himself with his work. He may not have been the most upstanding gentleman, but his novels will endure," she said, realizing how much she enjoyed these literary jousts with Leslie.

"I beg to differ. He never sees the significance of things. He never gets below the surface."

"But what a gorgeous surface it is."

"If you like sentimentality, heavy-handed characterization, and general muddle-headedness. He achieves his popularity by working upon the feelings with the cheapest of stimulants."

Anny knew that Leslie's objections had as much to do with jealousy as literary criticism. He was something of a snob, and a definite prude. He would never forgive Mr. Dickens for taking up with an actress thirty years his junior, an open secret at his club.

"Your father was different. He was not only a great writer, he was a great man. You are the only person who can present him in all his dimensions."

"I gave him my solemn word that I would never write his biography."

"But he's no longer alive."

"All the more reason to keep my promise. He is not here to renegotiate."

IN THE FALL, THEY MOVED TO A house next door to Julia Duckworth on Hyde Park Gate. Anny was glad to leave the house on Southwell Gardens. Everything reminded her of Minny—the furnaces her sister had designed, the special tiles she had so lovingly painted for Leslie, the stained-glass window in the stairwell that she had had fashioned from dark green bottles.

Shortly before the moving date, Leslie presented Anny with an envelope.

"What's this?" she said.

"Open it and see," he said, watching her closely.

She did. Inside was the deed to a house in Wimbledon.

"I don't understand," she said, staring at the document.

"I purchased it for you."

She was flooded with unpleasant feelings. How dare he do this behind her back without her approval. The color rose to her face.

"You want me to move to Wimbledon?" she said, coldly.

"Good gracious no. It's for your mother and her caretaker. I thought it would be good for her to have a permanent home closer to you."

She was stunned. He had never even met her mother and only spoke of her in the most pejorative terms. Yet here was this incredible act of generosity, made more touching since he was such a penny-pincher.

"I . . . I'm overcome. I don't know what to say," she said.

"It's my way of paying you back since I inherited Minny's share of your father's estate."

BECAUSE OF ANNY'S WEAKENED financial situation, she had abandoned plans to build a house on the Isle of Wight, but The Porch was still available to lease. She made arrangements to visit with bittersweet emotions—the place would not be the same without Cammie. Her spirits improved considerably when she learned that Richmond had arranged to come to Farringford with Lionel and his fiancée Eleanor.

On the island, Anny settled herself in the cottage. From her writing desk, she could watch rabbits scamper across the field. Ducks rooted for slugs in the garden and swam in the nearby creek. The red squirrels with tufted ears, native to the Isle of Wight, fed on the bread she left at the base of the bird feeder.

She had recently started three love stories, set in Freshwater, that featured characters inspired by the Camerons, Lewis Carroll, Alfred Tennyson and George Frederic Watts. She didn't know yet whether the project would turn into a novel or interlocking short stories, but she was planning on calling it *From an Island*.

For inspiration, she walked on High Down, passing by Cammie's empty house on the way. At first, she avoided it, but after a few days, she stopped by Dimbola and wandered about the grounds. The bones of the garden were visible, but weeds had overtaken it. Dried brown blossoms remained on the hydrangeas, and orangish pink hips ornamented the roses that climbed the trellises on the side of the house facing the sea. Like a body laid out for viewing, the house looked the same, but all the life was missing.

She peeked in a ground-floor window. Cobwebs had formed on the built-in cupboards, and a few abandoned items were strewn on the floor. She heard a cat meow inside. Perhaps it had been left behind, or given away, only to come home again.

She went around back and tried the door to the glass house. To her surprise, it opened. The overcast sky filled the room with mote-filled light. Gone was the large square camera that stood on legs, like a piano stool base. Gone was the vast array of costumes and props. A few stray pieces of straw remain stuck in the metal armature that held the glass siding in place, a remnant from the days when it was a hen house.

She could feel, floating about her in the silence, the ghosts of the titans who had posed for their portraits in this space: the astronomer John Herschel, the philosopher Thomas Carlyle, Charles Darwin, Alfred Tennyson, and Robert Browning. Cammie's gift had been to disarm these great men and capture on the glass plates images that made them seem both intimate, yet illusive. Anny wished her father had been alive for Cammie to photograph, but he had died on Christmas Eve, the very same day that Cammie's daughter presented her with the gift of her first camera.

She remembered the portrait Cammie had taken of her in the year that Minny married Leslie. It showed her in three-quarters image, turned slightly to the side. Her hair was fixed on top of her head and four strands of pearls adorned her neck. Anny had always loathed that portrait. The most interesting thing about it was the dress. The camera picked up every detail of that fussy, overwrought frock: the sheen of white satin, the light glinting off the pearl buttons, the intricacy of the lace bodice, and the panels of ruffles inset from shoulder to hem. In her lap she held a bouquet, like some kind of aspiring spinster bride.

Missing from the photograph were all the qualities that she admired most in Cammie's work: the dramatic use of light and shadow and a blurry focus that created an evocative mood.

Some of Cammie's fellow photographers criticized her for her unfocused images, but the truth was, she could make a perfectly focused photograph when she wanted to. Anny's portrait was evidence of that. But what became clear to her, in the silence of the abandoned glass house, was that Anny had neither of the qualities that fired Cammie's imagination: beauty or greatness.

She had spent her life within arm's length of greatness,

starting with her father and his circle of friends. But she had never achieved it herself, nor had she aspired to it. She did not have Leslie's obsession with producing a work that would last through the ages, the way her father's novels surely would. Her goals were more modest. She looked on great thought and great literature as a mighty river, to which her output was but a tiny feeder stream. Yet her work made her life rich and brought her a sense of fulfillment and occasional joy.

So why, if she had not aspired to greatness, did it hurt so much to realize that in Cammie's mind, she had not achieved it?

The wind slammed the door shut and she jumped. Shuddering, she left the ghost-filled studio and closed the door behind her.

THAT NIGHT, SHE DRESSED WITH great care for dinner. The Tennysons had invited her to Farringford to meet Eleanor, Lionel's fiancée. Richmond would be there, too. Anny had seen him a few times over the summer, but she longed to talk to him, away from the critical eyes of the family.

At Farringford, the guests gathered in the great drawing room. Anny surveyed the room but did not see Richmond, and mingled with the other guests. From a distance, she observed Lionel's fiancée, Eleanor, talking to Mr. Tennyson. She was a flirty, flouncy thing, Anny thought—a woman accustomed, by virtue of her breeding and beauty, to attracting attention wherever she went. She wondered how the girl would get along with Lionel's mother, Emily, who had a modest nature and dressed with studied plainness. His father, despite an intellectual bent, had a weakness for the attentions of young women, particularly pretty ones. Eleanor, familiar with his celebrity if not his poetry, was busy working her charms on him.

Richmond came in and smiled at Anny from across the room. He led Eleanor over and introduced her.

"This is Anne Thackeray, the famous writer. Perhaps you've read some of her novels," Richmond said.

"Oh, I don't have much of a head for books," Eleanor said.

Lionel will be bored within a year, Anny thought. But she could not help but notice Eleanor's skin, as fresh and soft as a newly opened magnolia blossom. The young woman held the stem of her glass between the tips of her fingers. Her hands were flawless, with fingernails the blush color of the interior of seashells. Anny became acutely aware of her own hands, puckered at the knuckles, with swollen veins. She set her glass down and hid her hands in the folds of her skirt.

"Perhaps you know my mother, Lady Charlotte?" Eleanor said.

"I don't believe I've had the pleasure," Anny said with a weak smile, glancing at Richmond, who seemed oblivious.

"Then you must be a friend of Lionel's parents."

"And Lionel." She resented the feeling Eleanor gave her of being cornered by one of her parents' cohorts.

She was glad when dinner was announced, but unhappy to find herself seated near Eleanor and Lionel, and far from Richmond. Eleanor changed the tenor of the table, favoring coquettish banter to substantive conversation. Anny missed the old Lionel and vowed to talk to him when his fiancée was not around.

After dinner, the women retired to the library and the men went to the rooftop to look at stars through a telescope. Anny much preferred the company of men but, being a good sport, she followed the ladies.

Before Richmond joined the stargazers, he managed to speak briefly to her alone. They agreed to meet on the flagstone terrace by the spiral staircase.

Later that evening, after taking leave of her hosts, she waited for Richmond at the appointed spot. Shadows from the leaves moved against the terrace flagstones. She felt jittery, thinking of all the ways the plan could go awry. What if Richmond forgot her, or she had misunderstood the plans? She had dismissed her servant, and didn't want to walk home alone.

Richmond emerged from the back of the house as quietly as a cat, and she felt relief wash over her. He always kept his word. If she knew nothing else about him, she knew that. There had been no cause to worry. He proposed that they take the long route to her cottage, by way of High Down.

The midnight air was crisp and cool. As they passed the kitchen garden her skirt brushed against a rosemary plant, causing it to release its pungent scent. They walked past the sheep meadow and climbed the path to where the trees and shrubs gave way to an open expanse.

Moonlight fell on High Down, bathing it in otherworldly light. Stars bejeweled the sky at the outer edges, beyond the moon's reach. An hour before, the male guests had observed these same stars through the telescope, but Anny preferred the magic to the science.

She grew aware that Richmond was watching her. He gently took her elbow to stop her.

"Shhh. Be quiet. Do you hear that?" he said.

They stood side by side, neither talking, and she listened intently. The moon highlighted the frothy edges of the waves. At the base of the sheer cliffs, the sea nipped at the shore and, withdrawing, pulled the pebbles back, creating a pleasant crackling sound.

"The waves?" she said.

"No, a song thrush."

She was quiet again, and, sure enough, further inland, where the trees and shrubs marked the edges of the down, the notes of birdsong reached them from far away. She shivered at the beauty of it.

After a while, they continued walking. Richmond steadied her when she stumbled in a toe-size hole left by badgers foraging for worms.

"What did you think of Eleanor?" he said, after they had walked in silence for a while.

"She's very . . ." She wanted to say young, but she realized that the girl was the same age as Richmond. She chose her words carefully. Lionel was Richmond's closest friend and he would be best man at his wedding. "She seems a little immature. She's very pretty, though."

"Poor Lionel. He's marrying for beauty, and beauty can be a colossal bore!"

"You think so?" she said.

"The secret to staying vibrant," he continued, "is always growing and questioning and being playful. Those are the qualities I've always admired in you."

"That's sweet of you. But around Eleanor, I feel . . ." she sighed. "Ancient."

"You could be as old as Methuselah, and my feelings for you would not alter," he said fervently.

"Surely you don't mean that."

"Oh, but I do."

He turned his face toward hers and their lips brushed lightly. She pulled back, startled. Could this be the sign that she had been waiting for?

He didn't care that she was old. He didn't care that she was not a beauty. He loved her anyway.

And then, as if to assure her that the first kiss was not a mistake, he took her in his arms and gave her a more passionate kiss. His lips were soft and full and warm and her body yielded naturally to his, as if she had been doing this all her life when, in truth, there had not even been a dress rehearsal.

The hope that she had repressed for so long was released like a thousand gulls, flashing their white breasts in the moonlight.

thirteen

1877

ANNY WAS IN LOVE. NOW THAT the sentiment could be named forthrightly, she embraced the freshness and giddiness that came with it. So what if she felt like everyone else who had ever been in love? That didn't diminish the experience for her. She cast out the writer's curse—that tendency to cleanse everything of sentimentality and treacle. Irony was the enemy of love.

That January, Richmond made frequent trips to London. Leslie was gone for a good part of the month on his annual mountain climbing trip. The fresh air and physical exertion always helped chase out his worrisome blue devils.

While he was away in Switzerland, Anny became accustomed to having the house to herself. When Richmond visited one afternoon after Leslie's return, she forgot to be on her guard. She and Richmond were kissing in front of the fire when Leslie walked in on them.

"What . . . What do you think you're doing?" Leslie sputtered, backing up in horror.

Anny and Richmond pulled apart, startled by his entry.

"I thought you were at work," Anny said.

"I can't allow this . . . this . . . indecency in my house."

"I didn't mean to upset you, sir," Richmond said.

"I'm going to have to ask you to leave," Leslie growled.

"It's best," Anny whispered to him and gave his hand a squeeze.

Anny and Leslie stood in silence until they heard the click of the front door close behind him.

"I'm sorry that boorish young man has ill used you."

"I'm not," Anny said.

"You mean you were . . . surely you were not . . . you could not have been enjoying it?"

She didn't answer.

"I am . . . I can't . . . I'm speechless," he stammered. "How could you do this to me?"

"You're not responsible for me," she said.

"But I feel as if I am. I have an obligation to Minny."

She realized that they had fallen into a strange co-existence, with ill-defined roles. He was not her father. He was not her brother. He was not her lover. Yet they were tightly bound by mutual history and affection.

"I'm disappointed in you. Really, I thought you had better sense than that. Why are you interested in that boy?"

"He loves me."

"What can he know of love, that fledgling?"

"Enough to teach me a thing or two." She realized it had been a mistake to keep Leslie in the dark about Richmond.

"He's not worthy of you," Leslie said, in the lecturing tone of the Cambridge don he had once been.

"Could anyone live up to your standards? I've waited my whole life, and no one of sufficient worth has presented himself, except Mr. Hastings Hughes."

"Who was at least of suitable age."

"Apparently you prefer to consign me to a lonely life on my pedestal, with my sterling reputation and my irreproachable character as my sole companions."

"Has grief over Minny put you in a desperate frame of mind?" he said, pacing in front of the fire.

"Quite the contrary. Her death has made me realize what's important," Anny said quietly.

"How long has this been going on?" he demanded, stopping in front of her. His towering height was intimidating.

"We have always had tremendous respect for each other, but the friendship has deepened recently," she said, sensing that knowledge of the long-standing nature of their attachment would only serve to inflame him.

"How long? Weeks? A few months?"

"I couldn't say."

"You must have some idea."

"It's been so gradual, it's impossible to put a time on it, nor would I want to."

"There was a rumor some years back. Min and I both treated it as unpleasant nonsense, coming from the gossipy Ritchies. Surely . . . no, it couldn't be . . ."

Anny blushed.

"Preposterous!" He looked like a spurned lover. "Carrying on indelicately under my nose. The behavior is not worthy of you."

"I refuse to be bullied," she said.

"Well at least let me talk to him and find out if his intentions are honorable," he said.

ANNY WAS ACCUSTOMED TO LESLIE's outbursts and knew that he would calm down after a few days, but Richmond had to return to Cambridge to sit for exams. Leslie arranged for him to come over that evening when he was still in a rage.

She was not invited to be present, but after Richmond entered the parlor, she crept along the hall to a spot where she could overhear. The niceties, if they existed between the two men, could not have lasted long, for they were already in the middle of a row when Anny focused in.

"It is impertinent of you to act in such a . . . such a disgraceful manner if you have no intention of betrothal," Leslie said, using his sternest voice.

"I have every intention of marrying her if she will have me."

Anny's heart lurched. This was the first time she had heard him speak explicitly about marriage.

"The age difference is considerable," Leslie said. "You are exposing yourself to the ridicule and disapproval of friends and family."

"I would consider my commitment extremely shallow were I to let that influence my feelings or actions," Richmond said.

Anny could picture Richmond, jaw set, standing face to face with Leslie.

"I am confident the world has better things to do than participate in the scorn of two people in love," Richmond continued.

A moment of silence followed. To anyone else the pause would signify nothing, but she knew Leslie well. He was planning his next line of attack.

"And what does your family think?" Leslie said, with fresh vigor.

"How anyone who knows Anny can fail to envy me in my blessed fortune I cannot see."

"So your mother is aware of your intentions?"

"Not yet, but I am quite sure she can be brought around. She adores Anny."

"You do not appear to have thought this through."

"I have thought long and hard about the only thing that matters—my feeling for Anny. Of that, I have no doubt."

"Earnestness can be deadly, in literature and in life," Leslie said.

"I love her. If that be deadly, so be it."

Leslie seemed ill equipped to deal with Richmond's sincerity, but he was not ready to give up.

"It's rather simple-minded, don't you think, to presume that love is enough?" he said.

"Would that I were arrogant enough to think that."

"But you have nothing to marry on."

"Whatever you think of me, I am not irresponsible," Richmond said.

"And how, pray tell, do you plan to provide for her?"

"Why is this any of your concern?" said Richmond.

"Anny is my wife's sister. I have a responsibility to see that she is well situated."

"And you don't have enough faith in her to trust her?"

"Of course, but she is given to passionate enthusiasms and sometimes needs to be protected from herself. So enlighten me. How do you plan to support a family?"

Anny bit her lip. As she feared, Leslie had ferreted out a weakness and pounced.

"I'm not sure right now," Richmond faltered.

"Your naïveté is breathtaking," Leslie sneered. "As you must know, leaving Cambridge without a degree would be injurious to your prospects."

"Anny's father never finished at Cambridge."

"He was a genius. Surely you are not including yourself in such august company."

"Certainly not. But my point is, success in life is possible without a Cambridge degree."

"When I was in university, before you were born, we were interested in debating the big topics—the origins of war, the derivation of power, moral conscience, the nature of God. We tried to put off as long as possible the dreary prospect of earning a living. Once you start on that path, you've sold your soul to the devil."

"I thought you didn't believe in God," Richmond said.

"True. The devil, however, has proved himself to be a more durable fellow."

Anny felt proud of Richmond. It was not easy going up against Leslie.

"Are you quite confident that your feelings are reciprocated?" Leslie asked.

"You would have to ask Anny that. I can only speak for myself and yes, I can assure you that I love her with all my heart, with all my intellect, with all my being."

"So you're an expert on love? At age twenty-one?"

"Twenty-two."

"Pardon?"

"I'm twenty-two."

"Oh well, then. You're a *mature* expert."

"No, I only know what is in my own heart, and on that subject, I am the world's expert."

"Ah to be young and naïve again," Leslie said with a sigh.

"It's not so bad. I recommend it."

Anny smiled. Richmond was holding up remarkably well.

"I would much prefer your blessing and well wishes, but if you are unwilling to grant them, it will have no influence on my future plans. The decision is entirely hers. I respect her enough to accept whatever she decides."

Anny sensed the meeting was coming to an end and didn't want to get caught in the hall, so she slipped out through the back. She had heard all she needed to hear.

COMMUNICATION BETWEEN Anny and Leslie became strained beyond bearing. He could not get over "the Catastrophe," as he called the interrupted kiss, and continued to rail against the impending marriage once he learned from Anny that Richmond had given her a formal offer.

"What did you tell him?" Leslie demanded.

"I told him I needed time to think about it," she said.

"Surely you are not going to accept? What is to be gained by an infantile husband? The whole thing is ridiculous."

"I know of no special ordinance of nature that prevents women, or men, for that matter, from being ridiculous at times, particularly where love is involved."

Leslie was taken aback by her total disregard for his counsel. Over the next few weeks he tried pouting, raging, belittling, and moralizing. If one strategy didn't work, he tried another.

At a time when Anny by all rights should be experiencing unalloyed joy—what she had dreamed of for so long was finally within reach—she found herself beset by doubts. What had been so simple when she and Richmond had kept their love secret became infinitely more complicated when exposed to natural light.

Richmond had always been the golden boy in the family. At Cambridge, he had garnered scholarships and prizes and had a glittering future in front of him. She was asking him to cut short his education and find a job for her sake. How could she be sure he would not resent her later on?

And then there was the matter of children. Both she and Richmond adored them. He was always a favorite with the younger ones at family gatherings. But she would turn forty in a few months and had accepted the fact that her childbearing years were over. She had mentioned this, though perhaps not as forcefully as she might. Richmond shrugged off her worries. He was willing to take a chance. As an entitled young prince, he never for a moment doubted that he would get what he wanted. She knew otherwise. Could she live with the guilt of being unable to provide him with the children he deserved?

There remained yet another roadblock, one that she had not discussed with him. She had promised Minny that she would take care of Laura. Had she known at the time that she would be called on so soon to keep her word, she might not have given it. But she did, and her word was important to her, especially where Min was concerned.

Deep down, she knew that she could not ask Richmond to take on the responsibility of raising a difficult child like Laura, not when he was making so many other sacrifices for her. On the other hand, she knew that if she left Laura alone with Leslie, the child would lapse into a state of isolation and loneliness.

What was a promise worth? What was a life worth? A tiny life, which, though stunted, had the potential to flourish, given the proper love and attention. But was Laura truly her responsibility? The child had a father, albeit one who did not appreciate what was special about her. But to go back on her promise to Minny felt disloyal.

The more she considered Richmond's proposal, the more confused she became. Given her mother's history, Anny wondered at what point the magic glue that held her personality together would stop working and allow the united parts of her to break and scatter.

The mental anguish caused her health to decline. Minny had suffered from a weak constitution since birth. Anny had always been more robust. So when she took to her bed and did not get up, even Leslie took note. The doctor, alarmed at her deterioration, prescribed purgatives and bed rest.

Julia, who had been such a good friend to Leslie and Anny following Minny's death, now stepped in and offered to take Anny into her house and nurse her back to health. With a grateful heart, Anny accepted her offer, knowing how desperately she needed a separation from Leslie.

The first week at Julia's, Anny did not leave her bed. Julia floated in and out of the room with a crisp white apron over her black widow's weeds. As a nurse, she knew how to be efficient yet unobtrusive. She had a soothing hand and a gentle matter-of-fact manner. Anny thought of her as her own private Florence Nightingale, ministering during times of war.

For war was what it felt like.

She and Leslie aggravated each other's worst tendencies, and without Minny to smooth out the differences, their blazing rows had escalated. But the fact remained: she was closer to Leslie than any other person in her life, and for him to be so emphatically opposed to the marriage weighed upon her more than she liked to admit. She begged Julia to help smooth things over with him.

"He will listen to you," Anny said.

"I fancy that I understand him. Our likeness in sorrow has brought us together."

"Then can you explain his harsh reaction? He cannot speak of Richmond without erupting into denunciations."

"No man likes to think of an older woman with a younger man. It's human nature. Or man's nature. Mainly, though, he's afraid he'll be demoted to a lesser place in your affections, and that is painful to him."

"His opposition muddies my feelings for Richmond. I can no longer see things clearly."

"Do you love Richmond?" Julia asked.

Anny thought about all that he would be sacrificing for her and said, "Not enough to refuse him."

AT THE END OF THE WEEK, ANNY got up out of her bed and was able to receive visitors in Julia's black and gold drawing room, but she was not ready to go back to the house next door that she shared with Leslie. Her stay at Julia's extended to two months.

Leslie came over most every day to visit, often with Laura. Anny entertained the child in her room while Julia and Leslie talked downstairs. Julia had a calming effect on him.

"Leslie seems to have softened his position on Richmond," Anny said after a few weeks. "What's your secret? Did you slip him a special potion? Eye of newt and toe of frog?"

"I merely pointed out that, for all your happiness and all your sadness, you've never had an individual life. You have always lived your life for others. He has benefitted, as has Laura, your father, and all who have come in contact with you. But you deserve some happiness all to yourself."

"Well, you have great influence on him. I sense a change in his attitude. He will never be wholeheartedly in favor of Richmond, but I don't think he will stand in the way."

Being in the presence of Julia, who was so supremely organized, boosted Anny's creativity. She worked diligently on *From an Island*, involving characters loosely based on Freshwater's artistic circle.

She remembered her father's mulish approach to work. He took his motto from the Roman poet Horace: *Nulla dies sine linea*. Never a day without a line. Inspiration was for amateurs, he said. She now realized that the habit of writing pulled her over rough patches, the way the institution of marriage carried couples through hard times.

When she was working, she felt completely herself, only better. Paralyzed by her indecision over Richmond, she had lost touch with her authentic nature. Now her confidence returned. Even though the interlocking love stories she crafted had nothing to do with her own life, through the process of writing, she was becoming herself again.

During the two months she stayed at Julia's, Richmond had been busy with his studies. She kept track of his exam schedule in her journal: English at the end of March, French, Greek, and Latin in the days before Easter. She was grateful he had no time to come to London.

In her letters she avoided any mention of her emotional turmoil or her physical collapse. She didn't want to call attention to the seventeen-year age difference, or make him think he might be marrying a sick woman. Anny realized the extent to which, in letters, one could invent a character and a story as surely as one did in a novel. But the one true aspect of her correspondence was her continued affection for him.

One night she awoke from a fitful sleep and, without lighting a candle, padded to the open window. She looked out at the night sky and was overcome with the certainty that Richmond, at that very moment, was looking at the same sky. "Then it was you I seemed to see," she wrote to him the following morning, "for all the stars were lighted up and a silver crescent was dropping and a sort of faint flame seemed to come from the horizon. Oh, I hope you looked out of the window last night!"

IF LESLIE HAD SOFTENED HIS stance toward Richmond, his attitude toward Laura remained unchanged. He was perplexed by her waywardness and her strange ways of speaking and thinking. Now six, the child acted much younger, and adults responded with a mixture of pity and discomfort. She was an affront to the vain part of Leslie that sought the praise and envy of others. Anny was certain that he loved his daughter, but she knew he would never exert the patient, loving tenderness that the child needed to thrive.

Julia assured Leslie that his daughter's setback was temporary, and that once she healed from the loss of her mother, she would catch up to others her age. But Julia never suggested that Laura play with her children when Leslie brought his daughter to visit.

That suited Anny fine. She wanted to spend time with Laura, though she never knew which child would show up: the frenetic child who loved to twirl, jump, and flap her hands, or the focused child whose powers of concentration allowed her to sit still for long periods and shut out the world.

One activity that kept her engaged was painting. Anny had pencils, paper, paint, and brushes available for her to use when she came to visit. One day, Laura outlined a four-story house with a gabled roof. The house was completely empty, except for an oversize black dot in the third-floor nursery with half a dozen squiggly legs protruding. To the side was a big splotch of red.

"What happened to that bug?" Anny said.

"Somebody squished it. With a shoe," Laura said.

"That wasn't very nice."

"Bad bug. Bad." The child put her thumb on the black splotch of paint and moved it back and forth. "Squish, Squish."

"That big empty house is so sad," Anny said. "Don't you want to put some people in it?"

The child shrugged.

"Where's Nurse Louise?" Anny said.

"Gone."

"Where's your Auntie?"

"Sick."

"Where's Memee?"

"Hurt." She pointed to the bright red spot of blood.

"You mean the bug's name is Memee?"

She nodded solemnly.

"Where's your Papa?"

"Cleaning his shoe."

Anny looked at the beautiful child, her mouth set, her curls framing her face. She took a moment to collect herself before she said, "When your Mommee was a little girl, about your age, she loved to rescue things. One day she found an injured fly and put it in a doll's teapot and added rose leaves. We told her it was dead, but she would not hear of it and the second day she took off the lid to sprinkle some sugar and crumbs inside and out flew the little fly."

"Anny not give up on Memee?" Laura looked at her with wide eyes. Locked inside that strange mind was a child as subtle and complex and worthy as anyone.

"Oh my precious pet," Anny said, but was too afraid to hug her.

JULIA WENT TO VISIT HER PARENTS near Tunbridge Wells for several days, but before leaving, she gave Anny permission to receive Richmond at her house for tea. Anny couldn't wait to see him, now that she was finally feeling like her old self. Julia had played a great part in her recovery, and Anny was deeply grateful to her, but, as ambivalent as she was about resuming her old life with Leslie and Laura, she could no longer take advantage of her friend's hospitality. Two months was enough. She made arrangements to move back next door as soon as Julia returned from her travels.

In the meantime, she awaited Richmond's visit with great anticipation. He arrived one drizzly April day and Anny knew, as soon as he shed his raincoat and hat, that something was terribly wrong.

After a period of strained conversation over tea, he said coldly, "Have you come to a decision?"

"I am close," she said. Truth was, she hadn't wanted to spoil her excitement over seeing him by stirring up the worrisome problems involved in accepting his marriage proposal.

"I feel the fool. If the decision is that painful to bring to a conclusion, perhaps it was never meant to be." Cold fury lay behind his calm demeanor.

"Oh, no, my love. Please don't think that," she said, alarmed. It was the first time he had been harsh with her.

"Then give me your answer." He brought his hand down on the table. The china cups clattered. "I'm not a saint," he continued. "You have sorely tried my patience. You've had months to consider my offer. I tried to give you the leeway to make up your mind without interference. But in dithering so long, you have toyed with my affections. It makes me think less of you."

She was stunned. She, who had always so carefully considered the feelings of others, had neglected to do so for the most important person in her life.

"Are my feelings a mere trifle to you?" he continued. "Do you have no consideration for what I have been going through—the uncertainty, the waiting? I rush to the post every day, hoping for an answer, only to hear from you about some quotidian piffle."

She realized that, by avoiding all mention of her turmoil, she had unintentionally hurt him.

"You are keeping something from me," he said, in the tone of a police inspector.

"Please, believe me. There has been no change in my heart." She felt him slipping away and it terrified her.

"Then why are you having such a hard time making up your mind?"

How could she explain to him the many complications? Life for him was so simple. He had never wavered in his affection nor wondered about the wisdom of their marriage. She, on the other hand, had spent the past two months mired in self-doubt. She questioned herself, her responsibility to Leslie, and her obligation to Laura. She reproached herself for forcing Richmond to curtail his future prospects for her sake. What should have been a simple answer was anything but.

"Do you care for me?" He was practically yelling at her. Not a lover's tender query, but an accusation, a threat, a dare.

"You know I do."

"Then why, by Jove, is it such a bloody difficult decision?"

She was trembling. She searched for the words to smooth the situation over, but before she could, he jumped up.

"I cannot trust myself to continue this anymore, for fear of saying something I will regret."

He exited, leaving her ashen.

WHEN JULIA RETURNED THAT EVENING, Anny had already taken to her bed. The following morning she searched out her friend to thank her for taking such good care of her the past two months. She found her at her dressing table, her long hair loose over her shoulders. These were the riotous tresses that had been immortalized by Cammie's camera.

She had rarely seen Julia's hair down, and now, as she stroked it with the sterling silver brush, it crackled and seemed to take on a life of its own. Julia turned to her and said, "There's something I've been meaning to speak with you about, but I've put it off because I was afraid you would mind most horribly. Leslie has declared his feelings for me." She spoke quickly, as if afraid she wouldn't get it out.

"Oh." The jolt left Anny speechless. It made perfect sense. Had she been paying more attention, it would have been obvious to her. Leslie spent hours in the parlor talking to Julia while Anny played with Laura.

"As I feared, I have shocked you," Julia said, setting the brush on the dressing table.

"No, no. It's just—well, a surprise." Her immediate reaction was to feel cheated. She had shared her most intimate feelings about Richmond with Julia, while for days, weeks, or months, Julia had been withholding the contents of her heart.

"He wrote me a lovely letter and said that he knew his love could never be reciprocated, but he had an ardent desire to be my friend, and that he would ask nothing of me." She nervously wound a strand of hair around her finger.

"He didn't ask for your hand?"

"I think he rightly guessed that such a thing would terrify me. He took exactly the right tone and offered no pressure. His letter made me realize for the first time that I don't have to accept a life clouded by sorrow as my permanent portion."

"So you encouraged him?"

"He said he would love me as long as he had any love left in him, but he would let me to be guided by my own affections. He offered to stop seeing me, if that was what I wished, though it would do his heart irreparable harm. He was so restrained and respectful."

Anny barely recognized the person Julia was describing. Such was the distortion of love.

"In his reluctance to pressure me, he won me over," Julia said.

"I know you care deeply for him. But do you love him?"

"I feel something, though I'm not sure what I would call it. I've become so accustomed to my poor dead heart. I didn't even realize it was frozen until I felt the drip drip drip of its thawing."

Had Anny been more observant, rather than trying to avoid Leslie's rage, she would have noticed the change in him. She knew that, in time, Julia would marry him. Of that she was certain. She wanted to say: *Don't wait. It's ruinous. If you love him, act immediately or you will lose him.* Her face must have mapped her distress, for Julia said, "Just as I feared, I have upset you."

"On the contrary. I am delighted. Why should I be upset?"

"Because Leslie was your sister's husband."

Anny took both of Julia's hands in hers. "If Min loved him, and I am quite certain she did, she would want for him to be happy. And I'm sure the same is true of your Herbert."

"I hadn't thought of it in that way," Julia said, and a radiant smile came over her face, as if she had been given the permission she needed to love again.

AT HOME, ANNY UNPACKED HER writing slope, inkpot, and pens and arranged them on the desk with the items she had left behind: the mother-of-pearl box of sand her father had used to absorbed the ink from his *Vanity Fair* etchings and the precious pen she had found under the Christmas tree on the eve of his death. It was strange to be back in the house she shared with Leslie, now that their circumstances had so altered.

Anny was delighted for Julia. She recognized the spark in her eye, the vitality. Being in love meant being more alive than anyone else. She knew Julia would see her way to marry Leslie. She was happy for them. Why, then, did she feel so blue?

After she unpacked, she went to the park in search of Laura. It was a beautiful spring day. She found Laura at her favorite spot near Kensington Palace. Nurse Louise sat on a bench watching the child at play.

The sun through the trees cast scraps of light on the grass, even though the leaves had not yet fully pushed forth. A white butterfly danced in the hyacinth-scented air. Intent on catching the butterfly, Laura leapt up, clasped her hands above her head, and came up empty-handed.

Laura grabbed at the air again, but the butterfly easily eluded her. The child did not tire of the game, nor was she discouraged by failure. It was the chase that delighted her. In her white dress with a blue satin sash, she followed the butterfly's irregular path, jumping this way and that, white chasing after white, as if she were pursuing a piece of herself that she would never catch.

The butterfly alighted on a bush and Laura rushed at it. The butterfly darted off, leaving Laura laughing in delight. She loved nature. She loved light. She was completely absorbed and happy.

Anny didn't dare interrupt her, and slipped away, feeling a sense of contentment. Laura's future was secure, now that Julia would marry Leslie. Julia was a wonderful mother, and she was confident that Laura would be well cared for.

Taking the long way home, she walked along the high brick walls surrounding Kensington Palace, where she and Minny had played as girls, freezing in the niches and pretending to be statues. She passed the grand house her father had built, the one a friend had dubbed "Vanity Fair." Anny felt no nostalgia for the red brick mansion, but she knew how much pleasure her father had taken in it. He had never complained about the extra work he took on to support the extravagant house, even though, unbeknownst to her, his health was failing.

The windows of his study looked out over the elms of the Palace. She remembered the day she sat in his study and asked him if he loved her mother.

"Oh, my dear, it's so much more complicated than that," he had said, looking at her over spectacles that had slipped down his nose. "I'll say this: had I to do it over, I would do the same thing, for you must go with your heart, even though fate may not be kind to you. You have to start out with love, for if you don't, what's the point? I loved her then—dearly, deeply."

Out of her parents' tragic marriage, one thing endured, and that was love. This was her father's gift to her: not only his love for her, which was unquestionable, but also his love for her mother.

Richmond had every reason to be angry with her. She had been so wrapped up in herself that she had lost sight of his feelings. For that, she was deeply ashamed. But if he had loved her once, he would love her again. After all, forgiveness was an important part of love.

"DEALING WITH THOSE CHATTERY, gossipy Ritchies. I'd rather be stuck in a tree of magpies!" Leslie groused.

He had taken it upon himself to convince the Ritchies to allow Richmond to marry Anny, now that she had formally accepted his offer.

Whatever Leslie's reservations, he had taken over the role as Anny's advocate. It was his idea that she move quickly rather than delay the marriage for another year, as Richmond's sisters suggested.

"I fear your health won't withstand a year more of uncertainty and vexation with the Ritchies."

He abhorred drama, yet for Anny's sake he threw himself into the negotiations with the family.

"I won't stand their worrying you," he said. "His sisters work themselves up into such tantrums that they can't talk sense. They act as if years were of no importance, as if you had the strength of a rhinoceros and were a strapping young cook of five and twenty."

At Leslie's urging, Richmond took the civil service exam and applied for a clerkship in the India Office in London. Richmond's sisters did not think that the job was commensurate with the talents of an academic scholar studying for the Classical Tripos at Cambridge, even though both families had deep ties to India. Richmond's father had held an important post in the East India Company, and Anny's grandfather had made his fortune supplying the company with elephants.

"My life is torture," Leslie said. "I can't stand the scenes. They are accusing me of ruining Richmond's career. Mrs. Ritchie is incomparably the most sensible of the lot."

Her main objection was that Richmond would be leaving Cambridge without a degree. Leslie, with his ties to the university, determined that if Richmond finished out the current term, he could complete his degree in absentia, and that reassured her.

In May Richmond learned that he won the clerkship in the India Office. All obstacles had been cleared, and the wedding was announced for August.

Letters and telegrams of congratulations poured in. Anny particularly cherished the response from her elderly cousin Chattie in Paris:

> Richmond wrote me the most eloquent testimony of
> his love. He considers you the most charming creature
> alive. His only apprehension is on your behalf, that the
> inevitable talk of the age difference will hurt you, but,
> as he so rightly perceives, your true friends will rejoice
> in your rejoicing. In fact, the unusualness of the match

is, in and of itself, proof of the strength of your feelings.
If I had known your hearts in Venice, I would not have
wished for any alteration in them. I support your engagement with all my heart, and regret that my health
prevents me from making the crossing, but I will be
with you in spirit, and wish you all the happiness on
your wedding day, and in your life after.

Among Anny's friends, surprisingly little was made of the
age difference, and there was no scandal, as Leslie had feared.
Some negative mentions of the marriage appeared in the newspaper, but Leslie refused to show these to Anny, even though she
begged to see them.

"It will benefit no one for you to see how snide and narrow
some people can be," he said. "Women are not allowed to do such
unusual things without some criticism."

Anny was touched by his efforts on her behalf. "You have
been so good to me," she said.

"I wish I had Minny's and your father's power of making
you happy. But at least you must let me do what they would have
done had they been with us still."

"But you *have* made me happy. Very happy," she said.

"I acted abominably at the beginning of the year. It's no fun
being the third person."

Anny smiled. "Really?" For someone to whom irony was a
sacred rite, he showed a remarkable lapse.

THE WEDDING DAY ARRIVED, A beautiful Thursday morning in
August, with more blue sky than anyone had a right to expect.
Anny called it the bank holiday wedding, for Richmond had
started his job and could only get off on this day. For once in her
life, Anny arrived on time to the old stone church in Kensington.

The ceremony was so brief that some late-arriving guests met the bridal couple on their way out.

In the vestry, Anny signed her maiden name in the parish register, as required by law: Anne Isabelle Thackeray. She would always be William Thackeray's daughter, but from here on out, she would carry that identity in her heart, and not in her signature. She took on her new name with pride, knowing that she had chosen wisely. She blotted her signature and looked up into Richmond's radiant face. As a novelist, she knew that happy endings depended on where you ended the story. But if she were to die tomorrow, this one day of pure happiness would be hers forever.

The wedding breakfast was held at the house she shared with Leslie. He and Julia had seen to it that the rooms were filled with flowers and greenery, giving guests the sense of being inside a bower.

Anny had been too nervous during the ceremony to notice anyone in the church, but now she reveled in being surrounded by people she loved. There was Leslie, looking a little grumpy but content to be beside Julia, whose slight concessions to her severe mourning garb—in jewelry and flowers—signaled a change others might miss. Lionel Tennyson, who served as best man, was in attendance, though his mother was sick and his father had chosen to stay in Freshwater, ever wary of appearing in public. If Richmond's mother and sisters still had reservations, they were kind enough to keep them hidden. Their presence rounded out the celebration, which contained Anny's signature mix of intimacy and informality.

A crowd of children played underfoot. Anny noted, with some smug satisfaction, that her sweet Memee, in pink lace and organdy, was better behaved than Julia's daughter Stella, who started to cry when her brothers excluded her from the imaginary fort they had set up under the grand piano.

The only note of sadness came from the important people in Anny's life who were missing: her father, Minny, and Cammie.

But she felt their presence, as she would in all the important events of her life.

When Richmond entered with a bottle of champagne and flutes for the children, they clamored around him. He poured a small taste for each of them.

The other guests held their bubbling glasses and waited in anticipation to see what this tender young groom would have to say. Richmond stood beside Anny in front of the fireplace and looked into her eyes, as if she were the only person in the room. Making reference to the end of her father's novel, *Vanity Fair*, he raised his glass and said, "To my bride, my beloved. May I never say a word to you that is not kind and gentle, nor think of a want of yours that I do not try to gratify."

They clicked glasses.

the end

HISTORICAL NOTE

$\mathscr{A}$FTER HER MARRIAGE, ANNY gave birth to a daughter, Hester, and a son, Billy, named after his grandfather, William Thackeray. She kept her promise to her father never to write his biography, but she did write introductions for the thirteen-volume Biographical Edition of Thackeray's work and the twenty-six-volume Centenary Biographical Edition of his complete works. Drawing on unpublished letters, diaries, and personal memories, she used her charming anecdotal and impressionistic style to paint a warm and quirky portrait of the author of *Vanity Fair*.

Richmond spent a distinguished career in the India Office in London, culminating in his appointment as Permanent Under-Secretary of State for India. He was knighted for his service. Despite the seventeen-year age difference with Anny, it was Richmond who died first, at the age of fifty-eight, of pneumonia.

Leslie Stephen and Julia Duckworth were married the year after Anny and Richmond, in the same church. Together the Stephens had four children, including the artist Vanessa Bell and the writer Virginia Woolf, who based the characters of Mr. and Mrs. Ramsay in *To the Lighthouse* on Leslie and Julia. Anny continued to be close to the Stephen family and was the unofficial aunt to their children.

Today Leslie Stephen is best known as the editor of the multi-volume *Dictionary of National Biography*, which resulted in his knighthood in 1902. He died two years later.

Laura did not fit in well with the blended Stephen family of eight children, which included Julia's three children from her first marriage. Because of Laura's unpredictable behavior, she was cared for in a separate part of the house. At the age of fifteen, she was sent to live with a governess in the country. She was committed to Earlswood Asylum for Idiots and Imbeciles at the age of twenty-two.

Anny remained the main person interested in Laura's welfare. She visited her and occasionally brought her home for short stays. But Laura outlived Anny by many years. When she died at the age of seventy-five, having been institutionalized for half a century, the Stephen family had been out of touch for so long that the staff at the home where she lived was unaware that she had any relatives.

Anny never stopped visiting her mother, who remained with a private caretaker for the rest of her life. At her death, she still wore the moonstone and diamond mourning ring that William Thackeray had given her for their engagement. She survived him by thirty-one years.

Julia Margaret Cameron's photographic output declined dramatically after she moved to Ceylon, now called Sri Lanka. Only twenty-six of her photographs from this period are known to have survived, mostly of Tamil women. Three and a half years after leaving Freshwater, Cammie succumbed to a sudden illness. Reportedly, she was lying in bed, looking through the window at the starlit sky. "Beautiful," she said, and died.

The Victorian era marked the beginning of celebrity culture. Unlike today's, it was the poets, writers, painters, scientists, and thinkers who were the celebrities, and Julia Cameron was their chronicler. Her portraits of Alfred Tennyson, Thomas Carlyle, Anthony Trollope, Charles Darwin, John Hershel, and others define the age for us. "The history of the human face is a book we don't tire of, if we can get its grand truths and learn them by heart," she said.

Charles Dodgson, writing under the pen name Lewis Carroll, revolutionized writing for children. After the publication of his beloved books, *Alice's Adventures in Wonderland* and *Through the Looking Glass and What Alice Found There*, children's books became less moralistic and more playful. The Alice books have been translated into more than seventy languages, including Latin, Esperanto, Yiddish, and Swahili. After the Bible and Shakespeare, they are the most widely quoted books in the English-speaking world.

Dodgson died a bachelor at the age of sixty-five. His photography remains an important part of his legacy. The existence of a handful of nude photos he took of prepubescent girls has raised eyebrows, but no evidence exists that he ever acted improperly toward his many child friends.

Nelly Watts received a divorce from the artist George Frederic Watts in 1877, thirteen years after the end of their ten-month marriage. Reversing the typical Victorian story of moral corruption and illegitimate children leading to penury or suicide, she married an actor in 1877 to give a name to her two children. Reclaiming her maiden name, Ellen Terry, she went on to become one of England's most celebrated Shakespearean actors. Her "paper courtship" with George Bernard Shaw in the 1890s produced one of the great correspondences in the history of English letter writing.

Anny never built a house on the Isle of Wight. Her one long-term commitment was The Porch. After Richmond's death, she spent more and more time there with her children and grandchildren. In 1919, she died at The Porch in the arms of her daughter. She was eighty-two. She left behind an impressive body of work, including five novels, two novellas, five books of short stories, five collections of essays, two biographies, more than one hundred periodical publications, and numerous introductions, prefaces, and biographical essays about her father and his literary circle.

THE PORCH

ACKNOWLEDGMENTS

I WOULD LIKE TO THANK THE Eton College Library and staff, as well as the Provost and Fellows of Eton College who made it possible for me to review original letters from the Thackeray family. I did additional research in the archives of the Morgan Library, the Duke University Library, the British Library, and the New York Public Library.

Lydia Chávez offered me a place to stay in London as well as insightful suggestions on early drafts. Susan Permut helped me with British usage. Andrea Barnet has been a dependable reader of my work since our early days in a critique group. David Milofsky nudged me forward and offered valuable guidance. Ursula Hegi is wise in matters literary and personal. Elizabeth Bell copyedited the manuscript. Ann Weinstock and Kris Weber are responsible for the gorgeous cover and interior design. To all: I am deeply grateful for your friendship and support.

And finally, to Frank, my first and most important reader: You always make me laugh.

PHOTOGRAPHS

𝒯HE NARRATIVE OF *Anny in Love* takes place when photography was a relatively new art form. Many of the book's characters sat for portraits for one of the most important and innovative photographers of the nineteenth century, Julia Margaret Cameron, also a character in this novel. This collection of photographs taken by Cameron and her contemporaries offers a glimpse of the people and places in the book's fictional domain.

ANNE THACKERAY

Photographed by Julia Margaret Cameron in 1870.

MINNY THACKERAY

Photographed by Julia Margaret Cameron in 1865.

JULIA MARGARET CAMERON

Photographed by her husband
Henry Herschel Hay Cameron in 1870.

DIMBOLA LODGE

The Camerons' home in Freshwater
on the Isle of Wight.

ELLEN TERRY AT THE AGE OF SIXTEEN

Photographed by Julia Margaret Cameron in 1864.

"MY FIRST SUCCESS"

Photographed by Julia Margaret Cameron in 1864
within a month of receiving her first camera.

ALFRED TENNYSON "DIRTY MONK"

Photographed by Julia Margaret Cameron in 1865.

LESLIE STEPHEN AND HIS DOG TROY

Photographed in 1875 shortly after the death of his wife Minny.

JULIA JACKSON DUCKWORTH

Photographed by Julia Margaret Cameron in 1867.

VIRGINIA WOOLF AND HER FATHER LESLIE STEPHEN

Photographed by George Charles Beresford in 1902.
Leslie Stephen married Julia Jackson Duckworth in 1878. Their daughter
Virginia Woolf modeled the characters of Mr. and Mrs. Ramsay in
To the Lighthouse after her father and mother.

CREDITS

PAGE ii–iii

Freshwater Bay, William Russell Sedgfield, circa 1859 — in or before 1869.
Published in J. Redding Ware's *Isle of Wight*. Rijksmuseum, Amsterdam.

PAGE 278

Anne Thackeray Ritchie's house, The Porch, at Freshwater Bay,
Isle of Wight, circa 1914. Scanned from Anne Thackeray Ritchie's
From the Porch courtesy of the University of California Libraries.
This work is in the public domain.

PAGE 282

Julia Margaret Cameron. Mrs. Thackeray Ritchie, 1870. Gift of
Mrs. James Ward Thorne. The Art Institute of Chicago.

PAGE 283

Julia Margaret Cameron. Minnie Thackeray, 1865.
The J. Paul Getty Museum.

PAGE 284

Henry Herschel Hay Cameron. Julia Margaret Cameron, 1870.
Harris Brisbane Dick Fund, 1941. Metropolitan Museum of Art.

PAGE 285

The Camerons' house, Dimbola Lodge, at Freshwater Bay, Isle of Wight, circa 1871. Scanned from Colin Ford's *Julia Margaret Cameron: 19th Century Photographer of Genius*. This work is in the public domain.

PAGE 286

Julia Margaret Cameron. Ellen Terry at the Age of Sixteen.
The J. Paul Getty Museum.

PAGE 287

Julia Margaret Cameron. "Annie My First Success," 1864.
The J. Paul Getty Museum.

PAGE 288

Julia Margaret Cameron. Alfred Lord Tennyson "Dirty Monk," 1865.
Gift of Mrs. James Ward Thorne. The Art Institute of Chicago.

PAGE 289

Leslie Stephen with Dog Troy, 1875. Mortimer Rare Book Room.
Smith College Special Collections.

PAGE 290

Julia Margaret Cameron. Julia Jackson "My Favorite Picture," 1867. Gift of
David C. and Sarajean Ruttenberg. The Art Institute of Chicago.

PAGE 291

George Charles Beresford. Virginia Woolf and
Sir Leslie Stephen, 1902. National Portrait Gallery, London.

www.ingramcontent.com/pod-product-compliance
Lightning Source LLC
Chambersburg PA
CBHW022106310726
48972CB00007B/1913